THE BATH CONSPIRACY

Also by Jeanne M. Dams from Severn House

The Dorothy Martin mysteries

A DARK AND STORMY NIGHT
THE EVIL THAT MEN DO
THE CORPSE OF ST JAMES'S
MURDER AT THE CASTLE
SHADOWS OF DEATH
DAY OF VENGEANCE
THE GENTLE ART OF MURDER
BLOOD WILL TELL
SMILE AND BE A VILLAIN
THE MISSING MASTERPIECE
CRISIS AT THE CATHEDRAL
A DAGGER BEFORE ME
DEATH IN THE GARDEN CITY
DEATH COMES TO DURHAM

THE BATH
CONSPIRACY

Jeanne M. Dams

**SEVERN
HOUSE**

First world edition published in Great Britain and the USA in 2021
by Severn House, an imprint of Canongate Books Ltd,
14 High Street, Edinburgh EH1 1TE.

Trade paperback edition first published in Great Britain and the USA in 2022
by Severn House, an imprint of Canongate Books Ltd.

severnhouse.com

British Library Cataloguing-in-Publication Data
A CIP catalogue record for this title is available from the British Library.

ISBN-13: 978-0-7278-9250-8 (cased)
ISBN-13: 978-1-78029-776-7 (trade paper)
ISBN-13: 978-1-4483-0514-8 (e-book)

This is a work of fiction. Names, characters, places and incidents
are either the product of the author's imagination or are used fictitiously.
Except where actual historical events and characters are being described
for the storyline of this novel, all situations in this publication are
fictitious and any resemblance to actual persons, living or dead,
business establishments, events or locales is purely coincidental.

All Severn House titles are printed on acid-free paper.

MIX
Paper from
responsible sources
FSC
www.fsc.org   FSC® C013056

Typeset by Palimpsest Book Produ
Falkirk, Stirlingshire, Scotland.
Printed and bound in Great Britain
TJ Books Limited, Padstow, Cornw

AUTHOR'S NOTE

Most of the locations in this book are real places, their descriptions based on my visits to Bath and environs. It's been many years since I lunched at the Sign of the Angel in Lacock. I don't remember if that was its name then, but I certainly remember the atmosphere and the excellent food and friendly service. And I remember the delightful banties strutting around! I hope they, or their descendants, are still there, along with the cat.

The Bath Abbey shop is in the process of transition as this is being written. In a small, rather cramped space when I last visited, it was closed for a time and was then to reopen in a temporary location before moving back near its old location but in a larger, better space. I hope one day to see its new glory. Meanwhile, I have written about it as it was when I saw it last.

If the Jane Austen Centre has an outbuilding used as storage for the shop's merchandise, I am unaware of it. In short, I made it up. Certainly no one has ever, to my knowledge, set any fires in the vicinity.

If you've never visited this amazing city or nearby Stonehenge, I hope you can get there soon. Both city and monument are among the wonders of the world.

ONE

I was sitting in our parlour, reading a book and absent-mindedly petting Samantha, our Siamese, when my husband wandered in.

'You look comfortable, love.'

'I'm so comfortable I'm almost asleep. It's such a beautiful, balmy day, most conducive to slumber. I can hardly believe we're in October already. This is the kind of weather we used to call Indian summer back home.'

I'm American by birth, from southern Indiana, but I married an Englishman some years ago and now make the small city of Sherebury my home. Alan and I live in a modest seventeenth-century house right next to the incredibly lovely Cathedral, with our two cats (Esmeralda, the other one, is a portly British Blue) and a big loveable mutt named Watson. All of us are getting on in years, and our mostly sedentary life suits us down to the ground.

I yawned and stretched. Sam, who disapproves of human movement when she's trying to sleep, uttered a pungent Siamese comment, dug her claws into my knee, and jumped down. 'I've always been glad I was born in October. It's my favourite time of year. At home, though, we got a lot more fall colour, brilliant reds and oranges. And the sky in Indian summer would sometimes be the most amazing sapphire blue.'

'Why is it called Indian summer? What does it mean?'

'Oh, so there are still some bits of Ameri-speak you don't know! I have no idea where the name comes from, but it means the time of lovely warm weather that would sometimes come after a few frosts and one or two hard freezes. We didn't always get it, but when we did it was a great blessing. Winter was coming, but for a week or so we could pretend we didn't know that and revel in the beauty. Most of the flowers were gone, victims of the cold, but the chrysanthemums were glorious. Their perfume filled the air, along with the lovely smell of burning leaves. We were allowed to burn them back then, and I suppose it was hard on people with breathing problems, but I loved it. Raking them into big piles, and then jumping in them so they had to be raked up all over again, and then at night the big fires. We'd sometimes roast marshmallows . . .' I drifted off, captivated by a dream of my lost youth.

Alan sat down next to me on the big, squashy couch. Our furniture is extremely soft and comfy, and almost impossible for people our age to get out of. Oh, well. You can't have everything.

'You know,' he said, 'you didn't actually have to remind me about your birthday. I hadn't forgotten.'

I was too relaxed to retort. 'Never hurts to put in a good word. But as you seem to be in a considerate sort of mood, I don't suppose you'd like to get me a cup of tea, would you?'

'I just sat down, woman. It's too warm for tea, anyway.'

'That I would live to see the day when an Englishman didn't want tea! Do we have any beer, then?'

'We do. I'll pour us some in a bit. But first I want to "set a spell" as you would say.' He stretched out an arm and pulled me closer.

I sat up straight, or as straight as possible in the clutches of both Alan and the couch. 'Alan Nesbitt! Never in my life did I use such an expression!'

'You've sometimes quoted your elderly relatives saying it, though. Dinna fash yoursel'. I have a proposition for you.'

'Oh, well, then.' I settled back against him and grinned.

'Not that sort of proposition. Not this minute, at any rate. Though later . . .' He looked at me with what he fondly supposes is a leer. His handsome, rather distinguished-looking face is not made to leer, but I've never undeceived him. 'No, I've thought of something you might like to do for your birthday. It's been quite a long time since we had a holiday, a real holiday. Our last few outings have been at the behest of other people, and they've become a trifle fraught.'

I grinned again. A trifle fraught, indeed! Our recent travels, to Canada and the far north of England, had involved us in considerable danger and trouble, including murder and, in my case, physical assault. Trust Alan to understate the case.

'So my idea was: how would you like to spend a week or so in Bath? Have you ever been there?'

My first husband and I had travelled a good deal in England before deciding to retire to Sherebury, a plan he died too soon to complete. I moved here anyway, too numb with grief to make any decisions – and then met Alan, also widowed, and the rest is (delightful) history. 'No, in fact Frank and I had intended to get there, but somehow we never did. All I know about it is from Jane Austen.'

'Then you know quite a lot. Of course, it's changed some since Jane's characters walked the streets and took the waters, but less than you might think. The Regency architecture is all still there, and of course the Roman Baths are hardly likely to change in a paltry few hundred years. There's a great deal to see and do; I think you'll enjoy it. There's quite a nice hotel within shouting distance of the Pump Room. Shall I book us in?'

So it was that a few days later we set out on the rather circuitous route that would take us to the city of Bath. (I should say here that the English pronounce it 'Bahth'. I've learned quite a lot of Britspeak while I've lived here, but I cannot manage that one. To my American ears it sounds affected. So sue me.) The weather was not propitious. Our Indian summer had given way to grey skies that couldn't quite make up their mind whether to produce rain or not. But my spirits were not dampened. I was traveling with the man I adored through the country I adored. Grey skies couldn't spoil that.

We went through a number of enticing cities on our way. Alan overruled me on my desire to stop in Winchester, but I flat-out insisted on paying our respects to Salisbury Cathedral, one of my all-time favourites. We had a leisurely lunch at one of the lovely little cafés that cathedral towns seem to specialize in, and then made it to our hotel in Bath just as the heavens opened.

A valet appeared, with a huge umbrella. He helped Alan with our bags, gave him a chit in exchange for the car keys, and took off through the downpour. Alan smiled at the expression on my face. 'Yes, love, I know we don't usually indulge in the luxury of valet parking. In Bath, however, parking is at a premium, and in this part of the city, it's virtually impossible. It's part of your birthday present – enjoy it!'

Alan and I live modestly. We have sufficient means to satisfy, as Hercule Poirot once said, both our needs and our caprices, but we're both rather frugal by nature. This hotel was certainly a cut or two above our usual choices. The efficient desk clerk had no problem with our different surnames (I remained Dorothy Martin when Alan and I married) when we registered. Our room, to which we were escorted with old-fashioned courtesy, was large and attractive, with – I turned around to Alan with a gasp – a large bouquet of autumn flowers on the desk.

'Happy birthday, darling,' he said with a kiss.

We went down to dinner rather late.

Next morning, the fickle English weather had forgotten it knew how to rain. The streets, though, were still wet with a puddle here and there when we set out to explore the city, so Alan hooked my arm firmly in his lest I slip.

There were plenty of tours available, either on foot or by bus, but we decided against joining one the first day. 'If you have questions about what we see, I can answer some of them,' Alan said, 'but just now let's soak up the atmosphere without bothering about dates and people.'

The Pump Room was first on the agenda, as it was the closest 'site'. I don't know what I had expected – a grand room peopled with young ladies in high-waisted muslin dresses and bonnets, eagerly attended by young men in tight breeches, perhaps. Of course, the people I could see were definitely of the twenty-first century. They were dressed nicely, but there was not a floor-length, high-waisted gown in sight. The room was grand, certainly, but set up as a restaurant, with tables dotting the floor and a concert platform at one end. Alan pointed out a small but impressive fountain in one corner, with water pouring from four spouts into the mouths of four bronze fishes in the basin below. 'That's the famous Bath water,' he said, 'an all-purpose curative, or so they say. Would you like a sip?'

'What's it like?'

'To my taste, rather like the nether regions from which it comes. Sulphur and brimstone, or sulphur, at least.'

'Then no, thank you!'

He laughed. 'Wise woman. If you change your mind, you can have some later. We're coming back for tea this afternoon.'

I had glanced at the tea menu. 'Alan, after that breakfast we had, you're going to have to roll me home. No lunch!'

'Of course not,' he agreed blandly, knowing perfectly well that I'd feel quite differently after an hour or two. 'Do you want to tour the Roman Baths now? They're right here.'

'No, I don't think so. I'd rather see the abbey. It's near here, isn't it?'

'It is, and you'll love it. The ceiling is, I think, even finer than ours.'

'Our' ceiling, that is the ceiling of Sherebury Cathedral, is sometimes said to be modelled on that of Bath Abbey, though in fact ours is much older, so it may be the other way round. Both are perfect examples of fan-vaulting, that elaborate inter-lacing of supporting stonework that always reminds me of fountains in stone. 'Hmph! I'll have to see it to believe it,' I grumped. I'm a fierce admirer and defender of our Cathedral.

'And you shall see it in a minute or two. No, this way, love.'

I possess virtually no sense of direction; without a map I'm lost in any strange place. Thank heaven for Alan, who seems to have a built-in compass.

I had thought I ought to be able to see the abbey from a distance. Surely such a large, imposing building ought to rise above all others. And so it does, I saw when we reached the open square. But the abbey has no spire, and on all sides but one it is hugged closely by other buildings which block out the view. I thought rather smugly of our own Cathedral, situated in a large grassy close, so that its grandeur dominates the city.

However, when at last I stood before the abbey, my smug-ness died away before its beauty. I was struck especially with the patterns on either side of the west front, like nothing I'd ever seen before.

'Jacob's ladder,' Alan explained, 'with the angels ascending and descending. Look closely at that one in particular.'

I put a hand up to shade my eyes and peered where he pointed. I frowned. 'But surely . . . why is it upside down?'

'It's one of Bath's greatest jokes. Apparently the sculptor

had never seen someone climbing down a ladder. Of course, they look exactly the same as those climbing up, but he chose to send this one down head first. Droll, isn't it?'

'Oh, I have to have a picture of that!' I pulled out my phone, but Alan restrained me. 'It's too far away; it won't show well. I'm sure the gift shop will have postcards of it. Shall we go in?'

As we always do in a church, we stopped for a moment of prayer; the abbey, like most of the great churches in the UK, has a small chapel set aside for this purpose. My prayers centred on thanks for the magnificent church, and for my wonderful husband who had brought me there.

Then we wandered. I got a serious crick in the neck from looking at the ceiling. 'It's lovely,' I agreed. 'But I like ours better.'

Alan smiled and wisely said nothing.

The abbey was in the throes of a re-construction project. The ancient churches always are. This one wasn't especially old, as churches in England go. It was begun in the late-fifteenth century, but then fell into disuse after Henry VIII closed all the monasteries. Restored under Elizabeth I, it underwent restoration again (several times) in the eighteenth century – and then came World War II and bombing, requiring yet more repairs.

So what with one thing and another, the abbey is something of a patchwork of periods and styles, and of course something always needs repair. In this case it was the floor, with bits of it taken up here and there, which made for interesting traffic patterns. I finally got tired of dodging barriers and dragged Alan to the gift shop, where I bought postcards of the upside-down angel and a couple of books. I was hesitating over a large candy bar when Alan murmured, 'Do I remember you saying you didn't intend to have lunch?'

I put the candy bar back, trying to ignore the eager little rumblings in my stomach. Alan took pity. 'As a matter of fact, I have a plan. Why don't we pop into a pub for a pint and a bit of pub food? That will satisfy the inner woman for a bit, and you'll still have ample appetite for your splendid tea.'

So we had a pint and a Scotch egg apiece, and then did some more wandering and shopping. I found a lovely and inexpensive blouse and Alan indulged in a new pipe. 'You don't smoke anymore,' I pointed out.

'I know, but this is beautiful. I'll enjoy looking at it.'

And men accuse women of illogic!

Our carrier bags were beginning to be burdensome, and I was getting tired, so we went back to our hotel (Alan found it; I never could have) to dump our parcels and have a little rest before tea.

I changed my clothes. It was unthinkable to go to an elegant tea in jeans and sneakers! I put on my nicest slacks with an elegant cashmere sweater and a brocade jacket, and a pair of dressy flats. (I drew the line at heels for walking.) Alan helped me fasten my pearls (the one piece of nice jewellery I take when travelling) and I felt dressed to the nines.

It was obvious that nearly everyone in the Pump Room was celebrating some special occasion. We saw parties of giggling girls, plainly brides-to-be and her attendants. There were a good many elderly couples in the room; several of them looked like anniversary celebrants. We were seated next to the platform where an excellent string trio was playing show tunes and light classics, and when they launched into 'Happy Birthday' we were not the only people wearing self-conscious smiles.

It was a totally happy time: delectable food in elegant surroundings, delightful music, the company of my favourite person in the world – and a glass of champagne to top it off. Who could ask for more?

TWO

After that amazing tea, and a day of lots of walking, I was too tired for much, but I insisted on hitting the gift shop. I'm a sucker for church and museum gift shops. There's so much to find there that one can't buy anywhere else. I picked up a guidebook to the Baths, to prepare for our visit, and some prints of the city of long ago, and a couple of tea towels and a few chocolate 'coins' for Alan's grandchildren. I resisted a nice little bottle of the famous water, but did buy a small bottle of the 'Bath Botanical Gin'.

Alan was dubious about the gin. 'Botanical. What does that mean?'

'I've no idea. It may be flavoured with ancient Romans, for all I know. Never mind. Watered down with good tonic, it'll be drinkable. Anyway, I love the label. And it's my birthday, so there!'

That evening we planned the next few days. 'Now that you've had a taste of Bath—'

'Literally,' I interrupted, indicating my distended tummy.

'Indeed. What would you like to do tomorrow? We could take a guided tour, either on foot or by bus. We could, on our own, investigate the famous architecture of the Royal Crescent and the Circus and the nearby Jane Austen sites. There are some interesting Austen museums. And incidentally, the Royal Crescent Hotel does a splendid lunch.'

I groaned.

'Yes, but you'll feel differently tomorrow. And, of course, there's always Stonehenge, not too far away. Have you ever been there?'

'Once, at least fifty years ago. Considering its age, though, I can't imagine fifty years has made much difference.'

'It has, though. The feet of hundreds of thousands of tourists over the years threatened the stability of the stones. They've had to put up an enclosure. One can no longer wander into the circle.'

'Oh, what a pity! I'm not sure I want to see it that way.'

'They now have a large gift shop, however.'

He gave me one of his deadpan looks. I couldn't help laughing. 'Okay, you know me too well. Put Stonehenge on the list. But look, how about this? The Baths and the museums are indoor things, right?'

He nodded.

'So let's let the weather decide. If tomorrow is a lovely day, we can tour Bath or go out to Stonehenge. If it's rainy we'll do the Baths or the museums. I don't want to crowd too much into one day, or I'll just end up with a kind of Bath soup in my head. And we're here for a week.' I yawned. 'Alan, is it too ridiculously early to go to bed? I've had it.'

'Me, too. We can get an early start tomorrow.'

We woke before the dining room was open for breakfast. Alan made us coffee while I showered. This elegant hotel provided a cafetière with proper ground coffee instead of horrid instant. I was awake after I'd drunk a nice strong cup, but hungry. 'Do you suppose there's a café somewhere that's open?'

Alan handed me the cellophane packet of shortbread. 'This is a city for holidaymakers. It always has been, actually, ever since the Romans discovered the hot spring and built the Baths as a place to come and relax. That means things don't get under way really early. But it's only half an hour till they begin serving here. Can you hold out that long?'

'I suppose. We didn't have dinner last night, remember, and that lovely tea has vanished as though it had never been.'

My stomach produced a loud rumble, and Alan laughed. 'Rule number one when traveling with Dorothy: keep her adequately fed. You could break into your stash of chocolate coins.'

'Those are for Mike and Dennis,' I said virtuously. 'Never let it be said that I took candy from the mouths of babes.'

'They're teenagers, love, and would not appreciate being called babes.'

'The principle holds. No, I think I can manage not to faint from hunger. Just.'

Of course, when I did sit down to a full English breakfast I ate far too much. 'Have we decided on plans for the day?' I asked when I had at last stopped gulping my food.

'It's a splendid day. Shall we do the walking tour of Bath?'

'I'd love that, except I've eaten so much I really need to sit for a while and let it all settle. Stupid of me, I know. Such a pity to waste glorious weather.'

'Ah, but there's an alternative. Why don't we send for the car and set out for Stonehenge? If we dawdle a bit on the way we should get there shortly before they open.'

I shook my head to clear it. The idea of an ancient stone circle having 'opening hours' boggled the mind, but I managed to understand that the twenty-first century AD operates a bit differently from the thirtieth BC, or whenever the place was built.

'Right. I'll book us in straightaway for nine thirty.'

He pulled out his phone. Another culture shock moment.

While Alan waited for the car I went back up to the room to change into my sturdiest shoes. My memory of the Stonehenge of fifty years ago and more was a bit vague, and that visit had taken place at night, but I was sure that very uneven ground came into it somewhere. Also fierce winds. I picked up my coat and scarf and an extra sweater. A beautiful October day it might be, but it might not stay that way.

The drive was pleasant once we got out of Bath, which even at that hour on an ordinary Wednesday was crowded with traffic. The lambs were long gone from the meadows, having turned into stolid sheep that looked up as we passed, their silly faces looking even sillier as they chewed. I sighed with pleasure. Alan glanced at me.

'It's the sheep. I love them so. They're so very English.'

That prompted, as I knew it would, Alan's stock 'Yes, dear' response.

We dawdled, as Alan had proposed, and even so were among the first ones at the car park. Alan explained that under the recent arrangements, one had to park at this location a mile or so away from the stones and take the shuttle bus to the site.

Of course, the first thing I wanted to do when we got to the visitor centre was to shop. Alan reminded me that, though I was welcome to buy anything I liked, it might be better to wait until we came back. 'You won't want to carry a lot of bags while we're seeing the stones and all the rest. When we come back we'll sit and have something to eat and drink, and then you can shop to your heart's content.'

The shuttle was about to leave, so I reluctantly turned my back on the enticing array of goodies and climbed aboard.

It's impossible not to be awed by Stonehenge. The very size of the stones makes it incredible that prehistoric man erected them. Not feasible, one would think. And yet they did. How? And why? We don't know, but scientists and historians over the ages have made educated guesses.

'They think the stones came from Wales,' I read from the guidebook. 'But how? How on earth could they have moved those huge stones all that long way? Even nowadays it would take cranes and sturdy flatbed trucks. And why? I know there are timber circles here and there in England. That's so much easier! And the stones up in Orkney are of local origin. Why did the people here, whoever they were, feel they had to get enormous stones from *miles* away, and then go to the back-breaking work of setting them in place? So carefully, too, so that they're aligned with the movements of the sun.'

'The apparent movements, love. We know it's the earth that moves.'

I waved aside this pedantic objection.

'As for moving them,' he went on, 'one theory I've heard is that they floated them across the Bristol Channel and then up the River Avon. However, lately the people who research these things think they've found the quarry in Wales where they come from, and it's miles from the sea, so now they believe they actually were dragged on sledges overland. But as to why . . . ah, we will never know. The assumption of a religious and/or scientific purpose makes sense to me. A culture will go to almost any length in the service of its religion, and since astronomy and astrology were very much a part of religion in ancient days, I think the assumption holds water.'

'And of course the Druids had nothing to do with it.'

'Not unless our knowledge of Druidism is woefully inadequate. We can date them in Celtic lands back to about 400 BC – but that's millennia after the henge was built.'

'When I was here with Frank,' I said dreamily, 'all those years ago, it was on Midsummer's Eve. We'd booked a hotel in Salisbury and hitched a ride out here in the middle of the night. We wanted to see the sunrise over the heel stone. Back then we were allowed to walk in among the stones. There was quite a crowd, I remember, including a number of bobbies, there to keep order, I suppose. The only interesting incident was when a hippy – this was in the sixties – decided it would be a good idea to take off all his clothes and climb on top of the stones.'

Alan winced. 'Deuced uncomfortable, I'd have thought, in the nude.'

'That was my thought exactly! Anyway, a bobby came up and tapped him on the heel with his torch and told him he had to come down. Someone provided a blanket or something to cover him up, and they took him off. That was all, except that a lot of Druids were there in white robes, and they blew horns at sunrise. Actually, the sun didn't visibly rise, there being a thick cloud cover, but one of the Druids had a nice modern watch and checked the time so they could mark the right instant. That struck me as funny. I suppose it was that sort of thing, the climbing, I mean, that convinced the powers that be to close the circle off. Pity.'

'That, and to stop people chipping away bits and taking them home.'

'No! Who would do such a thing?'

'There are a lot of thoughtless people in the world, love.'

I shook my head over that and moved around looking at the displays. I had to admit that I saw a lot more of the place than I had on that memorable night years ago, and learned a lot more – but the incredible atmosphere of that long ago wonder would remain in my heart forever. That night the place was magic. Today it was just amazing.

When I had seen my fill, and had become too tired to respond with appropriate enthusiasm, we went back to the visitor centre, and after tea and sandwiches and the rock cakes for which the café was famous, Alan turned me loose in the gift shop.

He'd been quite right to make me defer that pleasure until the end of our visit. Weariness never keeps me from shopping. I was slightly distracted for a moment by what seemed to be an altercation between one of the shopkeepers and a woman who looked like a superannuated hippy. She was screaming at the clerk and brandishing something in her fist, but when she turned her head for a moment and saw us, she stomped off.

'There's one in every crowd,' I murmured to Alan, and turned to the important business of shopping. In rapid succession I picked out plum wine for Alan's daughter Elizabeth and a thousand-piece puzzle of Stonehenge for her sons. 'You got them the chocolate,' Alan objected.

'Christmas is coming.' I couldn't resist an adorable teddy bear for the youngest child of our friends Nigel and Inga

Evans, or a gorgeous teapot for our dear neighbour and pet-sitter Jane, or various T-shirts for some friends back home in Indiana. Et cetera.

The parcels were, as Alan had predicted, not only bulky but heavy. We staggered back to our car with them, and Alan put his share on the gravel of the car park while he opened what I'm learning to call the boot. The lid raised itself in its obedient way.

We stared. 'What on earth?'

The boot was full of boxes and bags of objects we had never seen before.

THREE

'Is there a problem, sir? Madam?'

A security guard had appeared at our side. I must have cried out in a louder voice than I'd intended. 'Well – not really,' I stammered. 'That is – yes, I suppose there is. These things – I don't know how—'

Alan took over. 'This is our car, but we did not put these things in the boot. We don't recognize them.'

'The boot was locked?'

'Of course.'

I moved to take a closer look, but Alan smoothly stepped in my way.

'Hmm,' said the guard. 'Has the car been under your control at all times?'

'No,' said Alan before I could reply. 'We live in Sherebury, a small cathedral city in Belleshire. We are visiting in Bath for a bit of a holiday, and our hotel provides valet parking. Until this morning, when it was delivered to us at the hotel, we had not seen the car for over twenty-four hours.'

'And you did not open the boot at that time? This morning, that is?'

'No. There was no reason to do so. We had no luggage. We are returning to Bath this afternoon.'

'I see, sir.'

He moved close to the boot and peered inside, poking into this box and that. 'Hmm,' he said again. 'Rather an odd assortment. One might almost think they were intended for a jumble sale, though there seem to be some items of value in with the— Oh.'

He straightened and looked at Alan with a much-altered expression. 'You came straight here this morning? No stops along the way?'

'No stops,' I said impatiently. I was tired of being ignored. 'And we're headed straight back. And I'm tired, and I'd like to get to the hotel as soon as possible. What should we do with all this junk?'

'I'll take it for now, madam, until the police can have a go. And I'm sorry, but I'll have to ask you both to remain here until the authorities have talked to you.'

'Police! What are you talking about? What right do you have—?'

'Dorothy.' Alan put a hand on my arm. 'There's an obvious misunderstanding, but certainly we'll cooperate. May we put our recent purchases in the backseat? They're a bit cumbersome. We have the receipt and will be happy to show it to you.'

I took a breath to speak. Alan's pressure on my arm increased. I held my fire.

The guard gravely inspected our bags and the receipt and allowed us to stash everything in the car. Then he and another guard carefully loaded the contents of the boot onto a handcart and wheeled it into some private place at the visitor centre. *Then* we were finally allowed to go in and sit down.

'And I don't care if it is the middle of the afternoon! I want a gin and tonic.'

'I don't believe they serve spirits, but you can have a nice pint.'

'Or two! Alan, why did you shut me up? What's going on, for Pete's sake?'

'I wanted to keep the atmosphere cool. You didn't notice, my dear, but I did, and the guard certainly did. One of those boxes contained a good-sized chunk of rock. I'm no expert, but it looked a great deal like the stones we saw today. The monoliths.'

'But – a piece of *Stonehenge*, you mean?'

'Exactly. And the rest of the "junk", as you put it, seemed to be memorabilia of various kinds. I'll get our beer.'

I was still in shock when he came back with two brimming pints.

'You're saying,' I muttered when I'd had a hefty swig and wiped the foam from my mouth, 'that that man thinks we stole a piece of Stonehenge? And a lot of other artefacts, as well?'

'Let's say he considers it a possibility. That was why I so rudely pushed you away. When the police get here I'm going to insist that they take our fingerprints.'

'Oh! And then when they're not on any of the stuff—'

'It won't absolutely prove our innocence. But I'm hoping that they'll be covered with other prints. Whoever the malefactor is, he doesn't strike me as very professional. Hiding his loot in someone else's car was not a brilliant move.'

'No. And I trust you'll flaunt your title and experience for all it's worth.'

'If it seems necessary, you can bet I will. And here they are, I believe.'

The two men introduced themselves, grimly but courteously. Alan introduced me and himself. The detective inspector in charge, a tall, wiry man who might have been almost any age, suggested that we move to a more private place, and we obediently tagged along to an office, recently vacated by the manager of the visitor centre. Everyone sat down. The detective inspector cleared his throat.

'Well now, Mr Nesbitt, you have been found in possession of some very valuable property, which you claim you have never seen before. I don't know how familiar you are with police procedure in such cases—'

'Forgive me for interrupting, sir, but I am in fact very familiar indeed with standard procedures. I was, you see, for many years the chief constable of Belleshire, and though now retired I have not forgotten the way things are done. For that reason, I request that our fingerprints be taken immediately, my wife's and mine, to establish that we have neither of us ever laid a finger on the items found in our boot.'

'Er . . . yes, of course. We've not brought that equipment with us, so perhaps a bit later on—'

'Now, Inspector. I insist. The sooner our lack of involvement in this matter is established, the sooner we can go back to Bath. My wife is very tired. Surely you must have the standard kit in your car.'

I endeavoured to look old and exhausted. It wasn't much of an effort.

The inspector was not best pleased, but he wasn't a stupid man. He recognized Alan's authority and inconvenient knowledge of standard procedures. He also noted, I'm sure, that Alan was taller than he and heavier by a good deal. Not that it would ever come to a physical struggle, but . . . He conceded. He nodded to his subordinate, who left the room and returned very quickly with a small box.

'Now, Mrs Nesbitt,' the sergeant began.

'Mrs Martin,' I corrected with a saccharine smile. 'This is a second marriage; I kept my former name.' I was enjoying this a good deal. Alan had managed, with very little effort, to establish control of the situation, and the sergeant's small mistake helped.

'Yes. Sorry. You've been printed before?'

'Often.' I hoped he might gain the impression that I was a habitual criminal, so that when the error was discovered, morale might be even further diminished.

With both sets of prints taken, the inspector opened his mouth, but Alan forestalled him. 'Now, of course, you'll want to check one or two of the objects from the boot.'

The inspector showed some irritation, and I, in turn, was wondering if Alan's tactics were a trifle heavy-handed, but now he began to lighten the touch. 'I suppose,' he said conversationally, 'it must be difficult for you here in high tourist season. Even with all the precautions laid down against theft and vandalism, you must have your hands full. You have my sympathy.'

The inspector thawed a trifle. 'It's a constant battle, as you may imagine. And of course there's the ordinary run of crime to deal with as well, with insufficient staff.'

Alan groaned. 'The perpetual problem! It's no wonder the wide boys sometimes seem to have the upper hand. Their profession can be a good deal better paid than ours, and with less risk.'

'It does sometimes seem that way, Mr Nesbitt.'

'Please call me Alan.'

'Thank you, sir. Alan. My given name, I'm sorry to say, is Cedric.'

'Oh, dear,' I couldn't help saying. 'What do your friends call you?'

He smiled. 'Rob. My surname is Roberts. Although, when they're upset, there are sometimes other terms. Ah, Sergeant. Any joy?'

'Prints all over the shop, sir. Our crook was too stupid to wear gloves. And none of them that I could find looked anything like . . .' He nodded to Alan and me.

The inspector heaved a sigh of relief. He hadn't looked forward to interrogating a retired chief constable. 'Well, then, that's fine. Of course, we'll have to have everything properly inspected, but it's apparent that you had nothing to do with this, sir – Alan – beyond the unfortunate circumstance of the goods being found in your car. Er . . . do you have any idea how that might have happened?'

'Very little, I'm afraid. As I told the security guard, I surrendered the car to the valet at the Royal George Hotel when we arrived.'

The inspector's eyebrows rose at the name of the hotel.

'That was on Monday in mid-afternoon, about four thirty,' Alan continued. 'We spent yesterday exploring Bath; my wife had never visited that remarkable city. This morning, quite early, we decided to visit Stonehenge, and rather than take the coach tour we sent for our car. It was delivered to us, we drove it here – and you know the rest.'

The inspector had listened carefully. 'Have you any idea where the car was parked while it was in hotel custody?'

'None. I would assume that it was in a secure carpark, or perhaps a garage, but I don't know.'

'We'll have to check with the hotel, then. Do you recall how much time it took for the car to be delivered?'

'Not with any accuracy. Somewhat longer than I thought it should, but that may be simply because I was impatient. We were both eager to set out.'

'I think it was about twenty minutes,' I put in. 'Because I went upstairs to change my shoes and hurried back down, not wanting to keep anyone waiting. And we still had to wait a bit.'

'This was at what time of day?'

'Around eight,' said Alan. 'That was one reason I was surprised at the time it took. The traffic wasn't yet horrendous.'

'Yes, I see. One last question. Was the driver who returned your car the same as the one who picked it up on Monday?'

'No. I did notice that, though I didn't read either of their name badges. But the chap this morning was Indian, or perhaps Pakistani. The other was English.'

'Right.' Rob closed his notebook and rose. 'I am so sorry to have delayed your return to your magnificent hotel. Enjoy the rest of your stay in Bath.'

Alan pulled a card out of his wallet. 'Here's my contact information. I'd appreciate your keeping us informed of developments.'

'Certainly, sir.' The inspector in turn gave Alan his card. 'You'll phone us if you remember anything else?'

'Of course.' They parted with cordial handshakes, with a grin from the sergeant, who had been effacing himself in the corner, and we traipsed back to our car.

FOUR

'Well! I've never before been accused of theft!' I slammed the car door with unnecessary vigour, and buckled my seat belt, looking smugly virtuous.

'Accuracy in all things, love,' said Alan. 'We weren't actually accused.'

'Oh, don't be pedantic! We certainly were, if only by innuendo.'

'Ah, but you can't sue over innuendo. And you must admit, appearances were suspicious.'

'I suppose.' I was reluctant to abandon my snit, but Alan had a point. 'What else was in the trunk? The boot? Besides that chunk of rock. Was it really a piece of Stonehenge?'

'I didn't look at it closely. If I had to guess, I'd say it was stolen not from the henge itself, but from the Welsh quarry where the monoliths originated. There's been a rash of thefts from there lately. As for the rest of the loot, I saw only a little before they whisked it away, but it was very odd. There was a snippet of cloth, for one thing. Not big enough for any practical use. I thought I spotted a bottle of the Bath spa water that you're so rude about, and a replica of a Roman coin.'

I got excited about that. 'What if it was the real thing? That would be worth a fortune!'

'Sorry, love. It was much too shiny and new-looking to be real. Oh, and I also saw just the corner of a booklet, thin and paperbound. This was all in the box. I couldn't check the bags without touching them, and you know why I didn't want to do that.'

'Fingerprints. Yes, I would have dived right in if you hadn't stopped me. You know, my dear, just occasionally it's useful to have a policeman for a husband. I think I'll keep you.'

'I'm relieved to hear that. Now. Straight back to Bath, or repair to a pub for a little rehab?'

'Straight back. We don't know the pubs along the way, and the classiest one we could hope to find is at our . . . What did the inspector call it?'

'"Magnificent hotel". It's all of that. I trust you don't plan to become accustomed to that sort of luxury. Don't forget this is a very special treat.'

'No, I'll happily accept re-entry into real life when the idyll is over. But for now I intend to live it up.'

We didn't dawdle on the way back as we had in the morning, so it wasn't very long before I sat at a comfortable table in the George's elegant bar with a perfect gin and tonic in front of me, along with a Scotch egg, my favourite bar snack. I told my conscience to shut up. Those rock cakes were but a distant memory, and I deserved some comfort after the recent trauma.

'But I can't help wondering,' I began, when my drink was half gone and spreading a warm glow inside. I stopped when Alan made a great show of consulting his watch. 'What? Are we late for something?'

'No, I was timing how long it would take you to start worrying at your bone.' He smiled blandly.

'Did I say I was going to keep you? I take it back. It's not fair the way you can read my mind!'

'As I've told you before, your thoughts are written on your face.'

'I know, I know. Never play poker. Which is wasted advice, since I don't know how anyway. However, before I was rudely interrupted, I was saying: I wonder about that very odd collection of objects. There doesn't seem to be any pattern. Do you suppose Inspector What's-his-name would tell us what else is in there, if you asked nicely?'

Alan shrugged. 'We're in an ambivalent position. We were initially suspected of theft, and although that suspicion is nearly dispelled—'

'What do you mean, nearly? They didn't find our fingerprints. And they won't, of course, since we never touched the stuff.'

'We could still be accessories, allowing the loot to be stored in our car. Or we could be fencing it. There are several possibilities.'

'But you're a chief constable, for Pete's sake!'

'I was. I am still a sworn police officer, but I no longer hold any rank. And as you well know, love, policemen have gone bad before now. It's a frequent plot element in your preferred reading.'

'Well, but can't they *see* you're a respectable citizen?'

Alan just shook his head pityingly.

I finished my drink and thought about another, but reluctantly decided I'd had enough. 'But it's so *frustrating*! There must be something we can do. Couldn't we at least ask for a list of the stuff? They can only turn us down. I mean, they wouldn't think that was a suspicious request, would they?'

'One wouldn't think so. I very much doubt they will grant it, though.'

I slid my empty glass around on the table, thinking. 'Well, at least we can ask about the parking situation, where the car is kept, that sort of thing.'

'Aha! I did ask, just now when I turned the car back over to the valet.'

'Oh, was it the same one?'

'Not the same as either of the others. I did get his name, this time; it's Ben.'

'Oh, English, then.'

'South African, actually, at least from the accent.'

I shook my head. I'm still bemused by the vast diversity of cultures one finds in England. Such a small country, but with a rich history of empire, which I suppose accounts for some of the mix. South Africa, though, was a Dutch colony . . . I brought my attention back to Alan.

'. . . on the outskirts of town, which is why there's a bit of a wait for the car.'

'I'm sorry, Alan, I got distracted. You're talking about where they park the car?'

'In a garage just on the edge of the city.'

'A parking garage?'

He smiled. 'We don't have many of those on this side of the pond, love. No, a repair garage, but with a separate area that's used by the hotel. I told Ben I might want the car very late at night, and he said that would be no problem; the hotel has a key to the facility.'

'Key! So it's kept locked?'

'At night, at least. I didn't enquire about the daytime hours when the repair garage is open.' He held up his hand as I opened my mouth. 'Yes, of course we want to know that, but I didn't want to push too far this time. We can find out more later. Of course, the police will be looking into it, too, very thoroughly.'

'Assuming they don't still think we're the villains.' I picked up my glass, remembered it was empty, and set it down again.

'Even if they still have doubts about that, they need to establish who had access to our car during the relevant times.

Don't underestimate them, Dorothy. The inspector who questioned us, Roberts, is with the police here in Bath, and he will be cooperating closely with the World Heritage people. Though some of what was in that box was obvious rubbish, that piece of stone, if it is bluestone, is a precious artefact. They're not going to rest until they find the thief. And that means they're going to keep us in their back pocket, so to speak, until they're quite satisfied of our utter innocence in the matter. Now. Are you going to keep on fiddling with that glass or have another?'

I was considering whether to be sensible or do what I wanted when the barman came over to Alan. 'A gentleman to see you, sir. A Mr Roberts. He's waiting in the lobby. Do you want to see him, or shall I tell him you've gone out?'

'Good grief,' I murmured. 'We've been here about forty-eight hours, and the staff know you by sight?'

'I ordered our drinks with our room number, love.' In a louder tone he said, 'Certainly I'll talk to Mr Roberts. In fact, I'll buy him a drink. Ask him to join us.'

He smiled blandly at me.

'That look,' I said quietly, 'always means you're up to something.'

'Ah, am I growing as transparent as you in my old age? It's nothing, really, just that . . . Ah, Rob! Do sit down. Would you prefer whisky or beer? I can recommend this' – Alan held up his glass – 'Highland Park. Got acquainted with it on a visit to Orkney. Well worth trying, if you don't know it.'

After that, the inspector could hardly refuse, and I caught on. With that one smooth move, Alan had taken control of the encounter. I lifted my glass in salute and grinned, and Alan signalled the barman for another round. I had noted earlier, with approval, that this was not the sort of place where one fetched them from the bar. Oh, no, not in this 'magnificent' hotel.

Inspector Roberts was, of course, not in uniform, but there was something about him that identified him as a person of authority. The barman was very quick with our drinks, but lingered a bit after he had distributed them. 'Anything else, sirs? Madam? Are the drinks to your liking? You would perhaps like some nuts? Crisps?'

He wanted to know what was going on; that was obvious. Alan had no intention of enlightening him, but sent him away with courteous firmness.

'And now,' he said, smiling at the inspector, 'I hope you have some news for us.'

The inspector smiled back a bit thinly. 'Nothing of any great interest, I fear. There's scarcely been time. We have at least learned where your car is kept by the valet service. It's in a locked facility at the edge of Bath.'

'Ah,' said Alan, 'that makes a good deal less likely that someone from outside put the stolen goods in our car.' Nothing in his voice or face betrayed the fact that he knew the car's location already. 'At least, I'm assuming that they were all stolen. Have you determined that?'

'Actually, no. We've not got far beyond unpacking everything, and really, it's the oddest assortment of riches and rubbish. There are trinkets from all the museum gift shops in Bath and environs, some of them made in China and vastly overpriced even at a pound or two; they still have the price stickers on them. One small bag actually had a receipt in it, so our boy bought them! And then there are the other things, quite definitely stolen. The chunk of bluestone is the most obvious, but there's also a Roman coin from the Baths museum, a glove that belonged to Jane Austen, from her museum, and a locket whose origin we have not yet determined, but it's gold and set with a small diamond.'

'Good grief! I begin to think, Mr— Rob, that we're dealing with someone who's not quite sane. This sounds like the hoard of a collector who's gone round the bend. As they sometimes do.'

Rob looked at me more closely, seeming to recognize for the first time that I was a genuine person. 'You have some experience with collectors, Mrs Nes— Er, Martin?'

'Dorothy, please. And yes, I had an unfortunate experience some years ago with a collector even more rabid than most, a woman who tried to kill me and succeeded in breaking my leg.'

'And in so doing delivered herself into the hands of the authorities,' added Alan. 'She had already been responsible for two murders, and it was my wife who figured that out. Dorothy has a remarkable insight into human nature, Rob.'

The man got that odd look on his face, the look of one who is peering at something in his mind. 'Do I seem to remember . . . Dorothy Martin . . . haven't I seen that name in the newspapers?'

'I suppose you may have. I've been involved in one or two criminal investigations. Strictly as an amateur, of course. And I've had the most amazing luck, sometimes.'

'Don't listen to her, Rob. Luck had very little to do with it. Dorothy is one of those gifted people who can take a seemingly meaningless bit of information and turn it into the linchpin of an investigation. If she had been born later, and in this country, she'd have been the chief constable in the family and I a lowly flunky.'

'And *that* is flat nonsense, and you know it, Alan Nesbitt. I never wanted to be anything but a teacher, which I was for years, Rob, back in Indiana where I lived all my life before coming to England. I think that's where I picked up a certain amount of knowledge about what makes people tick. I do admit to being as curious as a cat or the Elephant's Child. And . . . well, I care about people and like to help with their problems if I can.' I picked up my glass and sipped to hide my red face. Admitting to emotion is Not Done in England.

Rob's smile this time was genuine. 'I seem,' he said, 'to have fallen on my feet, rather than my face as I first feared. Am I to understand that the two of you are in fact an investigative team?'

'In a manner of speaking' said Alan. 'All strictly unofficial, of course. Back home in Sherebury, where we know nearly everyone, we are treated almost as police associates. Elsewhere, we try to interfere as little as possible.'

'We are, in fact, known to the police,' I said, almost giggling. Oh, dear. I put down my glass.

Alan patted my hand and murmured, 'Dinner, love, soon.' Aloud, he addressed Rob. 'Well, that's cleared the air a bit, hasn't it? Mind you, I quite understand that some suspicion must still attach to us until the real thief is caught. The swag was, after all, found in our car.'

'And we'll all be thankful when we find out how it got there!' Rob finished his drink, but before he stood up, he added, 'I hope . . . that is, if you . . . what I'm trying to say is that if the two of you should feel inclined to look into this matter, let me just say that my department and I won't stand in your way. Now that I understand the situation . . . well. I've kept you from your dinner quite long enough. Thank you for the drink, and for your time. I'll be in touch.' He gave us a little half-salute and faded out of the room.

FIVE

'He turned out to be quite nice,' I said in some surprise, when I'd eaten enough to be reasonably sober again. 'I'm sorry, by the way, for making a fool of myself. At my age I should know better.'

'It's been a trying day,' Alan said comfortably. 'No worries. Just make sure to take some ibuprofen before you go to bed, to stave off any possible after-effects.'

I smiled. 'I remember once, when I was very young indeed, I came to England by myself for the first time. It was before Frank and I were married. I was just out of college and got the chance of a very cheap flight. Of course I was sure I could cope brilliantly; one is so self-confident at that age. Anyway, I simply rambled, no plans, no booking ahead. I ended up one night at a pub in Chester whose proprietors were from Liverpool, and they took a fancy to this young American. Absolutely green as grass, I was, but I didn't know it.

'They decided to undertake my education in English beer, and since they were paying and I was a resident, I could drink till the cows came home. And did. I was having a good time and totally lost track of how much I'd had, until the wife sized me up and told me I'd better go to bed. She gave me a couple of tablets of something, I've no idea what, and told me to take them, without fail, before lying down.

'The amazing thing is that I woke in the morning with no

headache, no miserable stomach, none of what I so richly deserved. I wish now that I'd asked what the magic pills were. If they're still on the market, and legal, I'd like to lay in a stock of them, just in case.'

'And if you could buy enough of them, you could make a fortune selling them on the black market.'

'And you a policeman. For shame! Anyway, it sounds as though Rob has checked us off his list.'

'Provisionally. The stuff was still in our car. And as the facility was kept locked, that does limit the people who could have put it there.'

'We still need to find out if the people at the repair garage could get in during the day. What with customers coming in and out, that would widen the field considerably.' I yawned. 'Sorry.'

'Go up to bed, darling. I'll follow after I've had a word with the clerk at reception.'

'It's too early. I'll just wake up early, and tomorrow will be a reprise of today.'

'Without, one hopes, any nasty surprises. Off you go.'

I half-heartedly stowed away the day's purchases. We'd just dumped them on the bed earlier. I was too sleepy to speculate much about what Alan was doing at reception. He'd tell me when he got back. I yawned again.

'Morning, love. Sleep well?'

I opened the other eye and tried to focus on the lighted numerals of the bedside clock. 'What time is it? Looks like the middle of the night.'

'Just past six on a beautiful October morning. It's going to be a fine day, but the sun won't rise for a while.'

'Umph. And I'm wide awake.'

'No ill effects from last night's indiscretion?'

'Not a one. I have an errand, though.'

When I got back from the bathroom I crawled back into bed. 'I don't want to get up, but I know I can't get back to sleep.'

'Ah. I have an idea about that.'

* * *

'That,' I said an hour later, 'was a ridiculously frivol[...] for two people our age to behave.'

'Yes. Isn't frivolity fun?' He leaned over and kissed [...]

I kissed him back and headed for the shower.

'There was something . . . oh, yes, what did you want to talk to reception about last night?' I asked as I towelled my hair dry and pulled on my slacks.

'The garage, and the valets. I didn't learn a lot. It turns out that the valet service is not operated by the hotel. It's run by a private team, under contract, so the hotel people know almost nothing about the facility or the employees.'

'Oh, dear. So I suppose we'll be chasing that down today.'

'Right. After we have breakfast. I don't know why, but I'm unusually hungry this morning.'

I always fear that I'll gain weight on vacation, because I eat enormous meals, much more than at home. But thank goodness, Alan and I also walk for miles, it being our firm belief that the only way to see a city is on foot. These days we have to take it in small snatches with frequent rests, especially in a place like our last outing, Durham, which is *all* hills. Bath is a good deal more level, but as we're no longer young, we still decided to be conservative about our touring.

'Later we'll try to talk to the valet service people, but as it's another amazingly fine day, let's tour Bath this morning. On foot or by bus?'

'Oh, by bus, definitely. It's hop-on, hop-off, right? So we can spend as much time as we want when we find that a place is interesting, and very little time when it isn't. And we don't have all that walking to do in between.'

Alan eyed my plate, now emptied of bacon and sausage and eggs and mushrooms and fried bread.

'And don't you lecture me, Alan Nesbitt! I enjoyed every bite, so there!'

He spread his hands and grinned.

The bus tour left from in front of the abbey, among other places, so the first walk was a short one. The day being gorgeous, we chose to sit on the top of the bus, open to the

utumn air and with glorious views of the city. As we'd
y had a quick glance at the abbey, and planned to go
e for a proper tour later, we skipped that and also the Baths,
which warranted a leisurely visit. But we got out at the Circus,
that ring of lovely houses near the Jane Austen Centre.

A mannequin dressed like Jane was standing in front of the
door, as well as a genuine living man, also dressed in period
costume. When I greeted him, he told me his name was Bennet.
I took a moment to commiserate with him about his difficult
wife, to which he responded with a resigned smile, and then
we walked into the world of the early-nineteenth century.

Anyone who has not read the books would probably dismiss
the period as quaint, staid, and dull, but I could see Jane's characters lurking behind every corner, and quiet intrigues hidden
beneath every bonnet and top hat. Alan and I took advantage of
the invitation to try on the latter; I thought myself very fetching
in a particular poke bonnet.

'But nothing ever happens,' I heard one American
complaining to her companion in a muted discussion about
Sense and Sensibility.

'Well, no,' I said to Alan when we had left the couple
behind. 'Nothing like gun battles or kidnapping or the discovery
of the Rajah's diamond. It's all internal. Before you get to the
third chapter of *Sense* you've had enough nastiness and greed
and cowardice and betrayal to fill most modern novels. And
humour! My word, the first chapter of *Northanger Abbey* still
makes me laugh out loud!'

'Yes, dear,' said Alan patiently. 'You're preaching to the
choir, you know.'

We ended up, of course, in the gift shop, where I wanted
nearly everything. Some of the costume jewellery was lovely,
and affordable, but the gold and silver items were well beyond
my budget. Of course, I wanted lots of books. Alan had to
remind me that we had several more sites to visit, and were
riding a bus, so I contented myself with one small Christmas
tree ornament, a representation of Mr Darcy, and marked out
lots more in a mental list for purchase before we went home.

The shop was crowded. In negotiating a tight corner, I

bumped into a young man who was arranging a display. He apologized profusely, although it was certainly my fault. 'I'm sorry, I'm sorry,' he kept saying.

Something about his voice and appearance kept me from annoyance. 'It's all right,' I assured him, over and over. 'Don't worry. My name is Dorothy. What's yours?'

The boy smiled broadly. 'Sammy. I'm Sammy.' He solemnly extended a hand which I shook.

'I'm sorry, Sammy, but I must go now. It was nice to meet you. I hope I'll see you again.' I smiled and walked away.

Shopping a bit more, I picked up a handkerchief embroidered with my favourite quote, the famous opening line of *Pride and Prejudice* – 'It is a truth universally acknowledged . . .' – thinking that it weighed nothing and wouldn't be a burden on the bus. I didn't know what I'd do with it, though, as I always use tissues. I was still debating when Alan came up behind me and uttered a little exclamation.

'Dorothy, I may be imagining things, but I'd almost swear I saw a piece of that, or something identical to that, in the box of' – he looked around and lowered his voice – 'the box in our boot.'

'A scrap of cloth, you said,' I remembered. 'This, you think?'

'I do think. The green embroidery is distinctive. I saw only a fragment of something curved, but it looked very much like this.' He pointed to a curlicue on the handkerchief.

I made up my mind. 'I'm buying it. We can take it to Rob and compare.'

As we paid for our few purchases the clerk said quietly, 'I hope Sammy didn't bother you. He works here, part-time, mostly in the stock room. He's a little . . .' She gestured to her head.

'Down syndrome?' I asked.

'Yes. He does very well, really, but he's very friendly, and sometimes people think . . . well, you know.'

'He's sweet, and didn't bother me at all. Years ago, back in the States, I was a teacher, and we had a few special needs children. I thought them delightful people. I'm so glad he's found a good place to work. That's important to youngsters like him.'

We walked back to the Circus and strolled for a few minutes until the bus arrived. I looked at the arc of Georgian town houses, all nearly identical, and commented, 'This would be a terrible place to come home to at night if one had had a little too much to drink. You could only find the right door by counting.'

Alan nodded. 'Or reading the house number. Neither easy to do with a snootful.'

Our next stop, just down the street, was the Royal Crescent. 'My word, it's even worse!'

I spoke too loudly and our guide heard me. 'It's regarded as the finest example of Georgian architecture in England, madam, perhaps in the world.'

'Yes, yes, I didn't mean . . .' But he had gone on to describe some of the details, and I sunk down into my seat while Alan tried hard not to laugh out loud.

A moment later he nudged me. 'Look over there.' The guide was explaining that the lovely lawn in front of the Crescent was protected from wandering livestock by a ha-ha, a sort of invisible fence consisting of a sharp drop-off at some distance from the buildings, creating a barrier that was effective, but unseen from the houses, from which the lawn seemed to stretch on. 'We can see it, just barely, from up here, but it was designed to be invisible to the residents.'

I peered. I could just make out a slight change in colour from one patch of perfectly groomed lawn to the next, but I couldn't discern the change of level. 'Very effective,' I commented. 'I never knew what a ha-ha was. Though I imagine there's not a lot of marauding wildlife in Bath these days.'

We didn't get out at any of the next few stops. 'I'm suffering from information overload,' I complained. 'My mind won't take in much more history or architectural description. And I'm getting hungry.'

'Well, then, we'll jump ship when it gets to the High Street and seek some food.'

I suppose it's politically incorrect to say that the main shopping area of Bath looks just like shopping areas everywhere in the UK. Same shops, same merchandise, same crowds. I do enjoy shopping where there are interesting and unusual things on offer, but I'd done enough for one morning.

'Lunch first?' asked Alan when we had hopped – in a manner of speaking – off the bus.

I just looked at him.

'Then let's find Sally Lunn's. It will be crowded, probably, but we might just squeeze in. They do an excellent lunch, and as it's in a fifteenth-century house, and the special bun they make goes back to the seventeenth, you can wallow in history as well as good food.'

Even I had heard of Sally Lunn's. 'Sounds fine. As long as it's not too far away.'

Alan consulted the map he'd bought somewhere (he's amazingly well-organized) and found the little café, which was well hidden down a narrow alley. It was indeed crowded, but we were shown to a table after a brief wait and refreshed ourselves with a nice cold lager while we considered the food question. There were so many choices I finally let Alan decide for me, and ended up with far more lovely food than I thought I could eat, from soup right through to a warm apple cake with generous dollops of clotted cream.

'You're far away,' Alan commented as I was finishing the last bite.

'I was thinking about Sammy. The boy in the shop,' I added when he raised an eyebrow. 'People tend to feel sorry for the retarded, as we used to call them, but I'm never sure that's appropriate. In some ways they're better off than those of us who are called normal. They are capable of great, uncomplicated happiness.'

'Also great sorrow, though,' Alan mused. 'When they're unhappy, it's as if the world has come to an end.'

'Yes. Emotions are all on the surface. But I think the joy outweighs the sorrow.' I finished my coffee. 'You know I sometimes watch that live-cam feed from the kitten rescue agency in Los Angeles. I don't think I've ever showed you, but in one of their rooms they have four cats, not kittens any longer, who are severely handicapped with a neurological disease. They will never be able to walk, or even stand up. They spend their lives curled up on their blankets or sometimes scooting around the room a little – but never very far. They have to be helped to eat, and can't use a litter box. And yet every volunteer at the agency says they're the happiest cats they've ever seen. They love to be cuddled. They purr most of the time. They enjoy the company of their human caregivers, and of the other cats who come to visit. They have no idea, you see, that there's anything wrong with them. They have no worries, no frustrations.'

I picked up my coffee cup, found it empty, and put it down again. 'I think the Sammys of this world are like those cats. As long as their basic needs are met, including love, of course, and they have an interesting way of spending their days, they're far happier than most of us who have to cope with the pinpricks of everyday life. No, I don't feel sorry for Sammy. In a way I envy him.'

'You have a point. Now – more coffee? Or anything?'

I pushed back my chair and groaned. 'I may never move again. That was an incredible meal!'

Alan grinned. 'Shall we buy a few buns to take back to the hotel? For tea?'

I just groaned again.

'Right,' said Alan once we were back on the street. 'We're about equidistant from the hotel and the Baths. Shall we take that tour now, or toddle back to our room?'

'I'm not up for anything but a nap, after that feast. It really isn't far, is it?'

'Not far at all, love. Courage!'

He pronounced it the French way, which made me giggle and gave me the impetus I needed to 'toddle' along to my nap.

SIX

D rugged with carbohydrates, I slept heavily for over an hour, but woke refreshed and ready for action. Alan made us both some coffee to waken us fully, and asked, 'The Baths this afternoon?'

'First I want to see if we can't find out more about the

mysterious loot in our car. Good grief, that sounds like a Nancy
Drew title. The Case of the Mysterious Loot.'

'Or Perry Mason. Right. I could call the valet service
company. Or shall we go to their office and badger them in
person?'

'In person, of course. It's too easy for people to dismiss
you if you're on the phone. Much harder when you're standing
in front of them.'

'Agreed. You're going to wear a hat, I presume?'

'Of course. It's a pity I didn't bring that Queen Mum thing
with the violets all over it.' I'm not quite as devoted to hats
as I used to be, but I do wear them on occasion. To church,
of course (though I may be the only woman in the place
wearing one), and whenever I want to impress or, as in this
case, intimidate.

'That is a truly awe-inspiring hat, but not exactly seasonal.
How about the one with the autumn leaves and chrysanthemums? Did you bring that?'

I whipped the hat box triumphantly out of the wardrobe.
'Ta-da! Of course I brought it. We're going to church at
the abbey. Couldn't appear there bareheaded!'

Alan called the concierge to order our car. The man rang
us back before I had time to adjust my hat properly. Alan
listened with an inscrutable face. His end of the conversation
was not enlightening, consisting of variations of *yes* and *no*
and *I see*.

He hung up and turned to me. 'There are developments.'

'What?'

'I'm not entirely sure. The concierge said that there might
be a considerable delay in fetching our car, but if we were in
a hurry, we could use the hotel's limo. Free of charge, of
course. I agreed to that.'

'Hmm. Interesting. Are we going straight to the valet
company, or to the garage?'

'The valet company, I think. Meanwhile I'm calling the
inspector. I think he'll want to know what's going on.'

The hotel limo (or perhaps one of their fleet; it was that
sort of hotel) was a Rolls Royce. Never had I thought to ride
in such a vehicle. My hat was inadequate; it should have been

a tiara. 'Should I wave graciously as we go down the street?'
I whispered to Alan as the chauffeur, a good-looking, pleasant
man, gently closed the rear door on us. Alan put his finger to
his lips and pointed to the microphone discreetly hidden in
the decorative work in front of us. 'I don't know if it's turned
on. Hello?'

'Yes, sir. Where did you wish me to take you, sir?'

Alan gave him the address.

There was a brief pause. 'Are you certain, sir? That is not
– that is, you might not find that part of the city to your liking.'

'It's the address we were given.'

'Very good, sir.' I wished I could see the driver's face. He
muttered something inaudible and put the car in gear.

It was unnerving to drive off in a vehicle that didn't even
seem to have the engine running. No noise, no vibration. I
nudged Alan. 'I feel like Scotty just beamed me up,' I whispered. Alan grinned and found the switch that turned off the
mike on our side.

'Now you can talk freely.'

'I don't want to. This is the only time in my life I'll ever
ride in a car like this, and I want to sit back and enjoy it.'

The drive wasn't long, but it did indeed take us to the
seedier side of town. Nothing downright ugly, but a bit
rundown, a bit grubby. An empty store front here and there,
weeds growing in cracks, a general need of a wash and a
brush-up.

The office of the valet service wasn't actually shabby, but
it didn't have the bright polish I had somehow expected. It
was small, and right next to a garage. 'Is this *the* garage, do
you suppose?' I asked. 'Where the cars live when they're not
needed?'

'I wouldn't be at all surprised.' Alan sounded grim, and
pointed. I had not recognized the unmarked car as a police
vehicle, but now I saw it through Alan's eyes. It was so delib-
erately conservative, so obviously inconspicuous, it could only
be official.

'Oh. So something's up. And Alan, our car is in there!'

'Yes.' He turned the mike on. 'We need to stay here for a
little while. Will you wait for us, please?'

'There is no lawful place to park, sir. Shall I circle until you return?'

'I am a police officer. I retired some time ago, but my warrant card is still of use. Stay here and show it, if necessary.' He pulled it out of his wallet and passed it through the little communication slot. The driver unlocked the doors, and we stepped away just as an irate traffic cop strode up.

We didn't stay to watch the altercation.

The man at the valet office desk wasn't eager to talk to us, and would probably have been downright rude if we had not arrived in such splendour. He looked us up and down, plainly trying to reconcile our very ordinary clothing with our royal carriage – and my hat. He compromised.

'The office is not open, sir, but perhaps I can direct you to someone who can serve you.'

Alan ignored that ploy. 'I believe your employees serve the Royal George Hotel?'

The man gulped and looked around, as if seeking someone who could deal with this awkward customer. 'That is true, sir, but at the moment—'

'I was told a few minutes ago that I could not retrieve my car. That is most inconvenient. I wish to speak to your superior.'

'I . . . he . . .'

A very large man stormed into the room through a side door. From the background noises when the door opened, I assumed the service garage was on the other side. 'Whose bloody great Queen Mary is blocking my drive?' he roared. His voice was as massive as his physique; his temper as his ginger hair would suggest.

'If,' said Alan in his iciest voice, 'you refer to the Rolls-Royce, my wife and I are using it today because my own vehicle, in your garage, is for some unexplained reason unavailable. My card, sir.' He handed him the one bearing his title, with the word 'retired' in very small print. 'I presume you are in charge of the garage, and I require an explanation and an apology.'

He studied the card. 'You're a copper?'

The chill dropped another few degrees, approaching absolute zero. 'I am a sworn police officer, yes.'

'Then you're not quite on the job, are you, mate? You want to know what's goin' on, you ask your flippin' constable.'

'If you read the card carefully, you will see that I am not in charge of the force here in Bath. We are visitors here, staying at the Royal George, and I cannot say that we have been entirely happy with the treatment we have received.'

I mentally translated. *We're rich and well-connected and able to spend a lot of money to boost the local economy, and we'd better be handled with kid gloves, or else!* I seldom see Alan do his intimidation act; I was enjoying this.

The garage man, however, was not easily intimidated, nor easily impressed by supposed wealth. He looked us up and down. I could see the calculator in his head summing up the probable cost of our attire and comparing it with our luxurious transport. 'So that bus is the hotel's.' He jerked his head in the direction of the Rolls.

'It has been provided for our use while our own is apparently being held hostage.' Alan looked at me with a histrionic sigh. 'It appears, my dear, that this person is unwilling to assist us. I believe I shall have to go in and take matters into my own hands. Will you come with me, or would you prefer to wait in a rather more salubrious situation?' His nod at the limo was a lot more courteous than Garage Man's.

'Now wait just a minute!' The man stepped in front of the door. 'Seems I've got to let the police – the real police – on my private property, but you got no right—'

His back to the door, he hadn't noticed the approach of another man. He was wearing a suit and an air of authority. 'Mr Nesbitt, sir, the inspector would like to speak to you, if you have a moment.'

The garage man's face turned an unbecoming shade of puce. I refrained from chortling in triumph, but it took considerable effort. We swept past the blockade.

'If you'll follow me, sir, we can go directly to the parking garage. The area where the mechanics work is . . . um . . . not terribly clean.'

It was also quite busy. One car was up on a lift, with someone in overalls doing mysterious things to its undercarriage. Another was having a dent pounded out, loudly. A man, apparently a customer by his clothing, was arguing, also necessarily loudly, with one of the mechanics. The place was no grungier than any garage, but it wasn't a good place for my hat.

'Only to be expected,' said Alan, his usual manner restored now that he wasn't dealing with surly rudeness. 'Repairs always create muddle and disorder. Now, can you tell me what's going on here? The . . . er . . . gentleman back there was not forthcoming.'

The constable grinned. 'Bit of a rough diamond, our Slim. Knows his job, but his tongue needs a good tune-up.'

'His manners could do with one, as well,' I commented.

'Yes, indeed. As to the situation, sir, I'll let the inspector give you the details, but the fact is, someone's tried to break into your car, and done a bit of damage into the bargain.'

'I see.'

We entered the garage in silence, to find Inspector Roberts, with another man, looking over our car. They were standing by the back of the car. When we got close enough to see properly, I gasped with dismay. The trunk lid – boot cover, whatever you want to call it – was scratched and dented. Someone had obviously been trying to pry it open.

'We instructed the garage to keep all the cars locked in future, hoping that would prevent further problems,' the inspector told Alan. 'Plainly we were wrong.'

'But why?' I almost shouted it in my frustration. 'There's nothing in there except a small tool kit.'

The inspector nodded. 'But of course whoever did this thought that there was something, something valuable.'

'Something he put there.' Alan wasn't happy.

'Almost certainly, yes. And the amateurish way he tried to open the boot is all of a piece with the oddly assorted nature of the articles we found. Some of great value, some mere souvenirs worth a few pounds, some of no value at all. We're dealing with a very peculiar sort of criminal here.'

'Indeed. Any self-respecting crook these days can get into a car in ten seconds flat, leaving no signs at all. And once in, he can find the latch that opens the boot, or the bonnet, or wherever he likes. This chap plainly didn't know what he was about.'

'I don't know why you keep saying *he*,' I grumbled. 'Could just as easily be *she*. No, I'm not being feminist about it, or not only that! But you have to admit that, on average, women are somewhat less knowledgeable about cars. I, for example, wouldn't have the slightest idea how to break into one. There was a time, I believe, when a coat hanger would help, if a window was left ajar, but no longer. So I insist on equal opportunity suspicion.'

That made Alan laugh, as I thought it might. The inspector got a coughing fit just then.

'So,' I pursued, 'the cars have not been kept locked until now?'

'No. It wasn't deemed necessary, as the car keys are kept in a locked cabinet to which only the manager on duty has access.'

'Nor, apparently, was surveillance deemed necessary.' Alan looked up and around the room. 'No cameras?'

Roberts spread his hands in the universal gesture of frustration. 'There have never before been any problems. Now their insurers are insisting on cameras, but it seems a bit late to lock the stable doors.'

'Insurers,' I echoed. 'So someone will take care of this damage?'

'They are poised to do the work next door, as soon as our people have gathered the evidence they need. You'll remember Sergeant Blake, who took your fingerprints yesterday. And this is Sergeant Lewis, my right-hand man and photographer.'

I didn't care who was who. 'They're going to work on the car next door? I'm not sure I'm happy about that.'

Sergeant Lewis comforted me. 'Don't worry, madam. O'Hanlon may not be easy to get along with, but he knows his business, and he keeps his men up to the mark. The work will be well done. It's a matter of pride with him.'

I shrugged. I suppose it didn't matter if I liked the man, so long as he did his job.

'Very well,' said Alan. 'Rob, I was going to get in touch with you a bit later. Is there a place where we could talk for a few minutes?'

After some polite skirmishing the inspector sent his car back to the station, along with the two sergeants, and Andrew, our driver, conveyed the three of us in silent splendour back to our hotel. Over wine and snacks in a quiet corner of the lounge we discussed the odd situation.

'My first thought,' said Rob, 'was that we were dealing with an undiscriminating collector. You thought the same, didn't you, Mrs Martin?'

'Dorothy,' I reminded him. 'But it doesn't quite fit, somehow. A collector, no matter how broadly interested and un-particular, would hardly hold onto a torn scrap of handkerchief.'

'Unless it had belonged to a celebrity,' Alan pointed out. 'Teenagers would swoon over the very germs of one that had belonged to – and been used by – a rock star.'

'Ugh! What a thought!' I drank some wine to wash away the idea. 'But this one certainly wouldn't qualify in that category.'

'Quite,' said Rob. 'Nor would a few of the other items. Junk, pure and simple.'

'Like what, Rob? We really didn't see it all properly before you took it away.'

'Dorothy,' said Alan with a frown.

'No, I didn't mean it that way. No complaint intended. Of course it had to be taken away. But if we knew what was there, it might give us some ideas.'

'I don't have the inventory with me.' Rob took another sip of wine. 'But I can remember most of it. There was the piece of bluestone, of course. Valuable, though not in terms of money, or not as much as one might think. Thieves have been peddling them on eBay for a few pounds. In historic terms, though, they're priceless. Then there were a few Roman coins.'

I gasped. 'Oh, but they'd be worth—' I began.

'They would if they were genuine. These are replicas, quite good ones, but shiny and new. If they were to be sold as genuine, they'd have to be very carefully "antiqued". There were a few trinkets from various museum shops, value a few pounds at most. An earthenware goblet from the Roman Baths shop, along with a bottle of the spring water – though why anyone would want that is beyond my comprehension. A few leather-bound books, but replicas, not old or worth a great deal. The most valuable pieces were some jewellery in the Jane Austen period and style. They're nothing actually worn by Jane, which would be very valuable indeed – if such items exist – but quite nice replicas or souvenir pieces in silver with gemstones.'

'Oh, we saw those! At the shop, I mean. Remember, Alan? I really wanted that little cross set in topazes, but it cost more than I could justify spending on myself.'

'That particular item was among those in the stash.'

For a moment the remark hung there, vibrating in the quiet air of the lounge. I looked at Alan. He looked at Rob.

Rob smiled and ate a couple of crisps. 'It's a pity we intercepted the goods before they could be posted on the Internet. You could probably have had your cross for a good deal less than market value.'

'I was about to put my hands out for the cuffs.'

'Dorothy, I might, very reluctantly, come to suspect you of theft if a rare book were stolen. A piece of jewellery, no. Most especially not a cross, with its associations.'

'I do like pretty things, though. I admit it.'

'You do. And you wear them very well, if I may say so. That hat is . . . remarkable.'

It was adorned with large silk chrysanthemums and velvet oak leaves. Remarkable was certainly the word. I had forgotten I was wearing it and hastily removed it as inappropriate to the setting and the time of day.

Alan simply laughed. 'My dear, if you were ever to take to crime, you would be captured immediately.'

'Well, I like that! Am I so incompetent?'

'You are extremely competent. You are also conspicuous. Even when you're not wearing a hat, the ghost of one adorns your head. But to get back to our real discussion, you think, then, Rob, that the goods were being stolen for the market?'

He shrugged. 'The pieces don't all fit. I admit it. But unless we're back to positing a very strange sort of collector, I can see no other explanation. Do you, either of you, have a better idea?'

'I had thought perhaps a child,' I said hesitantly, 'simply taking things for the look of them. Like a magpie, stealing shiny things. But that doesn't explain something like a ceramic goblet. Or a chunk of bluestone.' I held up my hands.

Rob turned to Alan, who said, 'I confess myself at a loss. There is the possibility of two thieves, of course, but that raises more questions than it answers. You have, of course, tested everything for fingerprints.'

'Yes,' said Rob with a sigh. 'There were many sets found. The cache all came from shops, of course, or most of it, so many people handled the items. There was only one set found consistently, and unfortunately it matched nothing in our database.'

'Is it certain,' asked Alan, 'that all the items were stolen? They're all of local provenance, except the bluestone. Could they simply have been purchased?'

Rob sighed again. 'There's no quick way to check that, especially with the more-or-less worthless items. Shops expect a certain amount of "shrinkage". The Austen jewellery, however, was certainly stolen. It's worth enough that the shop keeps a careful check, and those items are missing from its books. We're positing that the rest was also stolen, but we can't say that with certainty.'

I shook my head and went back to the fingerprints. 'No surprise, is it, that you can't identify them? Since we're thinking an amateur crook, not a slick professional who'd show up in police records. And surely a check takes quite a long time.'

Both Alan and Rob smiled. 'Not these days, my dear. Technology has made the process quite rapid. Not, of course, foolproof. In the end, a human must still look at a comparison and make a decision. But the narrowing-down process is much faster with the aid of computers. And I take it you came up with nothing?'

'Nothing even close. Apparently these are rather unusual prints. I know too little about the matter to be more informative. We tend to leave these things to the experts.'

Now it was Alan who sighed. 'I've never been quite sure about the proliferation of specialization in today's world. There are benefits, certainly, but one can lose touch with the big picture.'

'Oh, and in medicine, as well!' I interjected. 'Even back in America, years ago now, the old-fashioned general practitioner was dying out in favour of internists and rheumatologists and neurologists and orthopaedists and heaven knows what, until I had the feeling that a lot of doctors knew about pieces of me, but there wasn't one who knew and cared about *me*, myself, a living, breathing human being with problems and worries and fears, rather than just a collection of symptoms.' I finished my wine to cool me off.

'Yes, well.' Rob stood. 'My wife is complaining that she never sees me, so I'm going to give myself the evening off and have a meal with her, for a change. I'll be in touch.'

SEVEN

At breakfast the next morning, I asked Alan, 'Do they have a business centre here at the hotel? Someplace where guests can use computers? Surely not everyone in the world has an iPad.'

'I'm sure they do. I'd guess that most of the hotel's patrons do own laptops of some sort, but as this is more of a holiday destination than a business-conference sort of place, they might not bring them along. Why?'

'Just a random thought. These thefts are so petty, at least most of them. I wouldn't have thought it would pay the thief to fence them in the usual way, so I'm wondering if they're being sold online, eBay or wherever. Not just bluestones, but the rest of the stuff.'

'That's assuming that the thefts have been going on for some time, that our stash was just the most recent of several.'

We hadn't been keeping our voices down. The couple at the next table rose in something of a hurry, leaving their meals half-finished. I couldn't keep back a giggle.

'It's not ours! Though those poor people must think they've

fallen into a den of thieves. But I know what you meant. Anyway, don't you think it's worth a try? The Net, I mean, not adopting a life of crime.'

Alan looked out the window of the breakfast room. The sky was leaden, promising rain any minute, quite possible with thunder and lightning. We could see people walking with their heads down against the wind, their scarves flapping wildly, their raincoats billowing. He shrugged. 'It's not the most congenial day for sightseeing. We might as well do some detective work.'

We stopped by the concierge's desk and were given directions to the computer room and an access code.

Alan was inclined to be grumpy. 'I must say,' he said as he sat down and made his way to the Internet, 'that I had not planned to spend this holiday surfing the Net.'

'Nor had I, but we might as well admit it, dear. Crime seems to follow us wherever we go. We've talked before about that cartoon character with the little black cloud over his head, Joe Whatever-his-name-was. Maybe it's that cloud you see when you look at me, not a phantom hat.'

He looked me up and down and then laughed. 'No. Definitely a hat. A Miss Silver hat, perhaps. You're right. We can't escape our destiny. Now, do you have any idea what we should search for among the several million offerings?'

I thought about that. 'Gosh. There are so many. How about *souvenirs*, for a start?'

After wading through a plethora of items from Disneylands all over the planet, I hastily refined the search to *Bath souvenirs*. I should have known better. Rubber duckies filled the screen.

Alan, seated at the next computer, suggested *Roman baths*.

Bingo!

Well, sort of. A wide array of objects were offered for sale. Postcards, soap, toiletries. A couple of guidebooks to the Baths. Bottles of the water, most at very low prices. 'The sellers must have tasted it,' Alan commented.

Various sellers were offering the goods. Sometimes two or three were listed by the same person, but none, so far as I could tell, by a business. And none were priced over ten pounds.

When we thought that vein had played out, I suggested *Jane Austen souvenirs*, and we went through the same routine, with variations. Lots of books, of course. Odds and ends. Videos – lots of videos. I was tempted; I've never seen any of them.

'Hmm,' Alan murmured. 'Dorothy, look at this.'

I slid over to get a better look at his screen.

'Is that or is it not one of the nicer pieces in the Jane Austen collection?'

I tilted my head to look through the bottom of my bifocals. 'I think maybe. These glasses don't help, but it looks like one of those charms made to look like one of her books. What does the description say?'

He clicked and scrolled. '*Sense and Sensibility* pendant – eighteen-karat gold – good grief, four hundred pounds!'

'Alan, that's less than half what it costs at the museum!' I sat up, excited. 'Who's selling it?'

He clicked and scrolled. 'Oh. Someone in the States. An individual, not a business. Not a likely candidate for our thief.'

'Oh.' I slumped back. 'No. I suppose some American was given it as a gift and didn't want it. Drat.'

'I hope the giver doesn't see this listing. I would be mightily upset if I bought you something that expensive and you turned around and sold it.'

'As if I'd ever do such a thing! But I take your point. Sad, but it doesn't get us anywhere.' I rolled my shoulders and stretched.

Alan logged off and pushed his chair back. 'It was a good idea. Too bad it didn't reap any rewards.'

He didn't sound very upset. 'You're used to this, aren't you? From your days as a working policeman.'

'Lord, yes. By far the greater part of police work is sheer waste of time. Can't be helped. One goes through all the motions, and eventually something works. Usually.'

When we went out into the hallway, we saw that the mood of the day had changed completely, unnoticed in the window-less computer room. In place of the surly clouds there were puffy white ones floating decoratively in a sky of piercing blue.

'Oh, Alan, let's go for a walk! I'm tired of being mewed up inside, and tired of staring at a computer. There's a whole interesting world out there!'

Alan smiled at me. 'You are a child of the sun, aren't you?'

'That makes me sound like a hippy, and they're generations out of date! But if you mean I perk up in nice weather, well, who doesn't? Where shall we go?'

'We've been putting off going to the Roman baths, the focal point of the city.'

'No. I don't want to be cooped up in a museum today, no matter how interesting.'

'Well, then, there's a rather attractive option, depending on whether we can use the hotel's car and driver again. Have you ever heard of Lacock Abbey?'

I frowned. 'Strikes a faint chord somewhere deep in my head, but I can't remember . . .'

'William Henry Fox Talbot?'

'Oh! Yes! Photographer! My husband was interested in the history of photography. I think he got into it by way of his botany studies, something about pictures of germination. Didn't Talbot invent the camera or something?'

'Close. He invented the photographic process that was used for many years, involving a negative, and made the first photograph in England, a view of a window at the abbey.'

'Was he a monk, then?'

'No, no. This was in the early nineteenth century, about three hundred years after Henry dissolved the monasteries, and in any case the abbey had been a nunnery. It was a private home for centuries and was then given to the National Trust. It's a lovely place, and you'll recognize parts of it.' He gave me an enigmatic smile and would say no more.

'It's not far?'

'Less than an hour. We can get to the village in plenty of time for lunch, and there are some good pubs.'

'Let's do it!'

The hotel people were happy to make us free of their car and driver once more, so off we sailed to Lacock in luxurious splendour.

'You know,' I commented as we were driven in the hushed

atmosphere of privilege through the streets of Bath, 'I could get used to this sort of thing. You'd better be careful.'

'I'd give you three days, absolute limit, before you'd be impatient for the freedom of your own car. And the ability to park in a space about a third as big as one this monster would require.'

I sighed. 'I suppose. But it's lovely for now.'

I've lived in England long enough to know that the picturesque villages beloved of postcards and tourist brochures are not to be found around every corner. Modernity has invaded even some of the loveliest of old villages, a BP station replacing the old smithy, the rectory turned into a B&B, council houses crowding or replacing thatched cottages. Thus it was with a distinct shock that I first saw the High Street of the village of Lacock.

'But surely I've seen this before somewhere? Or was it just in a dream? It's too perfect! Except for the cars. They look really out of place.'

'You probably have seen it before. The village has been used as a setting for any number of films and TV shows. Almost the whole place, you see, is owned by the National Trust, so it's kept up perfectly. The houses look almost as they did when they were built, and that would be several hundred years ago. Not all of a piece, as you see, but varying in style and period and building materials. That's why it looks so right. No Picturesque-by-Design here.'

The voice of our driver interrupted. 'Sorry sir, madam, but would you like me to stop here, or do you prefer to go on to the abbey?'

'Oh, here, please! I want to wallow in the atmosphere. And shop.' I saw some enticing signs.

'And have a bite of lunch,' said Alan practically. 'Why don't you have yourself something to eat, Andrew, and do whatever you like until . . .' He turned to me, eyebrows raised.

'Two, maybe?'

'Until two o'clock. Where shall we find you?'

'One can usually park near the churchyard, sir. I'll be there at two. If you'll ring me then, or at any time, really, I'll come and fetch you.'

He stopped, opened the doors for us, saluted, and was off before Alan could offer him a tip.

'As I said.' I dug Alan in the ribs. 'When is your great-aunt going to leave you that fortune?'

'As she died some years ago, I think it's past praying for. Let's try the Angel. I've not been there for years, but they had marvellous food then.'

Amazingly, on this perfect tourist day, the Angel wasn't terribly crowded. It was housed in a very old building indeed. 'An old coaching inn,' Alan told me. 'Built in fourteen-something, I believe.'

'It's beautiful. And look at the garden!' There was a passage through to an open back door, beyond which we could see flowers and, delightfully, a couple of bantam hens busily pecking away. 'Aren't they sweet? I do love banties and their miniature self-importance!'

The proprietors of the inn had plainly made a few changes to the ancient inn to accommodate modern tastes – and health and safety regulations – but they had managed beautifully to preserve the atmosphere. Among other amenities, a large black cat wandered from table to table dispensing hospitality and probably looking for a hand-out. Our waitress apologized for him. 'He's not really allowed in here, but on a fine day with the doors open, it's impossible to keep him out.'

'It's all right,' I assured her. 'We love cats. How do he and the bantams get along?'

'Armed neutrality,' she said with a laugh. 'He knows he's not to hurt them, so he just sits and stares at them, tail a-twitch. For their part, they ignore him. Chickens aren't the brainiest creatures in the world, are they? Now, what would you like?'

We ordered. The waitress brought our beer and left; the cat stuck around. We probably sounded and smelled like cat people. He rubbed my ankle.

'Sorry, puss, we've nothing to give you,' I said sadly.

He went away then, turning to give us a scornful look before flicking his tail and stalking off.

'That's you told,' said Alan.

'A cat can express more contempt with a single gesture than most people with a ten-minute oration. Cheers.'

* * *

'Right,' said Alan when we'd finished our meal. 'You'll be glad later that you decided against dessert. There are several lovely places for tea later.'

'Alan, I'm so glad you brought me here! It's my favourite kind of place. Not just this inn, but the whole village. It's not frozen in time, either. Old, but alive.'

'I thought you'd enjoy it. Now. Credit cards at the ready?'

Our first stop was the antiques shop. I didn't really want or need any of the lovely things they had on offer. They were real antiques, not the attractive junk that often masquerades under the term in America. Much as I would have loved a beautiful little piecrust table, or a Meissen shepherdess, all golden curlicues, the prices made it easier for me to resist.

Next stop was Lacock Pottery, a working pottery with the potter busy at his wheel. It's something I love to watch: a lump of clay turns, in a matter of seconds, into a beautiful shape, and then grows and changes.

'It's magic,' I said softly to Alan.

'And harder than it looks,' he replied.

'Oh, I know. I tried it once when the art department at Randolph offered free classes to faculty spouses. I could never even get the clay centred on the wheel. Which meant it flopped all over the place as soon as I tried to draw it up and shape it. I felt like an absolute fool.'

'Happens to every beginner,' said the potter, glancing up from his work. 'No need to feel foolish. Just takes practice, that's all. You're from the States, are you? Or Canada?'

'From the States, originally. I've lived in England for some time, now, but I guess I'll never get rid of the accent entirely. This is beautiful work you're doing here.'

He ducked his head in acknowledgement of the compliment. I grinned to myself. Typical English reaction to praise! The work was truly beautiful, though. Alan waited patiently while I tried to choose among all the lovely things, finally settling on a large tile glazed in bright colours. Alan eyed me quizzically.

'For a trivet, of course! I'll get someone to frame it for me, and when it's not in use it can hang on the wall. Thank you, Mr McDowell!'

We carefully negotiated the steps down to the courtyard and

greeted the friendly tabby cat who sat sunning himself on the wall and responded to our overtures with a medium purr before going back to sleep.

Alan looked at his watch. 'It's nearly time to meet Andrew. Shall I call him and say we'll be a bit longer?'

'No, I'm just about ready to sit down. Let's mosey back to the car and see if there's anything else we want to see along the way.'

There was, of course. I was drawn as if by a magnet to the shop window of Watling Goldsmiths and Silversmiths. 'Alan, look! I've never seen anything like these pieces. They're gorgeous.'

He pointed to a small sign. 'They're made here. The owner really is a jeweller. And have you noted the prices?'

'Mmm.' They were all in the thousands of pounds. Not even for my birthday was I going to try to wheedle that much out of my beloved husband. 'Oh, but look. There's a set called "Pretty Poison". I wonder what prompted that idea.'

'And you with your love of mystery would like to have the pendant, or the earrings.'

'I would, but don't even think about it. I'd never have a moment's peace owning such a thing. I'd be afraid to wear it in case I lost it somehow, and afraid to keep it at home lest someone steal it. No. They're perfectly beautiful and I'm glad I've seen them, but no.'

Still Alan lingered. 'I'm wondering,' he said quietly, 'if our light-fingered unknown would find these of interest.'

I mulled that over. 'If he really is a magpie, he'd be mightily attracted. Talk about shiny! But I don't think he is. I think most of the stash was stolen for the market, and a modest sort of market at that. Honestly, Alan, I don't understand any of it. And you'd better take me away from here before I drool all over the display window.'

Andrew was waiting exactly where he said he would be, taking up a good deal of space just a stone's throw away from the steps leading up to the churchyard. We stopped to look at the church, small but in excellent repair. 'Do you want to look in for a moment, love, or go straight on to the abbey? You did say you were a bit tired.'

'Oh, but it wouldn't be polite not to pay our respects. We don't have to stay very long.'

So we went in and looked at the various memorials to the Talbot family and picked up the leaflet giving the history of the church. 'Good heavens,' I said, reading. 'Eleventh century, bits of it.'

'Heavily restored, though,' said Alan with a frown.

'Well, if it hadn't been, it wouldn't be standing any longer, would it? I know purists disapprove, but it's still beautiful, so I don't care.'

We said our usual brief church-visit prayer of thanks and blessing and went out again into the sunshine of the church-yard, again thick with box tombs and headstones for Talbots. 'They really were a power in the land, weren't they?' I commented. 'Have they all died out now?'

'I think so, but we'll find out more at the abbey. There'll be a good deal of walking to do once we get there, so let's have Andrew drive us up.'

It was a very quick trip. Ten years ago I would have scorned the very idea of driving such a short distance. But age takes its toll even of the healthy and relatively fit. I was content to lie back in the well-padded cushions of the Rolls and purr along to the abbey.

'I suppose it's the usual story,' I mused as we drove. Andrew was taking it slowly, partly so we could gape to our hearts' content, and partly because of the hazardous combination of a large car, narrow streets, and lots of pedes-trians. 'Henry dissolved the abbey, the property went to someone in exchange for services rendered, and it became a private home.'

'More or less,' Alan agreed. 'I don't recall all the details, but I believe the nunnery was sold rather than simply granted. Henry went through a lot of money in his reign; one of his reasons for the Dissolution was to replenish the coffers. The Talbot family came into the picture several generations later. You can, I'm sure, find out more than you really want to know once we get there. And, in fact, here we are.'

I got out, aided by Andrew, though in fact it's a whole lot easier to get out of a Rolls than our Ford Fiesta, and looked critically at the building before me. 'Very nice, but it doesn't look medieval.'

'And in fact most of it isn't. It's been a living residence for centuries, and the owners made changes as styles of living changed. But wait till you see the cloisters.'

The house was very nice, but very nineteenth century. 'It's a home,' the guide reminded me. 'Members of the family lived here until quite recently. It's meant to look like a living place, not a museum. Of course, there is also the museum. And the old parts of the building are very old indeed.'

We looked through the house. Alan pointed out the famous window, the subject of the first photograph. 'You can take a picture of it yourself,' he said with a smile. 'It's the only place in the whole abbey where they allow photography.'

I kept my phone firmly in my pocket. 'I don't propose to compete with the world's first photographer, thank you.'

Much as I hated to admit it, I was getting tired. I find it vastly annoying, but I can't do as much as I once could. Alan saw that I was flagging. 'They have rather a nice tea room, if you're ready for a little sit-down.'

I smiled gratefully. 'More than ready. And a cup of tea sounds like heaven.'

So we did that. I allowed myself a self-indulgent piece of lemon cake, rationalizing that I'd taken quite a lot of exercise today. It's an excuse I make with alarming frequency. My bathroom scale isn't fooled.

'Better?' he said when I'd done everything but lick the plate.

'Much. I feel sorry for Andrew, though, waiting around for us all day.'

'I told him to get himself a drink, or whatever he liked, and that we'd phone when we needed him. And gave him some money for a bit of sustenance.'

I squeezed his arm. 'You know, there are times when I think I did the right thing when I married you.'

'Oh, I could have told you that! Now, are you ready for home, or our reasonable facsimile thereof in Bath?'

'No. I've revived, and I want to see those cloisters you've been tempting me with.'

Now, I've seen cloisters. Lots of them. On earlier English

visits with my first husband, and in recent years with Alan, I've visited a lot of cathedrals, with cloisters. There is a sameness to them. After a while they begin to blend. Long corridors, open on one side to a courtyard, paved or grassy. Arches overhead, Roman or Gothic, fan-vaulted or unadorned. Pillars, slender or sturdy. They're all slightly different, and all interesting.

But . . . these rocked me back on my heels, but not for any architectural or aesthetic reason. 'Alan,' I breathed, clutching his arm. 'It's Hogwarts!'

I'm a big fan of Harry Potter and have seen several of the movies. I never thought I'd be walking through Hogwarts, in person.

He chuckled. 'I thought you'd be surprised. The cloisters have been used in several films, but the Potter ones are perhaps the most recognizable. And a bit farther on . . . voilà!'

I stood transfixed. There, in a perfect medieval room, small, arched, rather dark, stood a large black pot, the very cauldron I'd seen on the screen. 'It's . . . it's spooky. The setting makes it all seem so real. I swear I expect to turn around and see Snape breathing down my neck.'

'This was the warming room. They kept a fire going in the cauldron, or so the story goes, so the nuns could get warm for at least a brief time every day. The winters were cold indeed, and there were no fireplaces elsewhere in the abbey.'

I shivered. 'I used to think the cloistered life had a good deal of appeal, but now I'm not so sure. Were they Benedictines? Working all day would have helped keep them warm.'

Alan looked at the guidebook. 'No, Augustinians. I'm afraid I know nothing about their rule.'

'Poor things. I wonder where they went, what they did, when Henry threw them out.'

Alan squeezed my hand. 'You always sympathize, don't you? Even with people you never met, who died centuries ago. You may be sure, my love, that they've been in heaven for lo these many years, safe and comfortable and happy. And warm.'

I smiled at him. 'I'm sure you're right, but *I'm* getting cold down here, and it's a beautiful October day. Let's go out into the sunshine.'

EIGHT

There remained the museum and the used bookshop. I was torn. A bookshop has a powerful attraction for me, but a museum shop is always special. 'Very unique', as a friend of mine used to say over my anguished protests that the word *unique* cannot be qualified.

'Flip a coin?' Alan suggested.

'No. Museum. I don't know that I care much about the exhibits, but the shop . . .'

I left the thought unfinished. Alan knows me very well.

The exhibits were very well done, but photography as such doesn't interest me a lot, and besides, the display was a bit too up-to-date for me. I wanted something more in keeping with the ancient surroundings. 'Frank would have loved this,' I commented to Alan, feeling a bit melancholy. 'I'm sorry we never got here.'

'He knows all about it now, love. Probably enjoying conversations with William Henry himself.'

I appreciate Alan's talent for making things better.

So we skimmed the museum, once over lightly, and ended up in the shop.

Ah, the shop!

'Alan, am I a shopaholic?' I was beginning to feel some qualms about my instant gravitation to all museum shops.

'Only in specialty shops,' he said indulgently. 'And we're celebrating your birthday, remember? When we get home I'll put you back on bread and water. For now, shop to your heart's content.'

So I did just that. There were books about photography, about the abbey, about the Talbot family, about the Harry Potter connection. I bought one of those for a young neighbour, Nigel Peter Evans, who was addicted to all things Potter. Of more interest to me were the gardening items, lovely little pots, seed packets, and even the occasional plant.

'There's a garden centre just outside Lacock, and a good one, too, but we won't have time to get there before they close,' said Alan, 'so you might want to pick up a few things here. I wouldn't suggest plants, though. Don't forget we have to get them home, and the poor things might not enjoy travel.'

'Oh, you're right, darn it. I had my eye on that.' I pointed to an attractive pot holding lots of slender green stems with tiny red flowers on top. 'I have no idea what that is, but I'll bet Bob could make it grow in our garden.' Bob Finch is our gardener, a green-fingered magician who, between occasional bouts of drinking, makes our small plot of land into a paradise.

'Bob can do anything except, unfortunately, stay away from the bottle. But I'm not sure that tender little thing, whatever it is, would enjoy a long ride.'

So I settled for asking the name and writing it down (the salesperson gave the proper botanical name – my husband the botanist would have approved) to give to Bob when we got home. Then there were a few trinkets for various friends, decorative pots, pretty plant labels, that sort of thing.

'This doesn't seem to be the kind of shop patronized by our thieving friend,' I said softly to Alan. 'No jewellery, nothing very expensive. Nothing here to attract a magpie.'

'No,' said Alan in an odd voice.

'What?'

'This.' He picked up a postcard. It was a reproduction of the famous 'first photograph' of the window, showing both the original negative image and a positive print made from it. I'd learned that it's perhaps the most famous photograph in the world, and the shop had them by the dozens.

I frowned. Yes, it was all very interesting, and the image was nice, but nothing to get excited about. 'So?'

'One of these postcards was in the bag in our car.'

We asked Andrew to take us back to the Angel, where we requested a quiet corner and pints while we considered this development.

'Alan, that makes no sense!' I said for the fifteenth time.

'And when has anything about this mess made sense? It

means, presumably, that the chap's thieving radius extended – or extends – beyond Bath itself.'

'Right. And he stole a postcard that sells for fifty pence. There's no way he could hawk that at a profit.' I took a healthy swig of my beer. 'Unless . . . no, that wouldn't work.'

'What are you thinking?'

'Well, we think he stole the reproduction Roman coins planning to "age" them somehow and sell them as real antiquities. I was thinking he could do the same with this photo somehow, but it wouldn't work.'

'No. Even if he copied it onto the right sort of paper and so on, there's only one of those negatives. He couldn't hope to pass his amateur effort as the one-and-only.'

'So that just reinforces one of our conclusions: the man is not the sharpest knife in the drawer. Alan, let's go back to Bath. It's getting dark. We've kept poor Andrew working all day and I'm sure he wants to get home. And I want to have a nice meal and go to bed and forget about all this for a while.'

Andrew dropped us at the hotel with assurances that the rather long day had posed no problems for him, and that he was at our disposal should we require his services again. Alan's handsome tip might have had something to do with his attitude, but again it might not. He struck me as the sort of person who genuinely liked people and took life as it came.

We chose not to explore dining options in Bath. Walking in a strange city after dark has limited appeal for our age group, and the hotel food was excellent. We had arrived at dessert (a heavenly fruit concoction of some sort) and coffee before I brought up our puzzling problem. 'Are we getting anywhere, Alan? It feels to me as if every new clue that turns up just makes the whole thing more confusing.'

'There are at least two possible reasons for that.' Alan tented his fingers in his lecturing position. 'The first is that we're looking at everything from the wrong angle. Find the proper one and the picture will upend itself, the kaleidoscope will form its pattern, and we'll see clearly.'

'If that's the case, I sure wish we could get some hint of

that proper angle. I'm getting frustrated. Is your second possibility any more optimistic?'

'Sorry, no, and I fear it's the more likely one. It may be that there is no pattern, no reasonable solution. If we thought some ill-balanced collector was amassing trophies from Bath, the Fox Talbot postcard spoils that theory. I'm leaning to the idea that someone was clearing out Grannie's attic.'

'And Granny was a thief with a taste for jewellery and Bath oddities.'

Alan spread his hands.

'And how does that theory explain how the loot – all right, the attic gleanings – ended up in our car?'

'Do you have any idea how many two-year-old Ford Fiestas are on the road? Many of them grey?'

'No, but I'll bet you're going to tell me, O Source of all Wisdom.'

He grinned. 'I have no idea, actually, but I do know it's the most popular car in England, so there are bound to be heaps of them. Well, you know as well as I do: every time we go to the supermarket there are several cars just like ours.'

'I know. I've had to use the panic button more than once to find it. I wish it were bright yellow, or fire-engine red.'

'So there you are. The cars in the garage were not, then, kept locked. Our not-too-bright friend simply made a mistake and put the stuff in the wrong car.'

'And was then so worried about it that he made an inept attempt to break into our car and get it back. An attic's worth of junk.'

Alan is a very patient man. He shrugged. 'No, it doesn't answer all the questions. But I think it's a better explanation than any other we've proposed. Now, do you want a nightcap before we go up?'

We had that nightcap, and after a long day I fell asleep almost as soon as my head hit the pillow. Towards morning, though, after I had to make the usual trip to the bathroom, I fell into a fitful sleep with the kind of dreams that go on and on, never very pleasant, never reaching a conclusion.

This time it was the familiar dream of trying to get some-where, but making constant wrong turns, that led me deeper into the neighbourhood, or the building, or whatever I was trying to escape from. It seems I was driving a grey car, but so was everyone else on the road, and we kept running into bags of trash that made us swerve into yet another wrong path. I knew that if I could only get out, everything would be wonderful, but I couldn't work out how. Then I wasn't driving anymore, I was in the back seat, but the person at the wheel was doing everything wrong, and I kept trying to reach forward and take control, but my arms weren't long enough, and anyway I couldn't reach the pedals, and someone was talking to me, distracting me, never stopping, trying to make me move my arms . . .

'Wake up, love. Wake up. It's all right. Wake up.'

I opened my eyes. 'But I was just about to . . . or . . . was I talking in my sleep?'

'Muttering. And thrashing about. Was it bad?'

'Not really. I couldn't get out, and I couldn't control the car. And there were trash bags everywhere.'

'Ah.'

'Yes. Our puzzle attacking me in my sleep. It's not fair!'

'No, indeed.' He sat up and put his legs over the side of the bed. 'Coffee?'

'Is it morning?' We had pulled the curtains last night, and there was no light coming through the chinks.

'Earlyish. Nearly seven.'

'Oh. Way too early to get up on a holiday. On the other hand . . .' I got out of bed and tottered to the bathroom.

'Lord Peter once said,' I grumbled when I returned, 'that he didn't envy the young their hearts, only their heads and stomachs. Me, I envy them their bladders.'

'Me, too. Are you going to try to go back to sleep, or shall I make that coffee?'

'Coffee, I think. I've had enough sleep, really. It's just getting up in the dark that makes it so hard.'

'And after a distressing nightmare.'

'Not actually a nightmare. Just a standard frustration dream. I used to have them a lot. The scene changed, but the plot was always the same. I'm trying to escape from somewhere, turning this way and that, but always just getting in deeper.'

Alan shook his head. 'Sounds like a nightmare to me. Here, chase it away.' He handed me the coffee.

I drank two cups, and on that stimulus showered and dressed. When I next looked out the window a sullen sort of light was visible. 'Oh, nuts. It looks like rain.'

Alan consulted his phone. 'Yes, they're saying rain most of the day. Let's go down for some breakfast and decide what to do on a rainy day.'

Mindful of the huge amount of food I'd been putting away all week, I opted for cereal and fruit for breakfast, and tried not to look askance at Alan's plateful of eggs and bacon and sausage and mushrooms and beans. Tried, and failed. 'The Full Cholesterol,' I commented sourly.

He just grinned. 'Want some?'

'Yes, blast it, but I'm not going to have any. Hurry up and finish, though, so I don't have to look at it. And smell it.'

'You will be rewarded for your righteousness, my dear.'

I was about to snap back when a faint chime rang out. 'Ah! The abbey speaks a blessing upon me. So there!'

'I heard it too, you know. And it's given me an idea. We haven't really seen the abbey properly. Let's spend part of the morning there, shall we? Nice and dry, and beautiful.'

'And I don't think they have a café, so I will not be led into temptation.'

The rain had begun, but not hard enough to keep us inside. We put on all the rain gear we'd brought with us and walked fast, and arrived at the abbey mostly dry under our coats.

It's a beautiful church. Of course, for Alan and me nothing can compare with our own Cathedral at Sherebury. It's home. But one of my favourite beauties at Sherebury is the fan-vaulted roof, and that's one of the famous features of Bath Abbey as well. It was worth a more careful examination than I'd given it on our first visit.

'The guide leaflet says the choir ceiling is the original, but the nave is a copy. I wonder if the coloured middle bits in the choir are added, or just restored? I'm not sure I like them.' The centre spaces where the fans met in the choir ceiling were brilliant with colour, but not those in the nave.

'You know the mediaeval cathedrals had a lot of colour,

love. It's only in the past few centuries that almost everything reverted to the original colour of the stone and wood.'

'Yes, well, you know I'm a mediaevalist at heart, but I like the colour best in the glass. This east window is magnificent!'

We wandered for a bit, carefully avoiding the roped-off areas where the floor had been taken up for repairs. 'That's the trouble with ancient buildings,' I said, catching hold of Alan's arm as I almost tripped over a stanchion supporting the ropes. 'Something's constantly in need of repair.'

'And in this case it isn't just repair,' said Alan. 'I read somewhere back there – one of the signs – that they're also reconfiguring the space, and putting in underfloor heating.'

'But isn't that terribly expensive? All that electricity!'

'Not in this case. They're not using electricity. It's really quite a clever idea. They're going to use the hot springs, diverting them from the Baths. At the moment that heat is just wasted, flowing straight from the Baths to the river. Which, incidentally, can't be very good for the river and its ecosystem. I didn't read the whole thing, but apparently there's enough heat for the Baths and the abbey and several other buildings. Bound to be very expensive to build, but think of the money they'll save in the end.'

'Not to mention using less coal or oil or whatever. I'm impressed.'

I turned back to the guidebook. 'I can't find out anything here about guided tours, except of the tower.'

'Apparently that's the only tour available. And as it involves climbing over two hundred steps, and there wouldn't be much of a view today anyway . . .'

'Say no more. I wouldn't climb that many steps for anything short of . . . I can't think of anything, actually. Maybe when I was twenty years younger. Not now.'

We wandered for a bit, stopped for a quick prayer and then, inevitably, ended up in the gift shop.

It was crowded. A good many people seemed to have found the abbey a pleasant shelter from the rain. There was only one clerk, and she was hard put to deal with sales, let alone answer questions and help customers find what they were looking for.

'You need some help,' I said when I finally got to the head of the line with several books and postcards, a pair of earrings I couldn't resist, and (trying to hide it from Alan) a large bar of chocolate.

'I usually have a couple of helpers,' she said, sounding frazzled, 'but Elaine called in sick, and the weather's a bit dire for Sammy on his bicycle. That's seventy-nine pounds fifty, please.'

I handed her my credit card. 'Sammy? That wouldn't be the same Sammy who works at the Jane Austen Centre, would it?'

'Oh, you know Sammy? Yes, he's a dear. A bit wanting, of course, but as sweet a boy as I've ever known, and a hard worker. If you'll just enter your PIN – thank you.' And she was dealing with the next person.

Alan saw the chocolate bar as it tried to slide out of the bag. I gave him a shamefaced look. He chuckled and put his arm around me. 'You know perfectly well I love you just the way you are, so you eat all the chocolate you want. It's nearly lunch-time, though, so I suggest you save that for later. We can find something more politically correct, I'm sure, if you insist on worrying about it.'

It was not the kind of day when a salad had any appeal, but we found a place that had really good soup to nourish both my body and my conscience. 'Now,' said Alan when I had polished the bowl, 'this is a perfect day for the Baths. The big pool itself is open to the sky, but everything else, including the walkway around the pool, is under cover. And we're nearing the end of our stay, so I don't want to put it off any longer. Right?'

I was really ready for a nap, but I saw his point. It's unthinkable to come to Bath and not see the Roman Baths. So we retrieved our brollies from the stand and went back out into the rain that had plainly decided to stick around until Christmas, and sploshed through puddles over to Bath's chief attraction.

NINE

I was a bit taken aback to enter a modern lobby with efficient young men and women selling tickets. I'm sure I don't know what I expected, but given that the site was fairly close to two thousand years old, I guess I wanted some sense of antiquity. Nor had I quite expected to be surrounded by crowds of schoolchildren. I said as much to Alan.

'The site is both older and much younger than twenty centuries,' he said. 'The hot springs, the only ones on this island, are said to have been worshipped by the Celts. The Romans did come here early in the first century, but almost nothing of what they built is still here. It's been ruined and rebuilt and restored, and almost everything above ground dates to the eighteenth century or later. And as for the schoolchildren, it's a very popular place for school outings.'

'Field trips, we used to call them when I was teaching. They were wildly popular with the children. Getting a day out of school was a treat! I'm not sure they actually learned anything. And of course southern Indiana didn't offer anything quite so interesting as this. Alan!'

'What? Is something wrong?'

'No. It's just that I thought I saw Sammy over there with that group. They've moved on now. It was probably my imagination. Surely he doesn't go to school.'

'I wouldn't think so. He looks to be in his twenties.'

'And he probably couldn't cope in a regular school, anyway. Oh, well. Now, what's first?' We picked up our guidebook and audio guides and set out.

Oh, my! I had assumed I was going to see a big pool of hot water. Yes, but so much more than that! Excavations over the centuries have laid bare so much information about the original temple that stood here, and have brought so many artefacts to light, that the site has become a museum of more than two thousand years of local history, some of it pre-Roman. I was fascinated.

'I never liked history much in school,' I commented to Alan as we studied a model of a temple, perhaps the earliest building on the site, and its surroundings, including the baths. 'It was dull, just a listing of dates and events that we had to memorize for tests and then thankfully wipe out of our memory banks. This is different. This is real! Real people built all this, and worshipped in this temple and bathed in these waters.'

'Yes, dear.' Alan's heard this speech before, and I suppose it's trite, but it's quite true. History on a page in a book turns me off, but living history fires my imagination.

After perusing the model and trying to work out where these buildings might have been, compared to modern Bath, we went on to a display of the pediment of the temple. Not all of it survived through the centuries, but there was enough for the museum people to reconstruct it, and impressive it was. A video animation was playing, showing just what it must have looked like, and we sat down to watch.

'Fierce sort of chap, eh?'

The man who had sat down next to us on the bench was middle-aged and pleasant-looking, and spoke with a faint Cockney accent. He smiled and pointed to the carved image at the centre of the pediment. It had a fine head of hair (only the hair was made of snakes), and a pair of piercing eyes. 'Indeed,' said Alan. 'And unusual, as well. A gorgon, they tell us, but the gorgons are traditionally female. This one is certainly male, if the beard and moustache are any indication.'

We talked a bit about mythology. 'It's all a bit confusing,' I confessed. 'This was a temple to Minerva, Roman goddess of wisdom. But I though the gorgons were Greek. And the snakes – wasn't that Medusa, or am I getting it all mixed with Harry Potter?'

'Mythology has a tendency to mix elements, doesn't it?' Alan contributed. 'The temple was dedicated to Sulis Minerva, adding in Celtic traditions as well, and there were develop-ments and blending of ideas through several centuries. You're forgiven for getting muddled. I think they sometimes did, too – the chaps who built this place, I mean.'

'Our religion can be a bit off, too, can't it? Then there's the Buddhists and them.' Our companion shook his head. 'No wonder people give it up, is it?'

'But it's interesting how many of the basic, core beliefs have persisted across the centuries and even across doctrinal divides,' I mused. 'Look at Minerva, goddess of wisdom. Granted, she was responsible for a bunch of other things as well, some not so admirable.'

Alan chuckled and pointed to a passage in the guidebook. 'The Greeks called her Athena, and she was also the goddess of war.'

'And then here at the temple, they say, her lot was thrown in with some Welsh dame who ran a fine line in curses,' said the other man.

'Yes, all that,' I agreed, 'but my point is that wisdom has been a quality revered, even worshipped, through the ages. The wisdom of Buddha is quoted again and again. And when we get to Judaeo-Christian thought, wisdom is thought to be a gift of God, especially one of the gifts of the Holy Spirit. And you can trace the other qualities deserving of worship through mythology into present-day creeds, too. At least I think you can, if you know enough about mythology and modern theology, which I don't really. The schools in southern Indiana, when I was a girl, didn't dwell a whole lot on pagan religions.'

'You're American, then? Me, I'm Simon Caine, from London. You probably guessed that, just like I guessed you were American.'

'Our speech gives us away every time, doesn't it? I've lived in England quite a while, long enough to identify some regional accents, but yes, I'm originally American. Dorothy Martin, and this is my husband Alan Nesbitt.' Alan looked up from his perusal of the book and nodded an acknowledgement.

'You live here in Bath, or are you here for the culture?'

'Neither, just on holiday, visiting from Sherebury,' said Alan. We shook hands all round. 'Are you visiting as well?'

'Oh, I'm a bit of a rolling stone. Staying here for now. I may settle here. Nice town, this. Of course, after London . . .' He gave a comic smile and shrug. 'I'll be moving on to the next room. Nice meetin' you.' He tipped an imaginary hat and left.

'Nice man,' I commented. 'Reminds me of London cabbies.'

Alan nodded. 'That easy friendliness. I've never met with it anywhere else in the world.'

'Ah, that's probably why he seemed familiar. The accent and the attitude.'

'Perhaps. Although I've certainly never met a cabbie who was interested in comparative religion. Now what have we here?'

We saw artefacts recovered when the baths were excavated over the years. I found some of them amusing. Pointing to a display case, I said, 'Looks like people have been throwing coins in fountains for millennia. Wonder if any of them got their wishes?'

Alan was consulting the guidebook. 'It's possible there was a little more to it than that. The coins might have been sacrifices to the goddess, or thanks for favours rendered.'

'Or maybe propitiation, if the giver had done something awful and hoped it would be overlooked. Although, come to think of it, I don't know if the idea of sin and forgiveness entered into the picture back then.'

'Hmm. It was certainly possible to offend the gods of the ancients, and they responded alarmingly, with thunderbolts and earthquakes and the like. They could be appeased with sufficient offerings, I believe, but not by mere repentance.'

'You know a lot more mythology than I do. I do wonder, though, what on earth some poor soul must have done that gold coins were required as tribute.' I pointed. 'Or else he was hoping for some whopping favour.'

'Or, as is possible, he was carrying the month's payroll for the legion that was encamped nearby, and fell into the spring with it. We don't know enough. But the speculation is interesting, isn't it?'

Besides the coins, various other oddments had been unearthed. There were gemstones, some of them carved, and an unusual brooch consisting of a circle of bronze and a large pin.

'It would probably have been used to fasten a cloak,' said

Alan. 'The circle goes on top of the cloth. Then the pin goes through the layers and is held in place by the circle.' He demonstrated with his fingers. 'Clever, yes?'

'Sure was. And look at the decoration. Are those garnets?'

Alan took the guidebook from me. 'Red enamel, it says here. And from the delicacy of the carving, the thing must have been expensive. Thrown in as an offering, one wonders? Or fallen in by mistake when someone took off his cloak to bathe?'

Then there was the impressive collection of notes inscribed on pieces of metal. 'Pewter, the guidebook says,' I murmured. 'And Alan, they're curses! Good grief! Somebody lost a pair of gloves and wants the thief to lose his mind and his eyes.'

'You read Latin?'

I pointed to the translation. 'Never learned it, but even if I did, I couldn't manage any of this.'

Alan was reading further. 'Some of them were written in a sort of code, anyway, with the letters printed backwards. So that none but the goddess could read them, one supposes.'

I shuddered. 'Let's hope she ignored most of the requests. Idiocy and blindness seems a pretty heavy penalty for stealing some gloves.'

There was so much to see at the large complex. We ended up, at last, in the large atrium that housed the Great Bath. On this coolish day, steam rose from the water in the vast pool. 'Olympic-sized?' I ventured.

'Bigger, I'd say. And water up to the chin, at least. Says here it had a roof, originally.'

'Makes sense. They wouldn't have wanted rain coming in to cool the water. Alan, what an amazing building and plumbing project for people two thousand years ago!'

'Don't forget that this is a Victorian reconstruction.'

'I prefer to forget it. I want to think about people in togas and tunics coming here to relax after a visit to the temple. Prayers and a swim. What an idea!' I leaned over to test the water temperature, but Alan pulled me back.

'Can't have you falling in, love.'

'Oh, pooh. It's not deep enough to drown.'

'No, but the water's polluted, you know. The temperature

is ideal for fungal and bacterial growth.' He pointed out the warning signs that were posted at regular intervals.

'I'll bet the schoolchildren ignore them.'

'I'm sure their leaders threaten them within an inch of their lives if they do.'

A warm bath, at that point, sounded wonderful. I was worn out by the time we had walked around the pool and talked with some of the costumed guides, almost too tired to enjoy the gift shop. Almost, but not quite.

It was very crowded, even more so than on our first visit. The school groups, having been coerced into reasonably good behaviour during their tour, were more than ready to kick up their heels, and their leaders had plainly given up the struggle. The younger children were shouting and pushing; the older ones stood stock-still staring at their phones and blocking the narrow aisles.

'You choose your battles,' I murmured in response to Alan's raised eyebrows. 'They can't get into too much trouble here, and they'll get a lecture about courtesy on the way home in the bus. Meanwhile the ones who want to buy something are having a hard time getting to it, which is punishment in itself.'

'Nor can you buy anything, or not easily.'

With some difficulty in the crowd, I pulled my phone out of my purse and checked the time. 'It's after five. They'll be closing soon, so the kids will be getting herded out in a few minutes. When I can get to that corner, I'd like to take a look at the jewellery. No, not for me,' I said in response to his look. 'I hardly ever wear anything except earrings, as you know. But they might have the sort of thing Elizabeth would like for Christmas.' Alan's daughter's taste in clothing and adornment leans toward the unusual and somewhat primitive. I thought that a copy of the brooch found in the spring might be perfect for her, if they had such a thing.

I was disappointed. When the last of the children had been shooed out and I could get to the jewellery, the collection was sparse and not especially interesting. 'Never mind, love,' said Alan, steering me toward the door with a firm hand under my elbow. 'Christmas is months away, and there will be other shops.'

'Yes, but I had my heart set on something from Bath.'

'We'll find a pub and a pint and think about it. I'm sure there are jewellers a-plenty in Bath that might stock just what you want.'

A pint sounded good, especially given my aching feet. Right in the heart of Bath, there was no shortage of pubs, and though they were crowded on a Saturday evening, we managed to find one that was reasonably quiet. We had just sat down with our beer when Alan's phone rang.

'Drat,' he said mildly, and answered. 'Nesbitt here.' After only a moment or two, he put the phone back in his pocket. 'Sorry, love. That was Roberts. There's been an incident at the Baths, and I have to go. Stay here and finish your beer, and I'll see you back at the hotel.'

'Don't be silly.' I took a long, lovely swallow and stood. 'Whither thou goest, et cetera.'

TEN

'W hat's happened?' I asked as I hurried along, panting a little as I tried to keep up with his long stride.

'He didn't say much, only that there's apparently been a theft of some magnitude from the shop.'

'Another museum shop theft!'

'Perhaps. There could be other explanations. I'm sorry, love,' he said as I tripped and nearly fell. 'Am I going too fast for you?'

'Yes, but I'll manage. Go on. What other explanations?'

'I don't know yet, do I? A good deal of jewellery appears to be missing. That's all I know.'

I wanted to pursue the matter. Either it was missing or it wasn't. But I didn't have the breath, and I needed to concentrate on where I was going.

We went straight to the street door entrance to the gift shop. The stolid uniformed policeman at the door stepped forward to bar our entry, but saluted and stepped back when Alan presented his warrant card. Inspector Roberts was just inside, with a little clot of shop employees and police. He took us aside and told us the story.

'They take a cursory inventory at close of business every day, but an exhaustive one on Saturday. Extra employees are on board every Saturday, to deal with the crowds and also for the inventory. The woman assigned to deal with the jewellery saw immediately that the display was decimated, and that the lock was missing.'

We nodded in comprehension. The case containing the more expensive items had one of those little sliding locks.

'It was, of course, possible that an employee had sold a large number of pieces and simply forgotten to replace the lock. So the till records were checked and the employees questioned. Some items had been sold, of course, but nothing out of the ordinary run for a Saturday.'

'And the lock?'

'Found under one of the display tables.'

'Where it had rolled, or been thrown.'

'Presumably.' He paused in case we had more questions, and then went on. 'As a matter of routine, all the employees were searched. I understand that there were no complaints about that.'

'The innocent are usually eager to be proved innocent,' Alan commented, and I thought about his insistence on our having our fingerprints taken at Stonehenge. 'And they found nothing, I gather.'

'One chocolate coin, with a bite out of it. And the receipt for it, both together in a pocket. Nothing else.'

'Two questions,' Alan said. 'First, have they a list of the missing items?'

'That will take a little longer, I'm afraid. The shop stocks a broad range of fine jewellery and trinkets, and records of purchases must be carefully checked against sales records and items still in stock.'

'Understood. Second, is anything else missing besides the jewellery?'

'Again, that will take a while to determine. They are going

ahead with the usual Saturday inventory, though with some difficulty amidst the chaos, and I understand that so far they've uncovered only the usual shrinkage.'

'And do they have any ideas about who might have done this?' I was tired of letting the men do all the talking.

Inspector Roberts was polite. If he was unhappy about my sticking my nose in, he didn't show it. 'They were inclined at first to blame an employee, though not any one in particular.'

'The business about the lock.'

'Exactly. Only the employees know where that key is kept.'

'There is only the one?' Alan asked.

'Two. The spare is kept in a safe, in case the one can't be found and a potential customer is waiting. And before you ask, on the one occasion when that happened, the locks were changed before the shop reopened the next day.'

'So if someone stole the first one, it wouldn't do them any good later.'

'You've got it, Dorothy. And in fact, in that one instance, the "lost" key was eventually found in a washroom, having apparently dropped out of someone's pocket.'

'But where is it supposed to be kept when the shop is open for business? The one key, I mean, the one that's in use.' I thought it ought to have a home. A place for everything and everything in its place, so to speak.

The inspector sighed. 'It starts out the day in a drawer under the till, and it should be returned there.'

'Not in the custody of a particular employee?' Alan frowned. 'That would seem to be a more prudent plan.'

Roberts sighed again. 'Quite right. Far more prudent. Unfortunately, it's impossible in a place as busy as this. You have been in the shop, haven't you?'

'Yes, just this afternoon as a matter of fact.' I made a face. 'It was jammed with school groups that made it almost impossible to move.'

'And I'm sure all the employees were frantically busy, and the till operating at warp speed. In circumstances like that, the key is simply passed from one employee to another, as needed. It's not ideal, but there has never been a problem before.'

'And I gather,' said Alan, shaking his head, 'that the CCTV was of no help?'

'Not with that mob. Well, you were here. You know what it was like. The thief would have had to be nine feet tall with bright green hair to be visible amongst all the rest. Unfortunately, it seems he was not so obliging.'

Alan smiled, but it was a wry smile. 'They seldom are. Very well, Rob, you've put us in the picture. How do you think we can help you?'

Rob shuffled his feet. 'I hope you won't mind, but I've learned . . . that is, I've been in touch with Sherebury. They – that is, the police and others, of course – have a high opinion of both of you. The present chief constable went so far as to say that Mrs Martin—'

'Dorothy, please,' I interrupted.

'Sorry – that Dorothy would have made a splendid police officer had she come on the scene when women were being accepted into the force.'

I sketched a little bow. I get almost as embarrassed by compliments as the English.

'All right, Rob,' said Alan patiently. 'Kudos received with thanks. And, of course, you checked us out. Now spit it out. What, precisely, do you want us to do?'

The inspector got a grip on himself. 'Whew! I'm relieved that you're taking it that way. In a nutshell, what I was told was that your forte, Mrs— Dorothy, was simply talking to people. All sorts of people. They seem to like to tell you things. I realize that's easier on your home front, where you're known, but do you think you could attempt something of the kind here?'

'Actually, Rob, it can be easier in a place where no one knows me. When I first came to Sherebury to live, and became embroiled in a nasty mess involving the Cathedral, I could ask all sorts of questions, and I was just the rude, ignorant Yank who'd go home soon, so it didn't matter what anyone said to me. Sort of like a shipboard romance, you know? You'll never see each other again, so anything goes?'

Rob smiled and nodded. Alan aimed a fake punch at me. 'Better not try that, woman!'

'Don't worry. I'm too old for that sort of thing, and besides it can't happen on an airplane. Anyway, the whole thing became harder once everyone realized I was here to stay, but the advantage works again when I'm in foreign climes, so to speak. It's getting harder, but I can still do a strong American accent when I put my mind to it, and if I'm wearing a silly hat I can get by with a good deal. Where would you like me to start?'

Alan laughed. 'Can you ask, dear heart? Start in your natural milieu, the museum shops.'

'Exactly.' Rob nodded. 'Talk to the employees, the customers, the lot.' He cast a quick glance at Alan. 'And it might be best . . . er—'

'If I didn't accompany my wife,' Alan finished. 'I take your point. I will never look like anything but what I am, an English copper. And regrettably, I have no silly hats. Now the trouble, Rob, is that we have already frequented most of the shops, together. That might make talking with the employees a bit dicier.'

I grinned and waved an insouciant hand. 'Not a bit of it! I've come back, I'll explain, having escaped your restraining leash, so I can indulge my whims as I please, while carrying on a good gossip with everyone I see. It might get just a little expensive, though.'

Alan pretended to groan. It turned into a chuckle. 'We may not have to buy Christmas presents for the rest of our lives! I can see a cupboard full of artefacts that our friends and family will have to pretend to enjoy. Feel free, love. Indulge yourself.'

'And bring back some information, if you can,' Rob reminded me. 'Meanwhile, Alan, if you will, I'd like you to look over the reports with me. There may be some detail that's escaped all of us. You bring a fresh eye to the matter.'

'As well as a personal interest,' he said a little grimly. 'It was my car that the villains used and then damaged. I'd quite like to see them found and dealt with.'

I was, by now, nearly ready to sit down on the nearest display table, regardless of the merchandise I might flatten. That beer I'd abandoned was calling me, as well. Alan read my face.

'Right. Rob, I need to get this lady some rest and sustenance.' We began to move to the door. 'Will you join us at the pub round the corner?'

'If I might suggest, sir, madam.' One of the shop employees, the man in charge, from the look of him, had stepped up to us. 'A pub might be very crowded at this hour of a Saturday night. As you've been kept from your refreshment by our problem, we would be most happy to offer you our hospitality at the Roman Baths Kitchen. They do excellent food, whether a light snack or a full meal, and the beer and cider are fine. It will also be crowded, but if you will allow me to call ahead, there will be a table waiting for you. It's only a few steps away.'

'That's very kind of you,' said Alan. 'A table for three, please, Mr—'

'Abercrombie, at your service.' He turned away and pulled his phone out of his pocket.

'I'll gladly join you,' Rob murmured, 'but I'll have to pay my own bill, you know.'

'Nonsense,' said Alan. 'We're not talking about bribery here. You're enjoying a meal with friends and colleagues, and if they happen to have been given a treat, so much the better.'

'But your poor wife,' I began. 'Will she—?'

'She has actually gone to Salisbury for the weekend, to visit our daughter, so I'd have been dining on bread and cheese alone. I give in!'

'So much for anonymity,' I said when I had drunk about half my beer, almost at a gulp, and was beginning on my fish and chips. 'At that shop, for one, I have no chance at playing the stupid, nosy, American tourist. The minute the employees see me, they'll see the invisible police badge and turn into clams.'

'True, with this lot,' said Rob, who had chosen the full English breakfast, served all day, and was making short work of the beans on toast that I find such an odd part of that meal. 'But they have many more employees, including a goodly number of students.'

'Students?' I finished my beer and raised my eyebrows at Alan, who nodded and rose.

'Yes, there's a large university here, just on the outskirts of the city,' said Rob, creating a forkful of egg, sausage and mushroom. 'Something like twenty thousand students, and of course like all students, they're perpetually short of money and in need of part-time jobs. The museum shops are a great boon for them, and they for the shops, because the work is to some extent seasonal, heaviest in the summer when the students' study obligations are lightest.'

'And, of course, they're bright,' I mused, 'and with so many museums to choose from, they can probably find one that matches their interests. So you think that when I go back to the Baths shop, there'll be a different crew, kids who won't see through my pretence?'

'It's term time,' said Rob. 'So the students will probably be there mostly at the weekends. And they don't usually work both Saturday and Sunday. I'd try tomorrow, if I were you.'

'Sunday? Not in the morning,' I said firmly. 'I do know that the police never get to choose their times off, but Alan isn't on the force anymore, and I never was, and we go to church on Sunday mornings. I can't wait to hear the choir at the abbey. The shop is open in the afternoon?'

'Till five, as usual,' said Alan, returning with another round for all of us. 'Open every day except Christmas and Boxing Day, with later hours in high tourist season.' He put down the beer.

I tried not to look impressed. 'You remembered all that?'

'I cannot tell a lie.' He pulled the guidebook out of his pocket. 'I looked it up. Cheers.'

It was still early when we'd finished our meal, but I'd had it. The day had been long and eventful, and I was every now and then forced to admit that I was no longer young. We bade farewell to Rob, whose day, sadly, was far from over, and toddled back to our hotel, stopping on the way to pick up a bottle of our favourite bourbon, or at least my favourite, Buffalo Trace. Alan prefers Scotch, or simply whisky as it's known here, especially Glenfiddich.

'Because,' said Alan when we had settled down in front of the TV with our small nightcaps, 'it looks as though we may not be going home tomorrow after all.'

I was inclined to pout about that. 'I was looking forward

to home. This has been an amazing birthday present, and I want to come back to Bath one day, but I miss the animals, and our friends, and our own bed.'

'I'm sorry, love,' Alan replied to what I hadn't said. 'I had hoped that this would be a holiday, pure and simple.'

'Next time we ought to plan a trip to some infamous trouble spot, the slums of Marseilles or the middle of a war zone somewhere. Since we seem to go by opposites, we might find peace and quiet there.'

'Mmm.' Alan put down his glass. 'Are you watching this, love?'

'No.'

We put out the lights and were asleep almost before the TV screen went dark.

ELEVEN

We'd left the window open a bit, the evening being mild, so the bells of the abbey woke us in time for the eight o'clock service of Holy Communion, But as we had planned to go a much later service, we had a leisurely cup of the excellent coffee they provided in the room. 'We need to make some plans,' Alan suggested.

'Yes. We can't stay in this ruinously expensive place forever. And honestly, it's beginning to feel a bit – I don't know – confining.'

'I feel the same. We can't drop a fork without someone rushing to pick it up. Pleasant, perhaps, but a bit stifling. And then there's the question of our mission.'

'Right. I've been thinking about that. Bath is a good-sized city, but most of the museums, and hence the museum shops, are within a fairly tight little circle. If we were seen coming into this place by one of the many employees, my cover could be blown.'

'You, my dear, have read far too many detective novels. They've tainted your style.'

I made a face. 'I'm still an American, no matter how long I've lived here. All right, if you're going to be a purist: "Questions might arise about the factuality of the persona I have adopted." Does that make you happier?'

'In other words, your cover might be blown.' He dodged the pillow. 'Let's go down for one more sumptuous breakfast and then do some research into a good B&B.'

We had plenty of time before church, so I opted for a good solid breakfast and then went up to pack while Alan had a talk with the concierge. He came back, finally, wearing a bemused look.

'An interesting conversation?' I folded my last pair of slacks into my suitcase.

'Very. Of course, there was a good deal of tiptoeing around at first. The hotel could certainly accommodate us if we wished to make our stay longer. Was there some problem with the service here? What could he do to make it right? After I reassured him that we had simply decided we wanted to see another aspect of Bath and live in a more intimate sort of hostelry, he tried to interest me in a stately home a few miles out of town. "Not quite the standard of this establishment, of course, sir, but very pleasant indeed." I had to call upon all my powers of invention to explain why that wouldn't do, and finally managed to imply, very subtly, that the question of finances might enter into it. That shocked him, of course.'

'Of course. Money, or the lack of it, is Not Talked About.'

'Especially in a place where everyone is assumed to have masses of it. At any rate, he finally found a small B&B right here in the city, with space for parking. He tutted a bit over the amenities, or lack thereof, but I assured him that we could manage to survive for a few days without a bar and dining room on site, and that if we needed to go farther than we could comfortably walk, or to a place where parking our own car was difficult, there were such things as cabs.'

I had been packing as he spoke and now looked around the room to see what I had forgotten. Alan checked the bathroom and the wardrobe and opened drawers. 'Right,' he said. 'I think that's the lot. Now, shall we demonstrate our ability to cope without constant servitude and take our own bags down for storage while we're in church?'

The church bells had begun to ring as we closed the door on the most luxurious digs we were ever likely to see.

The service at the abbey was lovely. The music was exceptional and the ritual uplifting. It was unfortunate that I had a hard time keeping my mind on worship. Our problem kept revolving in my head. What did we know? Almost nothing. What could I hope to learn by talking to a lot of people I'd never met? I didn't even know what questions to ask.

Alan nudged me to stand for the creed. I recited it, and slowly the meaning of the words penetrated my brain. I wasn't really in charge of very much, was I? If I really believed what my lips were saying, I could safely leave things to the one who *was* in charge. Do my best. That was all that was expected of me.

I went up for communion in a chastened and exalted mood.

There was no time of fellowship after the service; someone explained that the coffee-and-chat gathering met between the services. We decided to defer the abbey gift shop until another time, found ourselves a traditional Sunday lunch at a restaurant recommended by one of the vergers, and by early afternoon had checked out of the George, collected our car (repairs being completed), and established ourselves in our new room.

'A bit small,' was my comment. 'But perfectly acceptable. And look at the lovely little garden down below. We can bring our tea out there one afternoon.'

'The bed's comfortable,' said Alan, stretching out on it.

'Don't you dare! We don't have time for a nap this afternoon. I have to get to the gift shop at the Baths, or I'll miss talking to the students.'

'Right you are. It's a trifle far to walk, and the wind is chilly, even if the sky is your favourite bright October blue. I'll drive you as close as we can reasonably get and then go on about my own nefarious business.'

It was a beautiful Sunday afternoon, and the heart of Bath was thronged with shoppers and sightseers. Alan dropped me off on a corner near the Tourist Information office and said he'd pick me up there whenever I called him. 'You have your phone? And it's charged?'

I barely had time to answer before a traffic cop loomed, so I extricated myself from the car, waved, and set off on my mission.

I'd been smart enough to bring the city map with me, since without a map I can get lost in the smallest of towns. But even with a map I can run into difficulties. The problem in English cities isn't reading the map. The A-to-Z people do an admirable job of laying out large street plans, with an index to streets and places of interest, printed in big enough type for an old lady to read. No, the problem is figuring out where one is. It ought to be simple. Look at the street sign, find it on the map, voilà.

But street signs in England are often not where one expects them to be. I've lived in this country long enough not to look for signs on poles at corners. The English post them as large plaques on the corners of buildings. Sometimes. I have stood on corners looking at every building in sight. Nothing. Look farther down the street. Nothing. One might think that a city that was always a tourist attraction, that was *built* for visitors, all those centuries ago, would do better.

One might be wrong.

The kindness of strangers, however, is one of the things I like best about the British Isles. No one I asked seemed to think me stupid for having to ask directions to Bath's most famous landmark. One kind young man even pointed out on my map exactly where I was and showed me the best way to get where I was going, and was gone before I could even thank him.

Maybe my silly hat led them to expect ignorance from me. Good. Exactly the impression I wanted to convey.

The Roman Baths, gift shop and all, were around only a couple of corners. I straightened my hat, put my map carefully in my purse so that part of it stuck out, and opened the door into the shop.

And ran straight into difficulties. Literally. The man coming out wasn't looking where he was going, and my broad-brimmed hat obscured my view. We collided head-on. I dropped my purse, which opened and scattered its contents. He dropped his parcels. Apologies. We bumped heads reaching down for our scattered belongings. More apologies.

When we'd got ourselves straightened around, belongings restored, I finally got a good look at my companion in misfortune, and to my distress, recognized him. If I hadn't seen that he also recognized me, I'd have slipped away, but as it was I thought I'd better brazen it out. 'Oh! I've forgotten your name, but didn't we meet yesterday? Watching the video about the temple?'

'Why, yes! Simon Caine, at your service. And you're – wait a minute, I'll get it – Doris Something.'

'Dorothy, Dorothy Martin. You did better than I. I've a hopeless memory' I pointed to his laden carrier bag. 'Looks like this is a wonderful place for gift-shopping.'

He ducked his head in embarrassment. 'Got carried away, didn't I? I do like souvenirs, but I'm asking myself, now, if my mates will like this lot as much as I do. I . . . um . . . I don't suppose you'd like to come for a coffee with me and give me some advice?'

No, that wouldn't do at all. I had only this afternoon to try to talk to the student employees. 'How kind of you to ask. And of course I'd be happy to help, but as I don't know your friends, or their tastes, I'm afraid I'd be pretty useless. And I've my own shopping to do – grandchildren, you know.'

'Oh. Oh, of course.' He sounded a little as if he didn't know what grandchildren were. 'Well, then, I'll leave you to it. Happy shopping!'

It was a beautiful Sunday afternoon, just the sort to lure people and their pocketbooks out. So the shop was very crowded, and as we'd stayed in a corner by the door, perhaps no one had paid us much attention. I arranged my face in an expression that would, I hoped, convey naïve enthusiasm combined with confusion, and drifted toward the display of jewellery.

It had been restocked since the theft yesterday, but the cases weren't anything like full. It looked to me as though the stock was seriously depleted. In particular, the brooch I'd hoped to find, the replica of the one found in the spring, was nowhere to be seen. Of course, that might mean simply that they had never stocked one, but somehow I doubted that. Something so distinctive would be sure to sell.

A young woman appeared at my side. 'May I help you, madam?' Maybe it was my imagination that she looked and sounded slightly suspicious, but the staff would certainly have been informed about the theft yesterday and might have been told to keep a special eye on anyone displaying interest in the jewellery.

'Oh, I sure hope so.' I put on my best American accent and tried to avoid the English idioms that had become second nature to me. 'I was here before, but my husband was with me, and he puts a damper on shopping! I was really looking for that pin they found when they dug everything up. You know, the funny round one with the rubies and that sharp pin to hold it on? I thought maybe you might have a copy of it I could get for a friend of mine back home in Indiana. She just loves antique stuff like that.'

The girl relaxed. She couldn't have been more than eighteen or so, but she recognized a ditzy American when she saw one.

'Oh, I'm so sorry, madam. We did have those replicas, but they . . . that is, they sold very quickly. They're very nice replicas, prettier than the original, actually. It's made of bronze and our copies are gold-plated.'

'Ooh! And do they have garnets, maybe, instead of the rubies?'

She shook her head. 'There were never jewels in the brooch. You're thinking of the red enamel decorating the place where the ends of the circle join.'

'Oh.' I pouted a little. 'Well, I guess that's okay, if that's what the real one had. But you say you don't have any more?'

She looked a little nervous. 'Not at the moment, no. Sorry.'

'But you could order one for me, maybe? I had my heart set on one for Janie.'

'We may be able to re-order, but I'm not sure how long it might be before they arrived. I can check for you. Meanwhile, can I show you anything else?'

'Hmph. You haven't got very much, do you? The other shops have a lot better selection of jewellery. If I were running this place I'd make sure we were fully stocked during tourist season.'

'I assure you, we make every attempt to do just that. But we were very busy yesterday, and—'

'Uh-huh.' I sounded as sceptical as I could manage, and leaned closer to her. 'You know what I think?' I said in a confidential whisper. 'I think maybe somebody got a little light-fingered, you know what I mean? I'll bet those cute little locks could be picked with a bobby pin.'

She gave me the sort of look that my brashness deserved. 'Our security system is excellent, I assure you. The locks on the cases are secure and there is only one key. I can get it from my supervisor if there is anything you'd like to see more closely, but if not there are other customers waiting.' She started to turn away.

'Not so fast! I didn't say I didn't want anything. Those earrings are kinda nice. You just get that key and show them to me.'

I had kept up the chatter until I could see that everyone who looked like a manager was busy. Now, if I was lucky, this poor hapless girl would fetch the key herself, and I could see exactly how carefully the opening of the case was handled.

I was lucky. She spoke to the woman at the till, who opened the drawer and handed her the key. She came back with it clutched firmly in her hand. 'Now,' she said brightly, 'it was this pair?' She applied the key to the lock, slid it off the bar, and dropped it in the pocket of her apron while she pulled the little white box out of the case. Before she handed it to me for inspection, she pulled the lock out of her pocket to re-attach it.

But she wasn't able to finish the action. There was a commotion. A few feet away, in the crowd queuing up for the till, someone had fallen against someone else, and in the domino-effect that ensued, my helper was shoved against me. I dropped my purse for the second time that day. She dropped the lock and the key, along with the little box containing the earrings. A supervisor came striding over, frowning.

'What seems to be the trouble here?' she asked, sounding

very much like every cop in every English mystery I've ever read.

'Someone fell against her,' I said quickly. 'It wasn't her fault.'

And from the little crowd a couple of feet away, where the trouble had started, came a childish wail. 'I'm sorry, I'm sorry, I'm sorry!'

It was Sammy.

TWELVE

'Alan, it was pathetic.' We were back at our B&B, sipping tea in the garden. Alan had bought a couple of Bath buns, but I didn't seem to have much appetite.

'Here he was, scared, miserable, and surrounded by noisy people. Some of them were being unkind about his mental disability, calling him ugly names. The supervisor did her best to calm him down and assure him the whole thing was an accident, he just slipped, none of it was his fault, but he was very upset.'

'He volunteers there, I take it.'

'I think so. There was too much brouhaha for me to ask casually, and I was concentrating on the jewellery case.'

'Good for you. I'll bet nobody else was.'

'Well, I did wonder if the whole incident was carefully designed. So I kept my eye on the open case.'

'Nobody grabbed anything?'

'I'd swear not.'

'But I suppose the lock and key disappeared in the confusion.'

'They did not. I stepped on them.'

Alan slapped his hand on the table. 'That's my girl! How did you manage that?'

'Well, they were right there in front of me, but I was afraid to pick them up. Too many people were milling around, and I didn't want my hand crushed.'

'So you got your foot crushed instead?'

'No, luckily. It wasn't very comfortable standing on the thing, though. It's lumpy and my Sunday shoes have thin soles.'

'So when the smoke cleared . . .?' he prompted.

'Yes, when everything had more or less settled down, I became suddenly aware that I was standing on something and handed it to the girl who'd been waiting on me, who by now was fairly frantic. "Oh, dear, was this what you were looking for? I seem to have stepped on it. I hope I didn't damage it." All in my best dithery style.'

'I'm sure it went down a treat. More tea?'

'If it isn't stewed, or cold. No, thank you, I won't have a bun.'

The tea was still acceptable. He poured out the last of it and studied my face.

'This whole thing upset you, didn't it?'

'It did. Not so much the commotion. I actually rather expected something of the kind, and nothing was actually stolen, as it worked out. Oh, but I had to buy the earrings. I thought it was the least I could do after being so difficult with the poor child. No, what bothered me was Sammy.'

Alan mused, sipping at his lukewarm tea. 'You think he could be involved in all this, don't you? The thefts.'

'I don't want to think so. I like Sammy, even though I barely know him. But I knew people like him, in my teaching career. Like them, he's sweet and so innocent. But he's a child, essentially, and children like pretty things. And . . . well, he does keep turning up. He seems to work, or volunteer, at all these museum shops.'

'You think that would give him an opportunity for the thefts.'

I nodded, miserably. 'I don't *want* to believe it, but there it is.'

'And do you think, from your experience in working with the mentally handicapped, that Sammy's moral sense would allow him to steal?'

I brightened a little. 'It's not likely, true. People like him are usually very trusting. They believe what they are told, without question. If Sammy's parents brought him up to understand that stealing is wrong, he would stick to that. But if he didn't have that kind of background, who knows?'

'Then I think a little information about Sammy is in order, if only to set your mind at rest. It shouldn't be too hard to come by. Everyone in town seems to know him.'

'But suppose we find that he is taking the things?'

'Then for his own sake, as well as for the sake of the merchants who are being defrauded, he needs to be stopped. But no judge on earth would send him to prison. It's an obvious case of diminished responsibility. He might be sent to a school. Most likely he would be reprimanded and would lose his jobs. Nothing worse.'

'For him, that would be quite bad enough. He needs routine. He needs his life to stay the same, day after day. To be sent away from his home . . . oh, it's not to be thought of!'

'Then we won't think of it, unless it becomes necessary. Meanwhile, did you learn anything else of value at the shop?'

'They were being very careful about the locked cases. The key was in the till where it belonged. The clerk had the lock in her possession from the moment she slid it off, never laid it down, just slipped it into a pocket for a moment when her hands were full and then got it out immediately. I'm sure she would have closed and locked the case even while I was looking at the earrings if the to-do hadn't arisen. And even in the middle of all the confusion, she managed to close the glass door and stand in front of it.'

'Hmm. That makes an opportunistic theft much less likely. Of course, security procedures might have been stepped up in the face of yesterday's funny business.'

'Of course. So I'm not sure my visit was of any use at all. Oh, but there was one rather odd thing, come to think of it. I ran into that chap we met yesterday, the Cockney one. Literally ran into him, I mean. He was coming out of the shop as I was going in, and we collided. I dropped my purse; he dropped his parcels. We tied up traffic in and out of the shop for some little time while we retrieved our belongings.'

'You dropped your purse,' Alan said sharply. 'Did you pick it up, or did he?'

'I don't remember, actually. I know I helped him pick up his

stuff. He'd bought a lot, and bits scattered all over the place.'
I thought about the scene and then did a double-take. 'Oh! You
think . . .?'

He stood. 'I think it would be a very good idea if you made
a complete inventory of the contents of your bag. Did you
leave it in the room?'

When he returned with my purse he brought along our bottle
of bourbon and a couple of glasses. 'I think we could use
something a little more sustaining than tea. Clear a space on
the table, love.'

He dumped the contents of the purse unceremoniously. A
pen, a bottle of pills, and a packet of tissues fell to the grass,
and several pieces of paper tried to blow away, but I retrieved
them and sat on them.

Alan has finally accepted my rag-bag habits, so I was
spared the lecture he used to deliver. ('Why on earth do you
need to keep month-old receipts and shopping lists? And do
you really need three packets of tissues?' Et cetera.) He does
have a point, though. 'Oh, dear. Time I cleaned out my purse,
isn't it?' I picked up an earring. 'I thought I'd lost this. And
I can't imagine how that card from the McKenzies got in
here.'

Alan helped me sort out everything, making neat piles and
putting our cups and glasses on them to stop them blowing
away. When we had finished, it didn't seem as if I was missing
anything. 'I never carry a lot of money, as you know, but
what's there seems about right. My credit card and debit card
are there, and my driving license and all that, and my passport
is right where it should be, in this pocket.'

'I still wish you wouldn't carry it all the time.'

'I'm a foreigner, remember. Oh, I know I'm officially a
Brit now, but I feel more comfortable when I can prove
it. Anyway, I think everything's here. You thought what's-
his-name might have staged that little accident to steal
something?'

'Simon Caine. The thought occurred to me. We know
nothing about him, after all, and he's turned up twice now.'

'But at the same tourist attraction. Not so surprising.'

'Perhaps not. Too many years as a policeman make me

suspicious of everyone and everything.' He stretched, picked up his glass, and finished his bourbon. 'It's getting chilly. And late. I think it's time we sought some dinner and forgot all about our problems for a while. It's Sunday, after all. Day of rest.'

'Right.' And if I sounded a little sarcastic, well, there was reason.

Next morning, we slept late. Our B&B was on a quiet street near the Circus and the Royal Crescent, but not so near that the traffic was constant. We made it down to the tail end of breakfast and contented ourselves with toast and cereal before taking coffee out to the garden to plan our day.

'What haven't we seen yet?' I asked Alan.

He spread out the map and guidebook. 'Many things. Bath has something for all tastes. It's another lovely day, so why don't we explore Great Pulteney Street and the Holburne Museum?'

'What's it a museum of?'

'Art.'

'Not antiquities? I think I've had enough of those for the moment.'

'No. Mostly Renaissance and Georgian, I think. The building is said to be impressive, and they have a café for when we get footsore and hungry. Of course, it probably won't help us with our problem. Not the sort of things our villain seems to like to steal.'

'I trust there's a gift shop, though.'

'Don't know, love. I've never been to the museum. Shall we find out?'

'I'm game. It would be good to get away from our problem for a while. Maybe not thinking about it will let our brains relax and come up with some ideas.'

Alan is not a great believer in the power of the unconscious. I'm a bit sceptical, myself, but I've sometimes dreamed things that ended up being useful. So I keep, so to speak, an open mind.

We drove as close as we could get, found a miraculous parking spot, and walked up Great Pulteney Street to the

impressive Georgian building at the end. 'Goodness, it must
have belonged to somebody important back when.'

'Actually, it says here,' said Alan, looking at the guidebook,
'that it was built to be a hotel.'

'Well, for really important travellers, then. Wow!'

Once inside, I forgot about the building and was drawn in
to the collection. Now I like paintings, don't get me wrong.
But it's the decorative arts that really speak to me, and this
was a splendid exhibition of glass and china and furniture
and knick-knacks. (Though I suppose at the prices these things
must command, it's insulting to call them knick-knacks.
Objets d'art, perhaps?) One large room had a table set with
gorgeous silver and china, just as though ready for a glam-
ourous banquet, all sparkling under a crystal chandelier.

Then across the hall my eye, always alert to small things,
was drawn to the portrait miniatures and especially to the
gems.

'Oh, my,' I whispered to Alan. 'Now here's something that
might appeal mightily to our larcenous friend! Good thing
they're well protected.'

'Hmm. But they don't have any special connection with
Bath, as most of the things seem to do. Maybe they're safe.'

He spoke a little too loudly, and a guard cast a suspicious
look our way, which set me to giggling. We left rapidly for
the next floor up.

I had barely begun to enjoy the paintings by some of my
favourite artists, and many I didn't know, when Alan's phone
rang.

'Drat. I meant to mute it. Let me just— Oh. It's Roberts.'

He moved out into a corner of the hallway and spoke quietly
into the phone, listened for a moment, and then came
back into the gallery. 'We need to go, love.'

I opened my mouth to question him, then shut it again at
his look that plainly said, 'Later'.

THIRTEEN

Once we were out in the sunshine, Alan gave me a quick update. 'Rob is coming to fetch us. There's been a fire at the Jane Austen Centre.'

'No! How awful! Was anyone hurt? It must have been full of tourists on this beautiful day.'

'I've told you all I know. And here's Rob. He'll fill in the details.'

Rob was riding in a marked patrol car, to my surprise. 'It'll be easier to get through the traffic,' he explained when I asked. 'There'll be fire trucks and who knows what at the museum, and it's a rather narrow street.'

'But tell us what happened!' My anxiety level was rising.

'The centre has a small outbuilding in the back, probably once a stable. They use it for inventory storage. Not for the more valuable items like the jewellery, but books and other bulky items. It is of course kept locked and well-secured: cameras, alarms, the lot.'

'So how did someone manage to set fire to it?' I interrupted. 'At least, I'm assuming we're talking arson. You wouldn't be involved if it were simply an electrical fire or whatever.'

'Quite right. The firefighters who responded to the call saw at once that it had started at several different locations round the building, and the smell of accelerant was strong. There was no doubt in anyone's mind that the fire was set, and amateurishly set at that. This was no experienced arsonist at work. The crew were able to contain the fire very quickly; little damage was done, and as no one was in the building at the time, no one was hurt. But the whole thing seemed so odd that, given the recent thefts from museums, including this one, they called in the police.'

'And has anything been stolen?' Alan asked.

'Not only was nothing stolen, but our friend with the matches did not, apparently, even attempt to enter the building. Here we are. Stay in the car for a moment while I have a word with the officers.'

Left alone in the car, Alan and I looked at the activity around the museum. Aside from the acrid smell of smoke, and the emergency vehicles and uniformed forces, I wouldn't have known anything had happened. No one seemed terribly disturbed. Mr Bennett stood at the door to greet visitors cheerily, along with his beautifully dressed non-human companion. Tourists came and went, smiling, having a nice day out.

'Alan, have we somehow followed Alice through the looking-glass?' I was only half joking. 'Nothing makes sense, everything is downright crazy. Can you think of any reason why someone would set fire to a building and then not even try to do anything else? Get in, steal something – whatever? It wasn't even some crazy interest group with a bone to pick, or they'd have left some kind of message.'

He sighed. 'It's all of a piece with the other things that have been happening. Of course, some splinter group may yet claim responsibility. Though it's hard to see a political motive, even one of the wilder ones.'

Roberts beckoned to us, and we were led through the museum to the back garden, where the smell of smoke was very much more pronounced. Here we could see evidence of the fire. The foundation stones of the outbuilding were black with soot, and the nearby grass was burnt. There was a sturdy wooden door in the wall nearest the main building, and it, too, showed some charring near the bottom. In several places there were little piles of ashes, looking very much like what Alan cleans out of our fireplace whenever we've enjoyed a fire.

One of the firefighters, a woman, came over to talk to us.

'They tell me you're looking into this,' she said a trifle brusquely.

'In a way,' said Alan. 'My name is Alan Nesbitt, by the way, and this is my wife, Dorothy Martin.'

She brightened a little at that, I thought maybe in approval of my keeping my own name. 'Smith. Station Commander Smith. And you are involved in this matter how?'

'Strictly unofficially, Commander,' said Alan with a sunny

smile. 'I am a retired chief constable from Belleshire, here on holiday with my wife. When our car was used, without my knowledge, for the transport of stolen goods, she and I naturally became interested in apprehending the thief. As the stolen goods were all connected in one way or another with various historic sites in Bath – including this museum – our thoughts led us to querying anything unusual happening at any of those sites. Inspector Roberts therefore asked for our help with regard to this fire. Which, by the way, you seem to have conquered with amazing speed and efficiency. Well done!'

I hid my amusement at how fast she fell for Alan's charm. She smiled and shrugged. 'It wasn't much of a fire. A kid's fire. She just put down newspapers around the perimeter and doused them with petrol. The building's solid stone. Except for the door, there was nothing to feed the fire. And that door's solid old oak and nearly as fireproof as the granite. The newspapers burned, but nothing else. It was nearly out by the time we got here, to tell the truth.'

'You said "she", referring to the arsonist,' said Alan. 'Have you any particular reason for supposing it was a woman?'

'Not really, except that competent arsonists tend in my experience to be male. However, I use pronouns impartially.'

'Good for you,' I couldn't help putting in. 'So many people, wanting to be politically correct, use "they" even for the singular. I'm not sexist, but I am grammatical!'

Alan and the firefighter rightly ignored that. 'And you've found nothing to point a path to the arsonist?' Alan asked.

'Not so far. To tell the truth, with no real damage done, we won't spend a great deal of time on an investigation. I said it was a kid's fire. That could be the literal truth – some little horror with too much time on his hands. Unless or until he goes on to bigger and better things, we can't worry about it much.'

Roberts came up just then. They conferred briefly, and the fire crew began to disperse. Excitement over.

'So they're not going to do anything about it?' I asked.

Roberts took the question as directed to him. 'From the point of view of the fire service, they're satisfied that there's nothing to do. A nuisance fire, nothing more. They get so many of those. The kids who used to play with matches now play with lighters. They burn their fingers and maybe the curtains and their parents warm their backsides and clean up the mess. Nothing to it.'

'And from your point of view?' Alan asked quietly.

'Dammit, I'm far from satisfied!' He spoke quietly, but with passion. 'It's another odd thing, apparently meaningless, and at a Bath museum.'

I looked at Alan and he at me. With a lift of his eyebrows he signalled me to continue.

'Rob, we have a theory, Alan and I. It's been proven true too many times to be discarded out of hand. Briefly, it says that when odd things keep happening around a certain place, or person, or subject, they're connected, and hook up with something nefarious. It comes from a book by Aaron Elkins—'

Rob slapped the wall of the outbuilding. 'Of course! Abe Goldstein's Theorem of Interconnected Monkey Business!'

'You read mysteries?' I said, incredulous. 'I'd have thought that would be too much of a busman's holiday!'

'No, because in the books, the sort I read anyway, things work out well in the end. The villains are caught and punished, and almost everyone lives happily ever after. It's a refreshing change from real life. And Elkins is one of the best, even if he is an American. He's very popular on this side of the pond, you know.'

'I didn't know, but I'm not surprised. He's terrific. Well, so you know about Abe and his theorem. And Rob, it works. Not always, but surprisingly often. And in this case, where so much seems either random or just plain silly, this is the sort of situation where the pattern will take a long time to surface, but there is one. I'm certain there is one.'

'I think so too, Dorothy. But I'll be that famous monkey's uncle if I can find it.'

'Then let's act like we think this fire means something, and have a really good look around. You two are the experts; tell me what I should look for.'

Rob grimaced. 'When you have no idea what you'll find,

you try to spot anything that doesn't seem to belong, anything foreign to the environment.'

'A poker chip in a day nursery,' I suggested. 'A prayer book in a . . . a brothel.'

Alan kept a straight face. Rob didn't quite manage it. I smiled innocently. 'Right. Got it. Let's get to work.'

It was a beautiful day, but it was late October. The wind had risen, and the temperature had dropped. I wasn't dressed for a long stint outside, and I'm never good at any activity that involves a lot of bending over and peering at the ground. My back was screaming in protest and I was ready to admit defeat and go someplace warm when I spotted a leaf near the building. It was lobed, like an oak leaf, and I wondered mildly. I could see no trees at all nearby.

I picked it up, groaning and clapping a hand to my back, and called Alan over. 'Something that doesn't belong. What's an oak leaf doing where there aren't any oak trees?'

'Hmm. And not an actual oak leaf at that. A picture of one, rather crudely drawn and cut to shape.'

'Oh. I thought it felt odd, but a dry leaf isn't all that different from paper. I didn't notice the crude drawing. Your oak trees are different from the ones back home. The leaves are smaller, and just . . . different.'

Alan wasn't really listening. He was looking more closely at the 'leaf'. 'And what's this? Is it supposed to be an acorn? I wish I had a magnifying glass.'

'Aha!' I fumbled in my purse and found my Swiss Army knife. 'Here you are.' I opened up the magnifying glass and rubbed a tissue over it.

Alan looked at the half-inch lens with no visible enthusiasm. 'And what exactly am I to do with that?'

'Stop being snarky. It may not be very big, but it's a perfectly good magnifier. No, not that way. Hold it up to your eye and then bring the leaf close.'

Squinting in his effort to see what he'd found, he finally handed the knife back to me. 'It did help a bit, I admit. That little extra bit of drawing is definitely not an acorn. It's some sort of pattern in a circle. Looks maybe like a bit of Celtic design. You take a look.'

I had to squint, too, and move into the light. 'We need a better glass, but it looks to me like one of those Celtic knot things, you know, that have no beginning and no end, just one continuous line in elaborate twists. Certainly it doesn't have anything to do with an acorn, or not that I can see. Let's ask Rob.'

Rob wasn't actually standing on one foot while he waited for us to finish, but he was obviously ready to move on.

'Rob, I want to take you to lunch, but first we need a good magnifying glass. Dorothy's found something, and we have only a toy lens.'

'It is not a toy! It's a perfectly good—'

'Yes, dear. But even you admit that it's rather small. The one that comes with her knife/cum scissors/cum screwdrivers/cum—'

'Ah. A Swiss Army knife. I've coveted one for years. And I've always wondered: do you suppose the soldiers of Switzerland actually carry such a thing?'

'I certainly don't know, but I do know I wouldn't be without mine for anything. I can't tell you how many times it's come in handy. Anyway, look at this. Your eyes are younger than ours; maybe you can figure it out.' I took the imitation leaf from Alan and handed it to him, showing him the tiny drawing on one lobe.

'No,' he said after a long look. 'Not just a scribble, but I can't tell what. Let's take it inside. They're bound to have a magnifying glass in the office here.'

Rob was tactful about asking the manager to use his magnifier. Somewhat bewildered, but eager to cooperate, he pulled it out of her desk and handed it to him.

It was a good big one, not much stronger than my tiny one, but much easier to use. We passed it around, and Rob found a piece of blank paper and drew a copy of the pattern.

'Definitely Celtic,' I said. 'I haven't seen that exact pattern before, but the general design is familiar.'

'Yes,' said Rob.

Alan looked at him sharply. 'This means something to you,' he said. It wasn't a question.

'Yes. This is a symbol used by the neo-Druids. It is said to

have ancient origins. Its meaning varies according to the inter-
preters, though the spirals are often said to represent the cycle
of life. But finding it drawn on an oak leaf has many
implications.'

I was beginning to see his point. 'Do I remember that the
oak tree was sacred to the Druids? The real ones, I mean?'

'Careful, Dorothy.' Alan shook his head at me. 'There are
a number of Druids in these parts, and they would be mortally
offended by your assumption that they are not "real". They
take their practices seriously.'

'Yes,' said Rob, 'and with Stonehenge so near, they abound,
as Alan says.'

'They had nothing to do with Stonehenge,' I pointed out

'No, not originally. But many of the present-day Druids
think they did, history and science to the contrary notwith-
standing. In any event, they have adopted it, and have rituals
there at various times of the year, along with other New Age
groups. Some of them are rather militant about it.'

Alan had caught on before I did. 'So. We were looking for
a sign claiming responsibility for this fire. You think this is
the sign.'

'I think it could be. Which raises the question: why would
the Druids want to burn this building?'

FOURTEEN

We repaired to a nearby pub and considered the
matter over beer and shepherd's pie.

'Are you going to tell the fire brigade people
about this?' I pointed to the imitation leaf, sitting there in the
table in front of us.

'Not until or unless we can establish some relationship
between it and the arsonist. You must realize, Dorothy, that
this might have blown there from anywhere. Perhaps a near-by
infants' school had a drawing lesson involving autumn leaves.'

'Right. With tiny Druid symbols added on for decoration.'

'A child could have drawn that simply because he liked the pattern.'

I raised my eyebrows and drank some beer. 'Getting back to the Druids, Rob, you said that some of them are militant. To the point of violence?'

'No. Never. They're not very patient, many of them, with those who make fun of their beliefs, and they'll wage fierce verbal battles online and in the media, but actual violence, no.'

'Well, come to think of it, I wouldn't be very patient with anybody who mocked my beliefs, and I suppose to non-Christians, some of them sound pretty strange. But you're pretty sure they're non-violent?'

'Non-violence is part of their . . . their creed, if you will, though many of them firmly deny that Druidism is a religion. They're flower children, for want of a better term. They espouse reverence for the earth, conservation, and so on.'

'You're very well-informed, Rob,' said Alan. 'Is this a part of police training here?'

Rob smiled. 'Not formally, but we are of course expected to keep ourselves abreast of local events and movements. One can hardly avoid knowing something about the Druids when they gather in such numbers at Stonehenge at the solstices and, in less numbers, at both the spring and autumn equinox. But I admit I've done some reading up. Some of the . . . er . . . less tolerant members of the force are inclined to dismiss the Druids as nutters, and if I'm to set them straight, I need to know whereof I speak.'

I finished my beer and plunked the glass down on the table, narrowly avoiding the object under discussion. 'Okay, if either of you can make any sense out of this, it's more than I can. I'm sorry I ever spotted the blasted thing. You're right, Rob. It blew in from somewhere, and as far as I'm concerned it can blow right back.'

Alan picked it up carefully and used his napkin to blot away the bit of my beer that had touched one edge. 'Not so fast, love. Who knows? This might be the key to our whole puzzle.'

'Then you're not dealing with the same sort of lock I am. That dratted thing doesn't fit any lock I've ever come across. I'm sorry, both of you. I'm tired and cross.'

'Nap time for you, my dear. Rob, sorry we couldn't help.'

'Oh, you may have helped more than you know. I'll be in touch.'

I was in a much better mood after a nap.

'Back among the living, then, love?' Alan handed me a cup of coffee, which completed the cure.

'I'm sorry I was such a grouch.'

'You're frustrated. Nothing seems to be going anywhere. Is it perhaps time to make a list?'

Alan used to laugh (at least inwardly) at my passion for lists, but over the years he's found them helpful in solving a problem. I always find them helpful, to my spirits, at least. Just setting things down on paper gives me a spurious feeling of accomplishment.

'Right! What did I do with my purse?'

Alan finally found it on a shelf in the wardrobe, such a sensible place for it that I would never have thought of looking there. I rummaged, found my little notebook and a pen, and sat down at the tiny desk, feeling efficient. 'Okay, where do we start?'

'I suggest where it all began, with the discovery of the contraband in our boot.'

I got a momentary mental vision of stolen loot stuffed into an extra-large wellie. Years of exposure to Brit-speak hasn't entirely overcome my American thought processes. I shook my head and wrote down: *loot in trunk*. 'I'll describe it, as best I can, though I can't remember everything.'

'Do it in categories,' Alan suggested. 'Stonehenge, Jane Austen, Baths.'

'And Lacock, remember? And under those headings, two more: valuable and cheap.'

That entry took some time and, when we'd finished raking through our memories, didn't tell us much. 'The bluestone fragment – if indeed that's what it is – is the only Stonehenge item, right?'

Alan frowned in concentration. 'I think I got a glimpse of what looked like a chess man that might have been from the set we saw in the shop there.'

'Just one piece?'

'Just one that I saw, and I'm not certain about that. The whole set was rather dear, as I recall, but one piece . . .'

I sighed and entered it in the cheap column, and looked at what we had. 'There's a lot more cheap stuff than valuable,' I commented. 'Some, indeed, worthless. That scrap of handkerchief, for instance.'

'So that's one pattern. Very little of intrinsic value. The Roman coins turned out to be modern replicas, so they're out. The topaz cross and the other pieces of Austen jewellery are fairly expensive, though not, one would think, enough to tempt a jewel thief. Some of the jewellery stolen from the Baths shop may be worth a bit.'

'But that wasn't in our trunk. Boot. Let's keep to our chronology. What came next, after that annoying discovery?'

'The still more annoying discovery that our car had been vandalized.'

'Oh, yes. The tr— boot pried opened. Or an attempt made to do that.'

'Presumably to retrieve the loot, which was no longer there.'

'But our villain didn't know that. Can we deduce anything from that, Alan?'

'Several things, actually. First, that our villain had access to the garage where our car was kept.'

'But we already knew that. How else could the stuff have been put in the boot?'

'Second,' Alan went on imperturbably, 'that the villain is an incompetent amateur, as he has no idea how to break into a car, a skill that the true crook learns at his mother's knee.'

I snickered. 'So that incompetence ought to make him easy to catch. But he's bamboozled us and everybody else for a couple of weeks now. Pretty good score for an amateur.'

'Actually, an amateur can be harder to track down than a career criminal, if I may use the term, as they tend to work in established patterns.'

'Ah, yes, the notorious *modus operandi.*'

'Oh, of course, you would know about that from your extensive research.'

'Don't scoff! I've learned a lot from the thousands of

mysteries I've read over the years. Oh, sure, the authors fudged occasionally, made up procedures to suit themselves, but especially nowadays, they do pretty careful research to make sure that what they have their characters do is logical and possible and conforms to established police practice. Of course, I know criminals stick to their habits – as do we all. But this guy – person – is a loose cannon.'

'And round the twist as well, it would appear. The more important to find him. So. Our car is vandalized. What next?'

'Wait a minute.' I wrote down our not-very-useful conclusions about that incident. 'Now. What did we do next?'

Alan's memory is much better regulated than mine. 'We had a pleasant day at Lacock.'

'Ah, yes. Where we learned absolutely nothing relevant to the problem.'

'Except perhaps that postcard of the famous photo.'

I waved that away.

'No. Put it in the list. It doesn't fit any pattern we've discovered yet, but it's often the things that don't belong that turn out to be the most important.'

'Page four-hundred-and-twenty-three of the Policeman's Guide to Catching Crooks. All right, all right. It's in. Probably our villain swiped it out of habit. Not nailed down, in the pocket it goes.'

'Perhaps. Then the next day the abbey in the morning, and in the afternoon the Baths.'

'Yes. Where nothing happened until we left, and someone burgled the gift shop.'

'Robbed, not burgled. Burglary involves forced entry.'

'Hey, I'm supposed to be the grammar maven in this partnership. All right, robbed, if you will. Thinking back about that, it must have happened just after we left, while all those kids were still milling around. The burglar – okay, robber – could easily have used that crowd as cover for what he was doing.'

'Write down everything you remember about your visit to the gift shop – that day, and the next when you were playing detective.'

'Our first visit wasn't memorable, really, except for that

crowd of schoolchildren. But then the next day there were two disturbing incidents.'

'Yes. Your encounter with Simon Caine.'

'Up close and personal. With all the stuff he was carrying.'

'I suppose you saw a receipt, so you know he bought and paid for everything.' Alan sounded like a policeman.

'No, I did not! But good grief, do you think I'm mentally deficient? Of course, I can't swear on a Bible that he'd bought the stuff, but if his behaviour and general demeanour are any guide, he was not an escaping thief! I've learned a thing or two about people in the course of a long life, some of it spent tracking down bad guys!'

I glared at him, and he looked at me for a moment with his stern policeman face. Then he held up his hands in surrender. 'You're right. Apologies. Of course you had a sense of the situation, and I accept your judgement. Still, I do think it's interesting that he bought such a lot.'

'We know he was interested in the Baths. And knew quite a lot about their history.'

'Yes, but we met him the day before your "close encounter". Would he have come back a second day to buy souvenirs?'

I thought about that one. 'Maybe he remembered a lot of people who needed gifts,' I said tentatively.

'Weak.'

'I know. But really, there could be a lot of reasons why he came back. Maybe he's a shopaholic.'

'Usually a female disease. And no, I'm not being sexist. There are reliable statistics. I think you should make a new list, titled "Persons of Interest".'

I did that and then, hesitantly, said, 'I think maybe there's another name we ought to note.'

Alan sighed and nodded. 'Sammy.'

'Sammy. We know nothing damaging about him, but he just keeps turning up. He's such a *nice* person! I don't want to think he could do anything bad, but . . .'

'Exactly. But. And of course he was the principal character in the other incident you were about to mention at the Baths gift shop. He caused a fall, when the jewellery cabinet was open. Could have been an intentional diversion.'

I nodded reluctantly. 'It could have been. Even at the time I didn't think it was and, mulling it over, I'm even less inclined to think so. Sammy is clumsy. Many people with his disability are. It was probably just an accident, and nothing was in fact stolen.'

'Perhaps because you were there?'

I shook my head, not in disagreement, but in bafflement. 'You've got me. Alan, I can't think any more. Pour me some bourbon and then let's go for a walk or something. My head is full of cotton, hay and rags.'

'Thank you, 'Enry 'Iggins. Here you are, love.' He lifted his glass. 'Confusion to our enemies!'

FIFTEEN

The next day we were ready to tackle our problem again. I restricted myself, at breakfast, to toast, a boiled egg, and coffee, on the theory that too much rich food puts the brain to sleep.

'Now,' I said briskly, when Alan had completed his more interesting repast, 'let's take a look at what we have.' I pulled out the notebook we had been too dispirited to study the evening before.

'It still makes no sense,' Alan said with a sigh after frowning at our efforts for a few minutes. 'There's no pattern. Full stop.'

I nodded. 'And we never even got to the fire at the Jane Austen Centre and the fake leaf.'

'Which only confuses the issue, in any case. Dorothy, it's time to put the DBI into operation.'

'The what?'

'Dorothy Bureau of Investigation. We've identified two individuals who just might have something to do with this mess, the Caine man and Sammy.'

I made a little gesture of protest, which Alan ignored.

'We know very little about Sammy, and virtually nothing about Caine. That must be remedied.'

'The police—' I began.

'You're waffling, love. You know quite well the police can't strain their resources by investigating two people who have been accused of nothing, against whom we have no evidence whatever.'

'You think we should go out and find out more about these two people.' I spoke with no enthusiasm.

'I do. I think you should deploy your strongest weapon, your ability to talk to people and get them to talk to you. And I think you're the one to find out about Sammy. Your strong sympathy for him will help you to get people to open up.'

'And I'll find nothing to his detriment, I'm sure. That boy is not a crook.'

Alan, to his everlasting credit, did not remind me of the famous president who once spoke similar words.

After some consultation, we agreed that I would start at the abbey gift shop. 'It's the smallest, but it may not be too crowded on an ordinary Tuesday in late October,' I reasoned. 'And I'll bet anybody working there will know Sammy well. Then . . . well, I'll follow whatever leads I might pick up there. And what are you going to be doing, meanwhile?'

'I'd like to know a good deal more about Simon Caine. I don't know where he lives, or what he does for a living, or anything about him, really, except that he hails from London. We have only his word for that, but I believe him. Accent, attitude – it all rings true.'

'London's a big place,' I said mildly.

'It is. And a place where most people are anonymous, as in any huge city. But I happen to know several people at the Met, including a few who owe me favours. I intend to call them in. It may get me nowhere, but if Caine is "known to the police" in any capacity, it should be relatively easy to find out a lot more about him.'

'And do you think he might be on their books?'

Alan ran a hand down the back of his head. 'I don't know. But there's something about him that rings alarm bells. Let's say I wouldn't be surprised to find him on the police blotter, probably for something very minor. He strikes me as a lad who would be very careful to stay on the right side of the law or, if temptation became too strong, to cover his tracks.'

'I agree. He seemed to me to be just a little too . . . I can't put my finger on it. But not quite genuine, somehow. Anyway, I'm off, if you'll give me a lift. Shall we meet for lunch somewhere?'

'How about that pub we liked, near the abbey? That's if I can park anywhere nearby. I'll call you about a time.'

He ran me into the heart of town, as close as he could get to the abbey. 'The sky's looking a bit unreliable. Did you bring your brolly?'

I nodded, patting the pocket of my sturdy jacket.

'Well, then, the best of British luck to you.'

'And back atcha, as the kids are saying these days. See you later.'

The abbey was an oasis of peace and quiet, a benison in the midst of the turmoil that seemed to surround me these days. I knelt for a moment, praying for wisdom to meet the task before me, and then made my way resolutely to the gift shop.

It, too, was quiet. There was one other customer when I came in, but when she left I was alone with the pleasant-faced woman at the till. 'Let me know if I can help you find something,' she said. Her voice was just as warm and friendly as her face.

'Actually,' I said, 'I was hoping you could tell me a little about Sammy, the boy who works here sometimes.'

'Oh?' Not quite so friendly this time; a note of suspicion.

I had my story ready. 'Yes, you see, I was a teacher back in Indiana. That's where I'm from originally, though I've lived in England for quite a while now. Anyway, over the years I met quite a few children with Down syndrome, and grew to understand them a little. And to like them very much, I might add. That is Sammy's handicap, isn't it?'

'I think so, though I'm not an expert in these things. What I do know is that Sammy is a sweet boy – well, man, but he's so childlike I think of him as a boy.'

'Me, too. And I agree that he's sweet, even when people aren't very nice to him. Really, I could wring some necks sometimes! Oh, not really, but when I see someone making fun of him, or calling him names, or even just turning away in disgust . . . well, it's like kicking a puppy, isn't it?'

By now she had melted completely. I was about to ask some of my questions when she asked me one.

'But how do you know Sammy?'

'I don't really know him, not well, but I have to admit I'm an addict when it comes to museum gift shops, especially on this side of the pond. We don't have anything back home that's more than about three hundred years old, so your amazing churches and monuments and so on just blow my mind, and I have to buy books and souvenirs to send to my friends in the States. And Sammy seems to work in many of the shops here in Bath, so I keep running into him. I've been wondering. Does he volunteer at all these places, or is he paid? He seems to be quite useful.'

'Oh, he's very useful indeed, and very hard-working! Limited in what he can do, of course. He can't read anything very complicated, nor do any but the very simplest sums. But he has a photographic memory. Show him a picture of what you want him to bring in from the storeroom, and he never gets it wrong. Yes, really, we couldn't do without him, and certainly we pay him. He only works here one day a week. As you say, he works at many of the shops, but we'd gladly hire him for more hours.'

'I hope he's getting paid at the other places as well. I don't imagine he has much in the way of resources, unless his family is well-to-do?'

My inflection made it a question, and I hoped I wasn't trespassing on one of those unwritten English rules of behaviour. In America it was impolite to ask someone about his or her financial standing, but usually okay to ask on behalf of someone who might be presumed to need some help.

The clerk hesitated, and then said (with reserve), 'I'm sure I don't know. I believe he lives with a grandmother.'

'Oh, then he has some support – emotionally, I mean. Back in Indiana he would be receiving Disability – that is, government aid to the disabled, those who can't work for one reason or another. Those who receive that aid, though, are not allowed to work at all – I think. I'm not really up on the laws; I haven't lived in America for years. Do you have any similar programs over here?'

But that was too specific. I saw her face shut down even before a family came into the shop. The two toddlers were under insufficient control, to put it mildly; the parents looked stretched to the limit. The clerk gave me a smile that tried to cover her relieved look, and turned to deal with the two little destroyers.

But I had learned two things. Sammy got paid for his work, and he lived with a grandmother.

That little chat had certainly not used up the morning. I pulled out my phone and checked the time. I decided I could do with a cup of tea and a biscuit, and there must surely be a tea shop nearby. The rain had begun, barely a mizzle, but enough to make me pull out my umbrella as I walked across the square. It was much less crowded than it had been last week. The year was beginning to draw in; tourists were seeking warmer climes, and the weather wasn't conducive to wandering. I found my tea shop and sat down gratefully to a steaming cup and a scone. (Well, I'd had a skimpy breakfast, I snarled at my conscience.)

The tall man who walked in just after me looked familiar. I was sure I knew him from somewhere, but I couldn't place him for a moment. Then my ragbag of a mind came up with the connection, and I waved.

'Andrew! How nice to see you!'

'And you, Mrs Martin. Mr Nesbitt is not with you?'

'No, he's off on his own today. Won't you join me?'

He brought his tray over and sat down at my little table with no sign of discomfiture. 'I hope,' he said, pouring his tea, 'that your car was repaired to your satisfaction? I must say I was not impressed with the owner of the garage.'

'Nor was I, but they did do a good job. You can't tell it was ever damaged.'

'I'm delighted to hear it, and, I admit, a bit surprised. I've suggested to the hotel management that they might consider contracting with another valet service. Yours is the first car I know about that was damaged, but one or two have, to my certain knowledge, been taken out without their owners' knowledge.'

'Good grief! Stolen, you mean?'

'Not precisely. Used for taxi service. Most of the drivers, the valets, are honest, but some are not, and they can make rather a nice thing out of providing rides when they know a car won't be wanted by the owner for some time. Hotel guests can be very trusting. They turn over expensive cars to people they don't know, for an extended period of time, and hardly ever check the mileage when they reclaim the cars.'

I finished my scone and wished I had another. I was, as Hercule Poirot used to say, given furiously to think.

'Andrew – I'm sorry, I don't know your surname.'

'Williams. But Andrew is fine.'

I thought for a moment about asking him to call me Dorothy, but realized he wouldn't care for that. There was a line I was not to cross. 'Well then, Andrew, do you know about what happened to our car before it was damaged?'

'The stolen goods that were placed in the boot? Yes, Mrs Martin.'

'Do you think it's possible that someone took it for one of these taxi runs you describe, and that's when it happened?'

'No. That's highly unlikely. For one thing, your car was brought to the garage relatively late in the day, and though it was unlikely you would want it before morning, the garage is locked at night. The window of opportunity was small.'

I studied his bland face, finding it difficult to read. But from his carefully non-committal expression I was quite sure of what Andrew was not saying, and I burst into laughter. 'And for the other thing, our car is far too nondescript to make a desirable target for the game. The crooks would want luxury cars. Oh, Andrew, you're so tactful!'

He gave in and smiled. 'Got it in one. Your car would be useful to criminals in another way, though. It's utterly reliable, and its "nondescript" nature, to use your word, makes it fade into the background. It would make a perfect getaway car.'

'You take my breath away! Were you a criminal in another life?'

This time it was a broad grin. 'No. I'm training for the

police. One must acquire a certain knowledge of the habits of criminals.'

'I think you'll do well. If in time you aspire to the Met, talk to Alan. He still has some contacts there.' I took it for granted that he knew all about Alan's background. Nothing much slipped by Andrew. 'But tell me. Where are you from? There's something about your accent . . .'

'Yes, it's still there, even after twenty years in this country. As is yours. My parents moved here from Jamaica when I was a child.'

'Oh, I should have guessed! You're far too young to remember Harry Belafonte, but his accent was just like yours. Jamaica overlain by American in his case, English in yours – but the lovely lilt is the same.'

'Thank you.' He stood. 'Excuse me, I have a class in a few minutes. Mrs Martin . . .' He hesitated. 'If I can be of service to you, in any way, I hope you'll call on me. Here's my phone number.' He handed it to me, picked up his tray, and was off.

Now what on earth was that about?

SIXTEEN

I was still wondering about it when I left the little café and debated my next move. The two other places where I knew for sure Sammy worked were the Jane Austen Centre and the Baths. I preferred not to visit the Baths gift shop just now. I thought I'd rather do that with Alan, after lunch. I wasn't sure why the place gave me the creeps, but there it was. It was a pleasant spot with a delightful selection of merchandise, but somehow I wanted Alan with me the next time I entered that shop.

And the Austen Centre was too far away to walk, I thought. I wasn't sure, since Alan had the map, but even if it was fairly close, I wasn't eager to walk in the rain, which was now much more determined. What a pity Andrew had left! He wouldn't have had the limo at his disposal anyway, though.

So I hailed a taxi. The journey proved, indeed, to be longer than I would have cared to walk on a rainy day. I thought about the days of yore when I walked four miles a day as a matter of course, and then decided not to think about it. Age happens.

'Mr Bennett' was standing just inside the door instead of on the stoop, and his faux companion was nowhere to be seen. The rain wouldn't have been good for her costume, I suspected. I explained to the jovial man that I just wanted to visit the shop, not tour the museum, and he evidently remembered me, for he smilingly pointed the way.

Then my luck deserted me, for the first person I encountered was Sammy, busily moving some books around on a table. He was humming tunelessly, but when he caught sight of me his face crumpled and he started to cry.

'No! I don't like you! Go away!'

His voice was rising. I tried to calm him. 'It's all right, Sammy. I won't hurt you.'

But soothing tones were no help. He was sobbing, close to losing control completely. The staff converged on us, talking gently to Sammy, easing him away into the back premises, all the while glaring at me.

'Madam, what did you do to upset him so?'

A man whom I recognized as the friendly manager we had talked to briefly on the day of the fire was now looking not at all friendly.

'I'm as confused as you are,' I protested. 'I said and did nothing. I walked into the store, saw Sammy, he saw me and . . . well, you heard.'

'He was distraught. Have you no idea why?'

I replayed the scene in my head, and suddenly I thought I knew why. 'Yes, now that I think about it, maybe I do. I was in the shop at the Baths on Sunday afternoon when there was an unfortunate incident. Sammy was the inadvertent cause of it; he tripped or something and fell against someone, and the domino effect ensued. I happened to be there, in his field of vision, and I must have said or done something that made him believe I blamed him. I didn't, and I don't. I like Sammy a lot, and I'd hate to think he now considers me a threat, or an enemy.'

The manager had been gradually relaxing as I told my little story, and finally sighed. 'Poor kid. He doesn't have . . . he can't always . . .'

'He doesn't have filters,' I suggested. 'Most of us filter emotions through experience and rules about behaviour and understanding of how people react. Sammy can't do that. When an emotion hits him, it's all that matters in that moment. It's as if he's missing a skin. Everything's raw and on the surface.'

Now the man looked surprised. 'You do understand.'

'I try. I should have introduced myself. My name is Dorothy Martin, I'm an American ex-pat, and I taught school for many years in the States. Over those years I knew several kids like Sammy, and found them all sweet and likable. They had tempers, of course, and could have tantrums, but they could also be very loving.'

'Oh, Sammy is all of that. Embarrassingly so, sometimes. He rather attaches himself to people, and some of them find it annoying.'

'Yes. At any rate, Mr—'

'Oh, sorry. Bates. Bill Bates, and I won't get upset if you get it wrong. Most people do.'

'Oh, but how delightful to be mistaken for the richest man in the world! Mr Bates, if you have a moment, I'd like to talk to you about Sammy.'

The suspicious look was back in his eyes, but as I was the only customer in the store, he could hardly say he was too busy. 'May I ask why? We do not usually discuss our employees.'

Not reminding him that we had been doing just that, I took a deep breath and made a decision. 'I have good reasons. You may remember that I was among those investigating your small fire the other day.'

He nodded, still wary.

'My husband and I, and the police officer who brought us to the fire, believe that it is a part of a series of incidents that began when we discovered a cache of stolen goods in our car. We did not put them there, and so far we have not discovered who did, or why. There have been other thefts from museum gift shops. In every case, Mr Bates, they have been shops where Sammy works.'

He recoiled. 'If you're accusing Sammy of theft, you can leave, right now! I refuse to believe that child would steal anything!'

'Nor do I believe it, sir. I am accusing Sammy of nothing, so hold onto your temper, please!' I allowed a trace of school-teacher to surface. 'I simply state that Sammy works at every place where the thefts have occurred, or almost every place.' I had suddenly remembered the bluestone, which had certainly not come from any shop. 'Items may have been stolen from other locations that we don't yet know about. But you must see that we need to know as much as we can about Sammy, his habits, his family, his friends.'

'Why are you meddling in this? You're not with the police.'

'"With the police" describes my position exactly, as a matter of fact. My husband was a chief constable, and maintains close contact with police forces all over England. I have helped him with a good many troublesome problems. And as the first thefts were found in our car, the investigating officer has no qualms about our helping with the investigation. Finally, it seemed to all concerned that I could better talk to Sammy, and about him, than a policeman, who might be intimidating.' I sighed. 'Sammy and I got on famously when we first met. Unfortunately I've lost that advantage, at least until he forgets about that last encounter, so I can't talk to him. But I do have some questions for you, if you'll allow me to ask them.'

He said nothing. He wasn't happy about this, but at least he didn't repeat his order to leave.

'First, I know he lives with his grandmother. Do you know her name and address?'

'Of course.'

I waited.

He scowled, but pulled a book out of his desk and read off the information. I jotted it down in my notebook.

'Second, do you know if he goes to school at all? Or did, when he was younger?'

'Why do you want to know that?'

'I'm trying to trace his friends,' I said patiently.

'I don't know that he has any friends, except the people he works with. Everyone loves Sammy!'

'I'm sure they do. So do I, Mr Bates. I repeat, I'm not accusing him of anything. Please believe that!'

He held up his hands in surrender. 'Very well. But you can understand why I was wary. Sammy seems so afraid of you.'

'I hope that will pass. Now, the last thing, I think. Have you noticed Sammy forming any special relationships with any of the customers?'

Bates frowned again. 'What do you mean, special relationships?'

'I'm not sure myself. I've been thinking that he might have met someone in a shop, someone who became a friend, who might be able to help me understand Sammy a bit better.'

That sounded weak even to me, and Bates looked very sceptical. 'Seems to me you understand him quite well. And no, I've never seen him making friends with a customer. He spends most of his time in the stockroom. When he's in the showroom, he often smiles at people and is friendly with them, but that isn't what you mean, is it?'

'No. He was friendly with me when we met here a week or so ago. That's why I was so disappointed today when . . . well, let it go.' I fished in my purse and found a card. 'I can't think of anything else. Thank you for your patience. If you think of anything else that might help me untangle this knotty problem, please do call me.'

I doubted very much that he would.

It was lunch time, and I was far from where Alan expected to meet me. I pulled out my phone and got his voicemail. 'Hi, love. I'm at the Jane Austen place. Don't know if there's a pub or restaurant near here. Where shall we meet?'

I waited in the hallway, not feeling very welcome in the shop but reluctant to go out in the rain, which had apparently set in for the day. Alan didn't call back for a while, and I was beginning to fret when our car pulled up in front of the door and Alan beckoned to me.

'Oh, I'm so glad you drove! It's really ugly out there.'

'Yes, November setting in a bit early.'

I was reminded of the Gordon Lightfoot ballad about the *Edmund Fitzgerald* and sang a bar or two as I settled myself.

'"When the winds of November come early . . ."' Alan looked mystified and I gave it up. 'So where are we going?'

'Rob and his wife have invited us to share a lunch with them. I have directions to where he lives, and I've programmed the satnav. Here.' He handed me his phone. 'The speaker isn't working properly, so if you will, watch and listen, and warn me when I need to make a turn.'

Well, what I wanted to do was tell him about my morning and ask about his, but we could do that over lunch. And it would be good to have a home-cooked meal for once. I was getting very tired of eating out.

Inspector Roberts turned out to live in a pleasant semi (or town house, in Ameri-speak) on the outskirts of Bath. The roses in the front garden were looking waterlogged and discouraged, but the chrysanthemums were still colourful and sturdy, and dahlias and asters were putting up a brave show. The bright green front door managed to look cheerful even through the rain, and the bay window showed a glimpse of a welcoming fire.

The woman who answered our knock was just as cheerful and welcoming. 'Dear, dear, what frightful weather! Such a horrid jolt after the lovely days we've been having. Do come in and take off your wet things and get warm. I'm Sylvie Roberts and of course you're Dorothy and Alan.'

She was round and rosy, not at all the sort of wife I had expected of her tall, rather taciturn husband. She bustled us into the sitting room and sat us down in front of the fire. 'The tea's just ready; I'll bring it in.'

I felt as though I'd been handed over to an efficient nanny. No more decisions to make, no more deeds to be done. I sank into the flowery chintz of the chair with a deep sigh.

Alan grinned at me. 'Are you feeling about three years old?'

'And a pampered three-year-old at that. Rob is a lucky man!'

'And he knows it,' said the inspector, coming into the room. 'Would either of you like a little nip in your tea, just to keep the cold out? Or instead of tea? We've some bourbon, Dorothy, if you'd prefer.'

'Tea with a tot of bourbon sounds perfectly wonderful, thank you!' Alan opted for the same mixture, and when Sylvie had brought in the tray and poured out, we sat basking in the warmth of the fire and the sweetness of the hospitality.

'"Even the weariest river . . ."' I began.

Alan finished, '". . . winds somewhere safe to sea." Indeed. Sylvie, we're most grateful for this respite.'

'I like to make people comfortable,' she said simply. 'Now I hope you like mulligatawny soup, because I've made a big kettleful. Seemed like just the thing on a horrid raw day.'

'Oh, so that's what smells so good. I was sure it was something curried. And I love all things Indian. In fact, that's one of the things I like best about England, the wonderful Indian food you can find almost anywhere.'

We kept up the gentle, idle chatter over lunch, which consisted of the thick, spicy soup, plenty of naan, and for dessert a warm bread pudding studded with raisins and served with thick cream.

'Comfort food,' I said with a contented sigh when I'd eaten absolutely all I could. 'Rob, how on earth do you stay so slim and fit?'

'Eating on the run, most of the time. A policeman's lot—'

'Is not a happy one,' we all finished, in chorus.

And that brought us back to the real reason we had met. Sylvie brought a tray with coffee into the sitting room and tactfully disappeared, and Alan and Rob and I sat down to compare notes.

'I'm afraid I didn't learn a whole lot this morning,' I began. I related the few facts I'd gleaned: that Sammy was paid by the several shops where he worked, that he was highly valued for his pleasant personality and his devotion to duty. 'I found out he lives with his grandmother, and got her address. You probably already knew that, Rob,' I added.

'I did not. We haven't got around to checking on Sammy yet. He seems so . . . so innocent, I suppose.'

'Yes, and certainly incapable of dreaming up any complex schemes. But he could, I think, be easily manipulated by someone he trusted. I knew a sad case once at the school where I taught. The boy – his name was Bert – was in a sixth-grade class, since he was eleven, but of course his learning ability was about that of a four-year-old. Those were the days when children of all abilities were taught together, though the children like Sammy could actually be taught very little.

'The child wasn't in my class, but his teacher and I were friends. She said that at the beginning of the school year things went fairly smoothly. The other children treated him kindly, for the most part, and they themselves dealt with the few bullies; the teacher didn't often have to intervene. Most children have a strong sense of justice, and their firm conviction that it wasn't fair to pick on Bert brought the others to heel. But then something strange began to happen. She, the teacher, couldn't quite figure it out at first. Two of the boys seemed to be making friends with Bert, special friends. They hung out with him at recess, gave him toys and treats, and so on. Of course he was happy. He wasn't used to so much attention. But the boys in question were usually troublemakers, the class louts.'

'Uh-oh,' said Alan. 'I think I see what's coming.'

'Yes. The teacher guessed when she began to notice things missing from her desk. Nothing terribly important. A pen or two. Some marbles and a squirt gun she had confiscated. Then some of the students reported missing items. Lunch money, trinkets. One little girl, in tears, said her brand-new watch, a birthday present, was gone. She had taken it off for an art lesson that involved paints, lest it get spattered, and put it in her desk. The lesson finished just before recess. When she got back to her desk, the watch was gone.'

'And, of course, the Usual Suspects had perfect alibis,' said Rob, who could also see the end of the story.

'Of course. Once she was alerted to the problem, she started keeping a close eye on Bert at times when he thought she was out of the room, and sure enough, he was the one who was doing the pilfering, and handing it over to the louts in return for candy and, as he thought, friendship.'

'I hope Bert wasn't punished.'

'No. The teacher took him aside and suggested that he might want to make some other friends. She'd already talked to one or two of the nicer kids, asking that they get closer to Bert. The louts were sent to the principal with a full explanation of what had happened. Their desks and coat pockets were examined, and the principal called their parents asking for a full search at their homes, in lieu of which the police would be called in. Everything was found except the lunch money and the marbles.'

I picked up my coffee cup and found the beverage cold. 'Okay, I've been talking too much, but of course you see the point. Sammy isn't much older, in terms of mental age, than that child back in Indiana. And he could be influenced as easily. He takes an instant liking to many people.'

'He took an instant liking to you,' Alan said, nodding.

'Yes, and that's why I hoped I could talk to him this morning, if I found him at one of the shops. Direct questions about his friends wouldn't have worked, but I thought I could learn something indirectly. Well, I found him, but it was all for naught.' I explained about Sammy's reaction and the shop manager's consequent hostility. 'I think I soothed the man down in the end, but I may have lost credibility with Sammy forever.'

I looked at my cold coffee again, and Rob, reading my mind, produced the bottle of bourbon and a glass.

'I think you could use this.'

We all had a bit and then sat around in a morose silence.

SEVENTEEN

'However,' Alan said at last, setting his glass down briskly, 'all is not lost. I've had no chance to tell you about my adventures this morning.'

'I hope they were more productive than mine.' I finished my drink. 'Goodness, it's way too early to drink that stuff, but I needed a boost.'

'And you've enough food inside to offset more alcohol than that. Don't beat yourself up, woman.'

'Okay,' I said meekly. 'But no more. Rob, is there by any chance—'

Sylvie interrupted me. 'More coffee? Indeed there is.' She set down a tray with a fresh, steaming pot, whisked away my cup of disgustingly cold stuff, and beamed as she left us.

'I'll never, never be that kind of hostess,' I said with a sigh. 'I try to provide adequate food and drink, but I don't have that art of reading my guests' minds.' I poured myself a cup of the fragrant brew and sat back to listen to Alan.

'Unlike my dear wife, Rob, I've very little drama to report, but some interesting information. I spent most of the morning on the phone with old friends at the Met, and came up with nothing at all.'

Rob got it before I did. 'Nothing, eh? Yes, that is interesting, isn't it?'

Bewildered, I looked from one of them to the other.

'Drink your coffee, love, before it gets cold again. My information, or non-information, is interesting because the entire resources of the Metropolitan Police were able to turn up no trace of one Simon Caine. No police record, no address or phone number, no record of employment, nothing. Nada. Zilch.'

'But . . . I still don't understand. He said he was from London.'

'I don't believe he did, not in so many words, if you'll recall. He spoke nostalgically of London. He has a somewhat diluted Cockney accent. We were the ones who assumed a London background. But if the Met couldn't find him, then Simon Caine never lived there. Full stop.'

The penny finally dropped. 'Simon Caine isn't his real name.'

Both men smiled. 'Right you are, my dear. At least that's my working hypothesis. It's possible, of course, that we're wrong about his origin.'

I shook my head. 'No, I remember now. He did say he was from London, when he told us his name. Your head was buried in the guidebook, Alan, but he distinctly said it. And then we went on to talk about accents and how he guessed I was American. So he's a Londoner, all right. And that means he's operating under an alias, and that probably means he's a crook!'

'Not so fast!' Alan raised a hand in the *stop* gesture. 'It's not illegal to use an assumed name, and there are lots of reasons people do. We can't condemn him on that count alone.'

'Then we have to find out who he really is. And that shouldn't be hard. We have – well, Rob, you have – all those fingerprints, from the loot.'

Both men looked startled. 'Do you have some reason, Dorothy, to connect Simon Caine with the "loot", as you put it?' Rob asked.

'No, actually I don't. It's only that he's persistently been there when so many things happened. He was at the Roman Baths shortly before the jewellery was stolen from their gift shop. He was there again, his hands full of stuff he'd bought – or at least I assumed he'd bought it. And Alan, I just thought of this, but would you swear he wasn't at the garage the day our car was vandalized?'

Alan raised his eyes to heaven. 'Really, Dorothy! Your favourite reading material has softened your brain. What on earth makes you imagine he was there?'

We were not alone. I held on to my temper. 'There were a number of people there. One customer in the garage was having a set-to with one of the workers. His voice was loud, to carry over the other noise in the place. He had a London accent, and his general build was about right. And you remember I thought there was something familiar about him when we first met.'

Alan shook his head. 'Awfully thin, you know. How many million men are there in the UK with London accents?'

'And how many of them are in Bath?' I retorted. 'I know it's not evidence. I just think it's worth checking out. Surely it would be easy enough to find out if Simon Caine had his car worked on at that garage.'

'And we will check, Dorothy.' Rob spoke up quickly. I think he scented the beginnings of a row and wanted to stop it before it started. 'That's easy. One quick phone call. The fingerprint question, on the other hand, may be a little more difficult. With departments all over the country seriously understaffed, the Met may not take kindly to a request to check unidentified prints against their enormous database. If it were a question of murder, or some other major crime, yes. But a few petty thefts . . .'

I gritted my teeth but said nothing.

'I'm sure you realize that Dorothy and I don't consider them quite so petty,' said Alan, in a voice calculated to placate me. 'We have been used, or at least our car has been used, as unwitting accessories to this series of crimes. We want them solved. I do understand your problem about the fingerprints. Believe me, I do!'

I could hear years of dealing with understaffed and underfunded forces in his tone. 'Would it help at all,' I asked tentatively, 'if we could somehow obtain Simon Caine's prints? To use the only name we know.'

'Of course it would help, but how do you propose to do that? Invite him over for a drink? You don't even know his name, let alone his address or phone number.'

'Oh!'

They both turned to stare at me. 'Something wrong, love?' Alan asked anxiously.

'No, something's very much right! At least I think so. Alan, I can't get out of this couch. Hand me my purse, would you?'

'Oh, of course!' He'd got it. Rob looked mystified.

'And is there a tissue, or a napkin or something handy, Rob?'

He reached over to the coffee tray and handed me a lovely piece of damask.

Carefully, I dumped the contents of my purse on the cushion next to me. Carefully I sorted through the pile, using the napkin to move things aside till I found what I wanted and handed it to Rob, encased in the napkin.

Alan was grinning as Rob carefully unfolded the napkin to reveal a small mirror.

'I almost never use it,' I said. 'I don't even know why I still carry it in my purse. But I do, and it fell out when Caine and I collided.' I explained that incident briefly. 'And he was the one who picked it up and dropped it back in the purse. So it might have some old fingerprints of mine, but the ones on top, the fresh ones, will be his.' I sat back, feeling as smug as if I'd planned the whole thing.

Rob slowly shook his head. 'Were you born under some special star?' he finally asked. 'Or have you just been so truly virtuous all your life that your guardian angel hands you gifts like this?'

'No, it's my benevolent influence,' said Alan. 'She was never so lucky before she married me. Unfortunately it doesn't carry over to things like picking winners at the racecourse.'

'Since we never go to the racecourse,' I agreed, giving Alan a Look. 'Seriously, though, you could maybe compare these prints with the ones from the loot. Or somebody could. Then if there aren't any matches we can pretty well take Mr Unknown off our list of suspects, right?'

'Dorothy, my dear, you need to remember that he isn't officially *on* our list of suspects.'

Sometimes Alan sounds annoyingly like a policeman. 'For that matter, if you're going to be pedantic about it, we don't have a list at all, just some vague suspicions about a couple of people who are probably perfect citizens, next in line for knighthood. But since there's no one else even in our field of vision—'

I was interrupted by Rob's phone, which had a rather strident ring tone. He listened for a moment, spoke a couple of words, and rang off. 'I'm sorry, I have to go. Nothing to do with this problem, but urgent. I'll be in touch.' He strode to the kitchen where we heard him tell Sylvie to expect him when she saw him, and was out the back door.

It is a trifle disconcerting when one's host disappears with scant ceremony, and creates an interesting social dilemma. Were we supposed to stay and finish our coffee as if nothing had happened? Or get up and leave quietly? Or what?

Sylvia solved our problem. She came into the room, placid and unruffled, and sat down. 'I'll wager you're accustomed to this, too, Dorothy. Your man up and leaving you, I mean.'

'No, actually, Alan was in an administrative position when I first met him, and has been retired for years, now. We were both widowed when we met, you see. My first husband taught biology in a university in Indiana. Very little drama.'

'Helen, my first wife, did have to suffer through it, though,' Alan said. 'She learned to cook only food that could be kept warm or reheated. Sometimes the next day.'

'Ah, yes. Casseroles. Soups and stews. One does long for a lovely roast or chops, but we can enjoy that sort of thing only on holiday.'

'Will Rob – er, Cedric – be retiring soon?'

Sylvie laughed. 'Oh, Rob, please. He hates his given name. He always says his mother was frightened by a picture of

Little Lord Fauntleroy. Actually, his grandmother apparently loved the book, and had a hand in naming him, poor kid.'

'Poor kid, indeed! I'll bet he was bullied at school.'

'Actually, no. He was always lean but tough and wiry, and the first time some of the louts tried to give him trouble, he taught them the error of their ways.' She chuckled. 'And of course he soon showed how good he was at sport, and that took care of the problem once and for all. He was Rob then and forever.

'And as for retirement, he could, in a couple of years, with full pension. Certainly he's thought about it, and I've tried to encourage him, but the fact is that he loves what he does and hates the thought of giving it up. I'm sure you can understand that, Alan.' She smiled sweetly at him.

'Dorothy will tell you I've never quite given it up. Maybe by fate, maybe by some mysterious working of our own wills, she and I have become involved in a number of investigations, often when we've been off on what were meant to be peaceful holidays. Like this one.' He made a face.

'Yes, Rob's told me about this particular problem that you've fallen into. And I might be able to help just a little. I volunteer at the abbey gift shop from time to time, and I've come to know Sammy rather well.'

'Oh, good grief! Here I was making all these would-be subtle approaches to people who might tell me about him, and here you were all the time. I suppose Rob would have told us, in time.'

'He would if he had known you had a particular interest in Sammy. And if he'd known how well I know the poor lad. Though I don't know why I call him that. We may think of him as handicapped or disadvantaged, but most of the time he's quite happy and doesn't feel sorry for himself at all.'

'Oh, I absolutely agree with you,' I said vehemently, 'as I was saying to Alan just a few days ago. But you say you might have some information about Sammy that we could use?'

'I wouldn't put it that strongly. Sammy and I get on very well, and he talks more to me than to some people, I think because he knows I like him and will take him seriously. The trouble is that he doesn't communicate at all clearly.'

'Garbled speech?' asked Alan.

'Yes, to some degree, but it's more the inability to string thoughts together in any logical order. He just says whatever is in his mind at that second, and the idea may be derailed by almost anything: another thought, something pretty that he sees or hears, a voice in the distance – anything.'

I nodded. Exactly the kind of thing I'd often observed with the schoolchildren in Indiana all those years ago.

'So it's not so much anything Sammy has told me, as a kind of feeling I've noticed in him lately. He's been excited, in a way. As if he's hugging to himself some lovely secret. He'll start to say something, smiling that infectious smile, and then clap his hands over his mouth and shake his head, but never losing the smile.

'I asked him once if something nice was going to happen. And he shouted "Yes!" and then shut down completely, hands over mouth and shaking his head violently. I could see tears in his eyes, so of course I changed the subject at once to something about the shop, I forget what. And he was all smiles again, the bad moment forgotten, but I couldn't help speculating. I did ask the manager to look up his personnel record, to see if he had a birthday coming up, but no, it was back in March.'

'And this happened . . . when?' asked Alan.

'Let me think. Mid-October, I believe.'

So not long before we found the loot in our car. 'Did you have any idea of what the secret might be?' I asked. 'Since it wasn't anything to do with his birthday?'

'Not a hint. Except that he was extremely pleased about it.'

'Sylvie, what kind of thing pleases him, in your experience?' Alan leaned forward.

'Oh, almost anything. A candy bar. A sweet puppy. A compliment. A new and interesting task to do. As I've said, he's a very happy boy.'

'But would he make a secret of any of those things?' Alan persisted.

'I wouldn't have thought so, no. He's usually very . . . I suppose transparent would be the word.'

'So this was something different.'

'Is something different. I saw him yesterday, and he was . . . I'm not sure what the right word is. Glowing, perhaps.'

'And yet today,' I said, 'he broke into tears when he laid eyes on me.'

Sylvie looked astonished. 'But why? What did you say to him?'

'Not a thing. I walked into the shop at the Austen Centre. Sammy was in the shop, I think arranging a display. The moment he set eyes on me, he fell apart.'

'But that makes no kind of sense!'

Alan sighed. 'Nothing about this matter, from the very beginning, has made sense. Truly I begin to wonder if we've lost our collective minds, or been removed by aliens to some parallel universe.'

Sylvie laughed at that. 'I don't suppose it's either of those things. You both seem to me to be extraordinarily sane. Nor do I believe my husband has suddenly gone round the twist. There must be a pattern somewhere.'

So we sat and hashed out everything we knew, everything we had guessed, trying to weave the wildly disparate threads into a tough, resilient fabric that would help us wrap up a crook. We didn't succeed.

Sylvia had made pot after pot of tea until my trips to the loo had nearly worn a path in the carpet. She had brought out luscious scones and jam tarts to fuel our weary brains. Nothing helped. We had talked ourselves to a standstill, and Alan and I had exchanged 'time to go' looks, when Sylvie's phone rang. She left the room and came back just a few moments later. 'That was Rob. He's going to be tied up with this new matter until dinner time. He'd like us to meet him for a meal and talk about some new ideas.'

'When?' I said cautiously. It was late afternoon by now, and I was in urgent need of a nap.

'Eight or so, he said, at The Scallop Shell. It's a fish and chips place, not fancy, but the best fish you'd find anywhere.'

'That sounds great! I'm tired of fancy restaurant food.'

Sylvie gave Alan the address. He programmed it into his phone, and we drove home for what we felt was a well-earned respite.

EIGHTEEN

Eight o'clock found us in a bright, modern room, cheery and crowded with people enjoying themselves and their meals. Rob insisted on our sharing a plate of mussels with our drinks; Sylvia and I opted for cider while the men had beer.

'All right,' I said finally, after the small talk had petered out, 'I'm dying by inches. What was your new case about, and how come you think it might be useful to us?'

'Ah,' he said maddeningly, neatly extracting the last mussel from its shell, 'well you might ask.'

'I *am* asking, and I warn you I'm growing dangerous!'

'My new case, as you put it, was nothing more exciting than a traffic accident.'

'C'mon! They don't call men of your rank in to deal with traffic accidents.'

'Not ordinarily, no. However, this one was a bit out of the ordinary.'

Alan covered my hand with his, silencing me as I was about to blow. 'All right, Rob, you've teased us long enough. Tell us.'

He sobered. He had enjoyed playing with us, but it was time to stop playing and get down to business. Serious business. 'They called me in because the accident appeared not to be an accident at all, but a deliberate attempt at harm. And also because the car and driver who were indeed harmed turned out to be the Rolls Royce limousine owned by the Royal George Hotel and its driver, Andrew Williams.'

'No! Not Andrew! Is he okay?'

'They took him to hospital, but the latest report is that he's not seriously injured. A broken right arm seems to be the worst of it, along with cuts and bruises. No internal injuries, amazingly, nothing life-threatening. The car, on the other hand, may not survive. The other car ran a stop light and rammed into the limo as Williams was attempting a right turn. It didn't hit the driver's side square on, thanks be, or Williams would probably not be with us. The limo was clipped on the right rear wing, which spun it about so that it crashed into a shop on the other side of the intersection, causing extensive damage to the left flank of the vehicle. The insurance people will probably write it off completely.'

I brushed off that information. 'I don't care about the car! That hotel can afford to buy a new one, even if the insurance doesn't pay a cent. But why would anyone try to kill Andrew? They – you – do think it was a murder attempt, right?'

'We do. The car that rammed him had stopped at the light, according to witnesses, and then revved hard as the Rolls made the turn. It was not accidental.' Rob's mouth set in a hard line. This one had roused his ire.

'I assume the criminal's car was also badly damaged,' Alan commented. 'That should make it, and the driver, easily found.'

Rob shook his head. 'The car was certainly damaged, to the point of being inoperable. That may be one reason why its driver simply left it where it stood, blocking the intersection, and fled.'

'Registration? Licence plate?'

'The car was reported stolen about a half-hour before the incident. From a deacon at the abbey,' he added before we could ask.

Our meal, for which we no longer had much appetite, was delivered just then. The waitress observed our glum silence and asked, 'Is something wrong? Can I get you anything else?'

'No, no, this is splendid, thank you,' said Rob, and she went away, unsatisfied.

I picked at my fried plaice, which looked and smelled delicious, and poured some vinegar on the chips. 'And why,' I asked, after biting into a chip and finding it cardboard, 'did you think this crime somehow involved us and our problem? Aside from the fact that we stayed at the hotel when we first came to Bath, and had made use of the limo?'

'Because Andrew mentioned your name, Dorothy,' he said, putting down his fork. 'When they were putting him in the ambulance, he beckoned me over and said, "Tell Mrs Martin to be very careful. *Very* careful! There's more than we know."'

'What did he mean by that?' I demanded. 'More than we know about what?'

'I don't know. They jostled his arm just then, getting him in, and pain cut him off. By the time he could speak again they'd closed the door. I couldn't follow him to the hospital immediately; there was too much to do at the site. Of course, other cars had been damaged, and that all had to be seen to, reports taken and so on, and traffic diverted, and the owner of the damaged shop interviewed. I did send a man to keep watch on Williams, in case there's another attempt on his life, but he'll be under sedation for most of the evening, while they deal with his arm. It's a clean break, but it will be extremely painful for a while. He won't be talking until morning at the earliest.'

'And you'll be there.'

'Probably not, Dorothy. There are too many other details to attend to. But I'll be sure the man on duty is told to note everything he says, verbatim, and to ask him some questions if he's well enough. Our first priority, though, as I'm sure you'll understand, is to keep his would-be murderer from making a second try.'

'And *my* first priority, wife, is to keep you from falling victim, yourself.'

'Me? But I'm not—'

'Andrew warned you, and he's an extremely astute and observant young man. You're not leaving my side until we get this cleared up.'

I would deal with that pronouncement later. Right now, I had another concern. 'Rob, does he have a wife? Family?'

'I don't know. You know he's studying to enter the force, but we don't have background info on him yet. My people will be looking into it.'

'Dorothy,' said Sylvie quietly, 'don't worry about that part. I'll visit any family he might have. I've always felt that to be part of my duty as a policeman's wife.'

I was immediately ashamed of myself for never having thought of such a thing. Of course, by the time I met Alan he wasn't actively working cases anymore. Still . . .

Alan squeezed my hand and gave me the look that always

brings tears to my eyes, the one that says *I love you and I think you're wonderful*. I blinked them back, cleared my throat, and said, 'Good. But Rob, you'll let me know how Andrew gets along, right?'

'And,' Alan added, 'exactly what he meant by that cryptic message. It will be far easier for Dorothy to protect herself if she knows what hazards to avoid.'

'For one thing,' I said briskly, 'crowded intersections. Rob, Sylvie, I hope you won't think us rude, but we have a lot to think about. Do you mind if we take this lovely food home? To the B&B, I mean. There's a microwave we can use, and I know it won't be quite the same, but it will still be good.'

The staff seemed astonished at our request. Apparently no one, but no one, ever failed to eat every scrap of their delectable food. But since they also did take-away, they were able to provide containers for our almost-untouched meals.

Alan waited until we were in the car before saying, 'That fish will be rather disgusting re-heated.'

'I know. I didn't want to hurt anyone's feelings. I'm not really hungry. We can throw it out, or give it to the cat.'

'Our landlady has a cat?'

'I have no idea. Probably. Alan, what are we going to do about this mess?'

'I don't know.'

That was the most devastating statement I'd ever heard from Alan. He always has ideas. He never gives up. When I'm tempted to throw in the towel, he always encourages me to give it another try.

I was speechless. What could we do?

A trite, silly phrase ran through my mind. Where would I go if I were a horse? The standard, not very useful advice for someone trying to find something. Where would I go if I were a kitten? Where would I go if I were a lost phone?

What would I do if I were a thief?

'Alan, I've thought of something we could try. Haven't you tried, at times in your career, to get yourself into the mind of the criminal? To try to work out his motives, or find him, or plan how to capture him?'

'Yes, on the odd occasion.'

'Well, then, let's take what we know about this guy, and see if we can't get into his mind.'

'You're sure it's a man.'

'I'm not sure of anything, but multiple pronouns are a pain. Besides, I'm of a generation that understood "he" could at times be non-gender-specific. So what do we know about him?'

'Damn all!'

'Now, now. We know a lot, actually. For one thing, we know he's extremely undiscriminating about his thefts. Expensive stuff, worthless junk, old, new – he doesn't seem to care.'

'There's one constant, though,' said Alan, getting a little interested in spite of himself. 'Everything he's stolen, or at least everything he stashed in our car – for which I'm pining to get even – everything there had to do with the history of Bath.'

'Or Stonehenge.'

'That can almost count as an extension of Bath.'

'Or the other way round,' I objected, 'since Stonehenge came first, by a few millennia.'

'All right, Bath and environs. History and prehistory, indeed.'

'From the bluestone, quarried circa 3000 BC, to the postcard of Fox Talbot's famous photograph in the mid-nineteenth century.'

'I think,' said Alan in his pedantic mode, 'we must remember that we have no idea when our particular chunk of bluestone was quarried.'

'Nit-picking. It was obviously intended to represent the Stonehenge monoliths. So we have the third millennium BC, and then a long gap until the first century or so AD, and the next few, and then another long gap to the Jane Austen era, late-eighteenth to early-nineteenth century, and then a very few years to Fox Talbot. Is there anything we can glean from that timeline?'

'Only that, if our thief is a historian, his interests are some-what eclectic. There is a good deal of history not touched, even if you discount the first couple of thousand years. The establishment and disestablishment of the abbey, for instance, and its later history of rebuilding. The whole Georgian era, with its remarkable architecture that shaped the face of Bath.'

'Hmm. Is there a museum of the architecture, I wonder?'

'There is. I have never visited it.'

'Maybe it doesn't have a gift shop with good stuff to filch. Or maybe our villain just isn't interested in architecture.'

Alan shrugged at that.

'What I do find very interesting, though, now that you've brought it up, is that nothing seems to be connected to the abbey. And they do have a gift shop, small but quite nice.'

'True. Now, what else is there to note about the thefts?'

We thought, silently, but neither of us came up with anything.

'All right. Now, I've written all this down.' I flourished my notebook. 'Do we have enough to understand our crook a little?'

'A little, perhaps. Not much.'

'No, but it's all we've got. So. I'm a crook, living in Bath. I decide that I want artefacts, no matter how trivial, from various important eras in Bath's history. The easiest place to steal most of them is from the museum shops. I don't care if they have intrinsic value or not. And that means . . . what?'

'That you have no plans to sell them. Either you want them for yourself, to build some kind of crazy collection, or you are stealing them for someone else, for the same reason – a daft collection.'

'And I'm not stealing anything from the abbey gift shop, because . . .'

Alan ran a hand down the back of his neck. 'I don't know. It could be that you're not interested in ecclesiastical history.'

'That won't wash. Stonehenge, it could be argued, is not ecclesiastical, exactly, but certainly religious. The baths were a part of a temple compound. I'd say religion is very much a part of his – my – focus. Anyway, if we're right, it isn't the thief's interests that matter, but those of whoever is going to get the collection eventually – who apparently is very interested in religion.'

'But only pagan religions, not Christian?'

'Possibly. Possibly.'

I put down my notebook and stretched. 'I'm thunk out. I don't know if we've made any progress or not, and I'm sure we haven't come any closer to figuring out why Andrew was attacked. Andrew, of all people! But I'm tired, and I'm hungry enough even to eat some of that fish and chips.'

'So am I. If washed down with sufficient alcoholic help. I'll see to the microwave if you'll pour the libations.'

So we had a meal that quieted our hunger pangs, if not our misgivings, and went to bed early. It was a long time, though, before I could stop worrying about Andrew.

NINETEEN

Morning came, as is its wont. It brought no light to my mind or my heart. And little, for that matter, to the bedroom. It was still raining outside; the sky was charcoal grey. I wanted to burrow back into my pillow and sleep until spring.

But: problems. Duties. The squirrel in my head took up his round on the wheel, making further sleep impossible. Anyway, I'd slept long enough. However little it looked like it, morning was definitely here.

Alan was still dead to the world, so I got up, showered, and made coffee for both of us. That tantalizing smell brought him to consciousness. We drank our coffee in the silence a nasty grey day imposed.

'Well,' said Alan finally.

'Yes.' I looked at the alarm clock. 'Breakfast? It's getting late.'

He yawned. 'Right. Ten minutes.'

A man can say that sort of thing and mean it. In exactly nine minutes he was showered, dressed, and awake. In that order.

Breakfast was as good, and as plentiful, as ever. We were both hungry after our unsatisfying dinner, but after a few bites I stopped eating. The eggs and bacon were apparently made of sawdust or chalk.

'Alan, what are we going to do?'

'We're going to see Andrew in the hospital,' he said decisively. 'We've got to have something solid to work with, and it sounds as if he knows some things we don't.'

'He might talk more freely if I weren't there. Man to man, you know.'

Alan set down his coffee cup very carefully. 'We are going together, or not at all. I know you don't like to be restrained. I know you think you don't need protection, nor do you want it. You're a free spirit, and I respect that. But until this villain is found and locked up, I am going to be by your side at all times. Period. Amen.'

Well, we've argued this point over the years until Alan finally abandoned his in-bred English male chivalry and reluctantly let me take my own risks. I looked at his face this time. It couldn't have been more set if it had been carved into Mount Rushmore.

I said mildly, 'You may raise some eyebrows when you accompany me into the ladies' room.'

That made him smile a little, but he wasn't going to budge one inch. 'I'll be just outside. With my ears tuned to any strange noise. Are you going to eat any more of that, or shall we go?'

'I thought I was hungry, but I don't want any more. Ready as soon as I go up for my raincoat and my purse.'

He was right behind me on the stairs.

I thought we might have trouble at the hospital, as it was well before visiting hours, but I'd forgotten the power of Alan's warrant card. He's not technically supposed to use it now that he's retired, but in situations like this he finds flourishing it to be more efficient than arguing.

The guard was seated just inside Andrew's room, with the door open. He stood up and came to the door as we approached. 'Sorry, sir, madam. This patient is not allowed visitors.'

'Well done, Sergeant,' said Alan *sotto voce*. 'If you'd like to phone Inspector Roberts, I believe he'll allow an exception in our case.'

Alan pulled out the warrant card again. The young man read it carefully, then handed it back with a smile. 'Yes, sir. The inspector did order me to let you and your wife in. You'll find Mr Williams still somewhat groggy, and in a good deal of pain. I think the nurses would ask you to limit your visit.'

Andrew looked awful. His skin, normally the lovely Jamaican coffee-cream, was greyish. His right arm was in a cast all the way from the shoulder, with only the tips of his fingers showing. He managed a smile, though, and nodded at the only chair in the room. 'Do come in. I've been expecting you. Sorry, Mrs Martin.'

It took me a second or two to realize that he was apologizing for not standing when I came into the room, and I very nearly lost my composure, but I hid my face for a moment and gravely took the indicated chair.

'I won't ask how you're feeling,' I said. 'I can guess, and I don't think you usually use that kind of language.'

'The drugs help a bit,' he said. 'It's only broken bones. They will heal.'

Alan, standing at the foot of the bed, said, 'Andrew, they'll only let us stay for a few minutes. So I don't want to be unsympathetic, but we need to know why you warned my wife.'

'Yes.' I nodded. 'It must be important, or you wouldn't have made the effort to speak through the pain.'

He pushed himself a little higher in the bed. 'It's a long story, and nothing is what you, sir, would consider evidence. But I'll try to summarize.' He paused for a moment. 'You know that the Rolls has communication between driver and passengers. You used it.'

We nodded.

'Passengers can control it, as you discovered, but not everyone realizes that. I usually speak up after a few minutes to tell them where the controls are, so they're not embarrassed by some indiscretion. Last Sunday I left it too late.' He coughed and swallowed. I handed him the glass of water.

'I picked up this man at the hotel a little before noon. He was talking on the phone when he got in the car, and continued before I could say a word. What I heard was this: "Trouble with the American woman. She is the prying, interfering sort." And then a pause, while he listened. Then: "Yes, I quite understand. Certainly this is too important to be stopped at this point, when you're so close. I'll see to it. She won't bother us any more, I promise." Another pause. "Yes, that will be splendid. I'll check with my bank tomorrow." Then he rang off. I looked in the mirror and saw him put his phone in his pocket. Then he laughed to himself, a nasty sort of laugh, and said, "Silly bitch." He was quiet the rest of the way, until I dropped him off at the Abbey. I thought at the time it was really stupid to hire a limo for that short way; he could have walked it.'

'And of course you never let him know the mike was on,' I said.

'No. But I think he worked it out somehow. Why else would he have tried to kill me?'

Alan leaned forward. 'You think he was involved in what happened later. Why?'

'I think he hired the limo to scope me out. If he's in on the thefts, as I believe he is, he would have known that you used the limo when your own car was unavailable. I think he thought you might have talked to me about them. Or something.'

He was tiring. Alan leaned forward and asked the critical question. 'Andrew, who was he?'

'The name he gave when he hired the car,' said Andrew in an expressionless voice, 'was John Smith.'

'Oh, no!' I almost wept. 'But what did he look like? How did he speak? Didn't he give you any clues at all? How about his credit card?'

My voice had risen. It was a shame I hadn't been able to keep quiet, for the noise brought a nurse into the room.

'I understood the police were allowing no visitors,' she said in her starchiest voice. Nurses no longer wear the starched uniforms and caps of my distant youth, but they do often wear the equivalent attitudes.

'We *are* the police,' said Alan. Well, it was only a little white lie. 'We have some important questions about his accident—'

She overrode him, not an easy thing to do to my husband. 'They can wait. Right now my patient needs quiet, and I intend to see that he gets it.'

'But I wanted—' Andrew began.

'We have only—' from Alan.

'Not now. Please be quiet as you leave. There are other very sick people on this floor.'

She had been edging us toward the door, and now shut it firmly, leaving us in the hallway.

'Well! That's the very first time I've seen you defeated by a nurse. When I was in the hospital in Durham, you routed her utterly.'

'I wasn't going to let some officious female get between me and my wife. This is a different situation.'

'But he was about to tell us something important. How frustrating!'

'Dorothy, try to remember he is a man with painful injuries. He's probably on a morphine drip. He truly should be allowed to rest. I'll give the sergeant some questions to ask when Andrew is able to deal with them. Meanwhile, I'm going to call Rob and give him a full report. He will be able to trace that passenger further.'

He pulled out his phone. A nurse walking by shook a finger at him. 'Not allowed here. Outside, please.'

I tried to think of something that would moderate his chagrin at being told off twice in five minutes. I couldn't. But I did manage not to giggle.

Once back in our car, Alan phoned Rob and told him of the conversation Andrew overheard, and asked him to try to trace the man who ordered the limo. I had settled down enough by then to control my reaction to his defeats.

'And now?' I asked when he had finished the call.

'We find ourselves some lunch, and then we wait.'

'Alan, I'm so tired of restaurant meals! Do you suppose there's a Tesco's someplace?'

Alan looked at his phone again, poked it a few times, spoke into it, and said in satisfaction, 'There are several, in fact, and one's not far from here. Walking distance.'

'Not in this rain, it isn't! Drive there, and if there's no place to park, I'll go in while you drive around.'

'You will not.' He pulled out of the car park. 'You keep forgetting. Siamese twins, my love. Joined at the hip.'

I made an exasperated noise. He ignored me.

There was no parking place near the shop. We might almost

as well have stayed in the hospital car park. We were both drenched when we got to Tesco, and I was in a very bad temper.

'So unnecessary!' I muttered. 'I'll only be here a few minutes! What could happen to me in a crowded supermarket?'

Alan continued to ignore me and kept scanning the crowd. He looked like a Secret Service agent, and I almost told him so.

His phone rang, and I thought I could escape him for a moment and slip into the frozen food aisle, but he took a firm hold on my arm and led me to a quiet corner while he listened, now and then making a face. He ended the call and sighed. 'The man booked the limo through the concierge at the Royal George, claiming he was checking in as soon as he got back from his little jaunt. Booked it under the name of John Smith, as Andrew reported. The concierge didn't check; the guy was fast-talking and plausible. There certainly are people named John Smith in this world.'

'Yes, but how did he pay? His credit card has to have a real name on it. Even if it's stolen, that would tell us something.'

'He paid,' said Alan heavily, 'in cash.'

I had planned a salad lunch, but the awful weather and the discouraging news demanded comfort food. I picked up my favourite brand of frozen lasagne and a large bottle of red wine, along with some plastic plates and heavy-duty plastic cutlery. I'm not a big fan of plastic, but paper plates are not sturdy enough for lasagne. I soothed my conscience with the thought that I'd wash them and take them home for many reuses. Alan picked out a huge bunch of grapes on the theory that a healthy dessert offsets a thoroughly wicked entrée. At least I had our trusty reusable bag, another sop to conscience, and we splashed back to our car. No one tried to ambush us. No one followed us. There was not the slightest indication that anyone was trying to do me in. I pointed that out to Alan. He grunted.

We nuked our lunch in the common room and ate it in our bedroom, clad in bathrobes after dumping our sodden clothes in the bathtub to deal with later. The food wasn't quite warm enough, but I was not about to get dressed again and go down to use the microwave. And the wine was lovely.

I didn't even take the wet clothes down to the dryer before succumbing to a nap.

TWENTY

When I woke, Alan had dealt with the clothes. Everything was washed, dried, and neatly hung up or folded. Really, I don't know what I ever did to deserve this man. 'Feeling better?' he asked, handing me a cup of coffee.

'Thank you, love. Yes, I'm warm and dry and rested. But still frustrated. We've been working away at this forever, it seems like, and we still don't know anything.'

'We do, though. The most important thing we know is that someone is willing to kill to keep us from knowing any more.'

'That's an inference,' I objected. 'The attack on Andrew could have been for some other reason.'

'Granted. But Andrew thinks it has to do with the thefts, and Andrew is a very bright young man. Don't forget he's planning to join the police and has been taking classes to that end. One of them had to do with accurate observation and logical deduction. You do that sort of thing by instinct, but he's trained to it.'

'Yes, and that's all very well, and maybe he observed some other things that would be useful. But he might as well be in Siberia, for all he can tell us or Rob.'

'Actually,' Alan dead-panned, 'I believe Siberia has excellent mobile service.'

I refused to respond to that. 'So we have to just wait? You know I'm not good at that.'

'No. There are a number of people we haven't yet talked to. You know as well as I do that most police work is boring routine. Talk to everyone who might have any information about the case. Most of the time those conversations yield

exactly nothing, but you never know. And the first person I
want to talk to is Sammy's grandmother. You have her name
and address. Why don't we go over there now?'

I fished in my purse and got out my notebook. It was a bit
damp, and some of the writing had blurred, but it was all
decipherable. 'Judith Campbell.' I recited her address and Alan
typed it into his phone. 'I wish we could call her first, but I
don't have a phone number.'

'Ah.' He poked the phone a few times. 'Rob, Alan Nesbitt
here. Can you have your people find me a phone number for
Judith Campbell at this address?' A pause while he poked the
phone some more. 'Right. Thank you very much.' Pause. 'No,
but we're ploughing ahead. We'll stay in touch.'

'I never cease to be amazed at modern technology. They
found that number in seconds!'

'I hate to tell you. He looked it up in the phone directory.'

'Oh, good grief! Then it must be a landline.'

'Yes. A good many people still have them, especially older
people. How old would you say Sammy is?'

'Hard to tell. Somewhere between twenty and thirty, I
suppose.'

'Then his grandmother could easily be seventy or older.
Not, perhaps, comfortable with a mobile. And if she seldom
goes anywhere . . .'

'Yes, I see your point. We're already making assumptions
about her, aren't we? I thought the police weren't supposed
to do that.'

'You're right, woman! Call her, and then let's go and see
for ourselves.'

'As soon as I've thought what to say.'

It took me a moment. I could hardly say that I suspected
Sammy of involvement in a crime and wanted to know more
about him. It wouldn't be quite true, anyway. Not quite.

Well, it would either work, or it wouldn't. Maybe we should
just knock on her door. But no. She was of a generation that
valued the small courtesies. I picked up my phone.

'Hello, Mrs Campbell?'

Her answer was tentative, the sort everyone makes to an
unknown caller who's probably a telemarketer.

'Oh, good. My name is Dorothy Martin. I'm visiting here in Bath and have met your grandson Sammy. He's a dear, isn't he?' The voice was slightly warmer, but still not conceding anything. 'Well, the reason I called is that I'd like to talk to you about Sammy, if it isn't inconvenient. You see, I'm a retired teacher and have worked with several children like Sammy, so I have some understanding of their problems. And the last time I saw him, he seemed troubled about something.'

That thawed her completely. 'Oh, yes, he is, and I don't know what. I'm concerned about him.'

'So am I. Do you think my husband and I could come and see you and talk it over? If it's not a terrible imposition. Yes, now, if you like. I'm sure we can find it.'

I clicked off. 'So far, so good. Lead on, MacDuff.'

Mrs Campbell lived in a tidy little flat in a Victorian house not too far from the centre of town. It would, I could see, be easy for Sammy to bike from here to his various jobs.

She met us at the door. Alan and I exchanged a quick glance. She was not what I had envisioned, and I could see Alan was surprised, too. Surely not yet seventy, she was slim, with short brown hair only touched with grey. She wore a nicely tailored pair of black wool pants and a bulky grey sweater, along with small, tasteful gold earrings. This was not the confused, possibly needy old lady we had imagined.

We got out of our dripping rain gear, and Mrs Campbell ushered us into the small, tastefully furnished front room and invited us to sit. 'I always have a glass of sherry about this time,' she said. 'I hope you'll join me.'

It was good sherry. Expensive, I was sure. More stereotypes were shattering by the minute.

She let us take our first appreciative sips before setting her own glass down with a decisive little click on the small piecrust table next to her chair. Both were period pieces. I don't have a good enough eye to tell if they were antiques or reproductions, but either way, they looked valuable. 'Now,' she said, 'you wanted to talk about Sammy. I take it, Mrs Martin, that you are aware of his disability.'

'Yes, I think so. As I said, I knew several Down syndrome children when I was teaching. That was years ago, and in the

States where I used to live, as you can probably tell by my accent.'

'It's faint, but yes, I assumed you were American.'

'Not any more. I was born in Indiana, but I've lived in Sherebury for several years now, ever since Alan and I were married, and I carry a British passport. However, conditions like Sammy's know no borders. He is in many ways quite typical, in his appearance and in his attitudes. He's so pleasant and friendly. And that's why I was surprised when, yesterday, I saw him at the Jane Austen Centre, and upset him terribly. He acted frightened of me, and I couldn't imagine why. Can you help at all?'

She looked us over thoughtfully before she replied. 'I can tell you very little. He came home very shortly after the incident you describe. The shop called to say he was very distressed and they thought he'd be better here.'

'He rode his bike? In the rain?'

'He doesn't mind the rain, and he's a good and careful biker. That didn't worry me. But his state when he got home did. He wouldn't say what was wrong, or couldn't. He just kept shaking his head and putting his finger to his lips, telling me he couldn't talk about it. So I gave him his favourite meal, spaghetti bolognese, and let him watch his favourite programs, and by bedtime he'd forgotten all about whatever it was.'

I smiled. 'Sounds like you know exactly how to deal with Sammy.'

'I should, given the practice I've had.'

'Has Sammy always lived with you?' asked Alan, who had been silent until then.

'Since he was a baby.'

Something about the look on her face told me there was a tragic story behind those few words. I had no right to ask, but somehow I had the feeling she might want to talk about it. Sometimes unburdening to strangers can be therapeutic. 'His parents . . .?'

'His parents abandoned him as soon as it was certain than he was "abnormal", as they put it. The pre-natal tests had indicated a strong likelihood that the baby would have Down syndrome, but my daughter-in-law is one of those people who believe only what they want to believe. She insisted the child would be perfect.'

She picked up her glass and took a sip. 'At first, of course, he looked like any other baby, except that he couldn't seem to hold his head up. Like most first parents, my son and his wife watched for all the usual developmental signs, and they didn't happen when predicted. The mother insisted that everything was fine, but Jeremy, my son, began to be more and more uneasy. They quarrelled. Jeremy wanted testing. Sharon refused. When he finally got his way and Sammy's condition was confirmed, Jeremy lost it completely: told Sharon it was all her fault, she should have had an abortion, he wasn't going to stick around to be father to an idiot – his term – and she could do as she liked.'

Her sherry glass was empty. Alan, nearest to the decanter, picked it up and raised his eyebrows. Mrs Campbell nodded, thanked him, and resumed her narrative.

'My son. I had always thought him a decent person. He left his wife and child without a qualm. We took Sammy in. My husband was alive then, and adored the baby. As I did. As I do. Sharon came to pieces. I won't go into all the sordid details, but in the end Sammy became our charge, legally. Jeremy contributed monetary support until Sammy came of age and then dropped it. There was never any emotional support, which was what the poor child needed most. And, of course, he will never come of age in any meaningful sense. His mental age, the psychologists tell me, is about ten.'

'But he functions very well in his jobs. And I believe he can read and write?'

'Yes, simple things. He went to school, you know, and stuck with it, even though the other children made life hell for him. He was so determined to do well. Of course . . .'

I didn't know what to say. It was such a sad story, but Mrs Campbell didn't seem to invite sympathy. Alan, as usual, found the perfect response.

'It must have been hard for you, Mrs Campbell, but you seem to have done a splendid job with Sammy. He's honest and hard-working, and Dorothy tells me everyone who knows him loves him.'

'He is quite likable. He has a raft of friends, and he's loyal. Would do anything for them. And he has a sunny disposition, always happy. But lately, I've had the feeling he's troubled about something. Oh, not just his fear of you yesterday in the shop, Mrs Martin. He was over that before he went to bed. But there's something else, something he can't or won't talk about.'

'Yes.' I nodded. 'I was talking about him to a woman who lives here in Bath and volunteers at the abbey gift shop. She knows Sammy quite well and said that she's had the feeling he was hiding something, some secret. She didn't think he seemed unhappy, though. More excited about whatever it is.'

'I've seen that, too, but it's changed the last day or two. And the more I probe, the less he will say. So I'm sorry I can't help, but really I have no idea.'

'And you know him better than anyone, so if he won't open up to you, he wouldn't to anyone.'

'That might not follow. I'm a parent figure to him, you see. When he was much younger, if he had got himself into some mischief, he might tell my husband about it, but not me. Douglas was always indulgent with him. So even now, if he's up to something, he might act wary around me, more than with other people.'

'So you think he might be "up to something"?'

She sighed and shrugged. 'It's possible. But I'd swear it's nothing really serious. Sammy's a good boy who knows what's right and does it. I'm proud of him.'

She didn't say it defiantly or apologetically, but as a simple statement of fact. She was proud of her grandson, proud of how he'd overcome his disability and become a productive, honourable member of society.

I started to reply, but she looked at her watch and stood. 'I don't mean to be abrupt, but Sammy should be on his way home, and I'd rather he didn't find you here. He's a creature of routine; guests upset him.'

I nodded. 'And you need to see to his tea. Thank you so much for talking to us. May we call you if anything else comes up?'

'Of course. Let me give you my mobile number.'

Alan entered it on his phone. She shook hands briskly with both of us, and all but pushed us out the door.

TWENTY-ONE

'Did we learn anything useful?' I asked Alan once we were back at our B&B. 'A lot about Sammy's background, and how sad it is! But is that any help to our investigation?'

'You never know what's going to help. But we now know, also, that several people have noticed Sammy's altered attitude. That is, I think, significant, and means that we, too, are justified in concluding that he's up to something.'

'But not alone, wouldn't you say?'

'Oh, certainly not alone. He was excited, remember? Excited about meeting a new friend. But something has changed lately. The excitement has changed to apprehension. I wonder why.'

I thought about that while I heated the water for tea. 'Hmm. Do Sammy and his grandmother go to church, do you suppose?'

'Good question. My guess would be not. She is very much not of the old school who went to church twice on Sundays no matter what. Nowadays so few people do attend, except for baptisms and so on.'

'Hatch, match, dispatch. Yes, sadly. But on the other hand she's careful about Sammy's moral attitudes. I'd like to know for sure. Do you think it's too soon to call her again?'

'You've got some idea buzzing around in there, don't you?'

'Hardly an idea. A half-baked notion. I think I'll call.'

Mrs Campbell evidently recognized my number. She was less than cordial when she answered.

'Mrs Campbell, Dorothy Martin again. I'm sorry to bother you again so soon, but I've thought of something I completely forgot to ask. Could you tell me where Sammy was christened, and when?'

'Yes, at the abbey, when he was six months old. We have always attended there. Why?'

'Just a detail I wanted to fit in. Thank you. I hope I haven't disturbed you.' And I clicked off.

I related this to Alan. 'Now what I want to know is whether they attended last Sunday. I didn't see Sammy, but it's a big place and there was quite a crowd. And do you remember anything about the sermon? I'm afraid I wasn't quite there most of the time.'

'A pity. It was a good sermon. The Gospel set out the two great commandments, and the sermon was about what it means to love our neighbour. He brought in bits of Psalm One, as well, setting out clearly that the righteous would be saved and the wicked would perish.'

I nodded. 'I thought it would be something like that. And it was that afternoon that Sammy caused that accident at the Baths shop, and was so dreadfully upset about it. And then the next time he saw me, he was almost hysterical.' I poured the tea. 'My theory is that Sammy *was* at church that morning, that he heard that sermon, and it awakened some doubts he was beginning to have about what he was doing.'

'And what he had been doing was . . .?'

'Stealing for his new friend.'

Alan frowned. 'Do you think he would do a thing like that? Honest, church-going, hard-working. He seems to possess all the virtues.'

'Including loyalty to his friends, remember?' I sipped my tea, the better to focus my thoughts. 'He makes a new friend and likes him very much. Or her, whichever. The friend asks him to bring some things home from the shops so friend can look them over and decide which he wants to buy as gifts. Friend doesn't like to shop, you see.'

'Very thin,' said Alan. 'More tea?'

'Thin to us, because we have more-or-less critical minds. Sammy doesn't. He's a trusting soul, and his thought processes aren't sophisticated enough to spot lies. Besides, friend has promised him something in return.'

'What? Money?'

'I don't know. Perhaps money, but more likely treats of some sort. Candy, maybe? The Down children I knew back in Indiana all had terrific cravings for sweet stuff. Or maybe it's a trip to the zoo, or some other outing Sammy would enjoy. Anyway, whatever it is, Sammy is delighted with it and with the friend.

'And then something happens. Maybe it was that sermon on Sunday, or something else, but Sammy begins to think maybe he's doing something wrong. He's not at all sure, and he doesn't want to lose the friendship, or the rewards, either. He becomes more and more unhappy, and people notice.'

'And then?'

'That's the question, isn't it? Alan, if other people have noticed the change in Sammy's behaviour, surely the friend has noticed, too. And that poses a danger. The boy has been told he mustn't talk about it, but what if his worries get the better of him? He might talk to almost anyone he trusts, like his grandmother. And then the jig is up. If I were a crook using Sammy as a cat's paw, I'd be very worried that he'd give the show away.'

Alan was silent. I looked at him and his face looked weary. And worried. 'So,' he said at last. 'Our villain has two options. He can close down his operation, take his profits, and scarper. Or—'

'Or, if he's not quite ready to do that, he can make sure Sammy doesn't talk. And there's really only one way to do that.'

Alan picked up his phone, but before he could make a call, it rang in his hand.

He listened, saying only 'yes' and 'no' and 'right away'. He clicked off, biting his lip.

'Bad news, darling. Sammy fell into the big pool at the Baths. They got him out, but they're not sure they can save him. I told Rob we'd meet him there.'

I had my raincoat on and we were out the door before he even finished speaking.

Alan drove very close to the Baths and parked in a spot which was quite clearly forbidden. A constable was at his door before he even shut off the engine. Alan waved his warrant card. 'We're here at Inspector Roberts' request. Would you like my keys, in case you must move the car for an emergency vehicle?'

'Oh. No, sir, it's just that . . . no, sir. It will be fine here.'

Rob came striding toward us, looking grim. 'Sammy's been taken to hospital. The prognosis isn't good.'

'The water surely isn't deep enough to drown in, is it?'

Alan didn't let Rob answer. 'Dorothy, you know better than that. It's about a metre and a half deep, but a person can drown in a bathtub. People have done. And even setting that aside, this water is so polluted that one could die just from ingesting it, am I right, Rob?'

'Unfortunately, yes. Sammy can't swim, and apparently he floundered about for some time, screaming and choking.'

'"Apparently"?'

'There were no witnesses that we can deem reliable. Most of the visitors were part of a large school group, aged ten and eleven. As you would expect, Alan, their accounts vary wildly. The two adults with them aren't much more help. Their attention, naturally, was on their own charges. They heard a splash, but the kids rushed to the edge of the water and blocked the adults' view.'

'And I suppose no one saw, or will admit to seeing, how Sammy happened to fall in.' Alan was sounding more and more grim.

'No.'

That was all, but it spoke volumes. 'What I'd like to know, Rob, is what Sammy was even doing here at this time of day. He wasn't working in the shop. We went to see his grandmother earlier this afternoon, and she was expecting him home from another job about half an hour ago.'

'We'd like to know that, too. We have the same information from Mrs Campbell. We phoned her, of course, the moment we found out about it, and she was already worried about him, because he hadn't come home. Apparently he was very good about that sort of thing.'

Yes, I thought, he would be. He would have a routine and stick to it, and be upset if anything didn't go according to plan.

'He was meeting someone,' I said with certainty. 'Probably the one who is at the back of all the thefts.'

Rob looked around. 'Not here. Come to my car.'

I would rather have repaired to the nearby pub, but I took his point. We needed to have assured privacy if we were to discuss theories and possibilities.

'All right,' he said when we were settled. 'You talked with the grandmother. Did you come up with anything?'

'We learned a lot about his background. Nobody wanted him, poor kid. His father opted out when Sammy's disability became evident, very early in his infancy. The mother had a nervous breakdown or something, so she was also out of the picture. That's when the grandparents took over, and Sammy finally got some love. Both Mr and Mrs Campbell cared deeply for him. Oh, Rob, it's going to kill her if Sammy doesn't . . .'

I couldn't say any more through the lump in my throat, so Alan took over.

'Mrs Campbell, like everyone we've talked to who knows Sammy, has noticed the change in his behaviour. From being utterly happy and content with his life, she saw him becoming secretive, even sly. That's an inference; she didn't use that word. She did say, quite specifically, that if her grandson was up to something – her phrase – he wouldn't tell her, because she's an authority figure.'

'Stern? Strict?'

'No,' Alan and I said together. 'Just the normal instinct of a child, as Sammy still is in many ways, to hide from a parent anything that might be a trifle dodgy.'

'So you and Gran think there *is* something dodgy?'

'And so do you,' I said flatly. 'You think he was pushed into that pool to keep him from spilling the beans.'

'And exactly what beans are we talking about?' Rob asked cautiously.

I related the plot Alan and I had deduced: Sammy as innocent tool of someone who had befriended him in order to use him as a thief. 'And now that he's been acting upset, his so-called friend is going to think he's likely to tell somebody about his woes. And that means it's time for friend to take off, or take action. And I'm very much afraid . . .' I lost it again.

'All right. I wanted to make sure we were on the same wavelength. I am operating on exactly the same assumptions. It's very likely that Sammy was pushed into the pool. With a large school group in the room, it would have been easy to do that unobserved. The staff keep a close eye on children, who are apt to ignore the rules and try to touch the water with hands or toes, or even to jump in. Adult visitors are not always so closely observed.

'Our villain almost certainly planned it that way. Wait for a large school group to appear. The Great Bath is usually the last stop for such a group. That would have given him or her plenty of time to call Sammy and arrange a meeting.'

'Does Sammy have a mobile?' I asked.

'Don't know. Probably. Almost everyone does. But even if not, our villain probably knows his work schedule and could call whatever shop he was working in today.'

There didn't seem to be much else to say. Rob would of course check on the phone situation. Mrs Campbell would know. Meanwhile . . . 'Can we visit Sammy?'

'He's unconscious, and in any case, no one will be able to see him until he gets out of the trauma unit. His grandmother is with him there.'

'Can we call and find out how he's doing?'

Rob shook his head. 'They won't tell you anything at this stage. You've dealt with hospitals; you know how they are. I was able to ferret out a few meagre bits of information about Andrew Williams because he's one of our lot, or nearly.'

'You've assigned someone to keep watch,' Alan said. It wasn't quite a question.

'Yes, as we believe he's in danger. Our resources are growing thin, though. I've had to remove Andrew's guard.'

This was depressing news. 'Perhaps, Dorothy, we should visit him. He might welcome the company, and might remember more about his incident.'

'I'm going to the station now. The hospital's on the way. Would you like me to drive you?'

'No, as I'm parked quite illegally, I'd best move my car before someone tows it away. Perhaps we'll see you there.'

'Shall we go straight to the hospital?' Alan asked when

he had driven away from his illegal parking spot, to the relief of the constable on duty. 'Or would you rather stop for a meal?'

'I don't think I could manage food at this point. And it's getting late. I don't want to miss hospital visiting hours.'

We got there with a half-hour to spare before they closed the doors to visitors.

TWENTY-TWO

Andrew was sitting in his recliner, in pyjamas and bathrobe rather than a hospital gown, and looked much more like himself.

'That was fast!' I said when he'd greeted us. 'This morning you looked like death warmed over.'

'Always complimentary, my wife,' Alan said with a grimace. 'Are you feeling as much better as you look?'

'I am, sir. There's no real reason for me to be here. The pain in the arm is manageable without opiates, and the rest works out to only cuts and bruises. I've had worse in a rugby scrum.'

'Are they planning to let you go home soon, then?' I realized I had no idea where Andrew lived, or what his domestic arrangements were. Married? Family? Or was he still living with his Jamaican parents?

'I think they're trying to work out the details of that. I live alone, you see, and they seem to think I might need some help managing with only one arm.'

That word *alone* set alarm bells ringing for me, and I could see, for Alan, too. He frowned.

'Andrew, you certainly ought not to be alone for the next few days. Have you a friend you could bunk in with?'

'I have very few close friends. It's kind of you to be concerned, Mr Nesbitt, but I'll be able to cope . . . Oh.' He stopped at the look on Alan's face. 'You're not thinking of my coordination, are you?'

'Not principally, no. I am thinking that your ability to defend yourself is severely compromised without a usable right hand.'

'And you believe I will have need to defend myself.'

'Oh, c'mon, Andrew! Stop being so cautious. You know perfectly well that the collision yesterday was an attempt to kill you. Rather an inept attempt, true, but it might have succeeded if you had been a less skilled driver. And you know Inspector Roberts ordered a guard for you because he was worried another attempt might be made, here in the hospital.'

'The guard has been called off.'

'Yes, because he was needed elsewhere.' I raised my eyebrows at Alan; he nodded. 'Andrew, do you know Sammy? I don't know his last name. Campbell, I assume.'

'Everyone knows Sammy. Everyone loves Sammy.'

'Someone doesn't. An attempt was made this afternoon to kill him, and' – I swallowed hard – 'and it may well succeed.'

'He— What happened?' Andrew's face had gone that pasty grey again.

'He fell or was pushed into the Great Bath. He can't swim. He's in the trauma unit here, under guard.'

'And he can't tell how it happened?'

'He's unconscious.'

'Witnesses?' Andrew was already thinking like a policeman.

'None that are of any use. Schoolchildren.'

'So,' I pursued, 'we've had two attempts at murder, all, we believe, connected with the peculiar series of thefts. At home, alone, you'd be a sitting duck and you know it. If we lived here, we'd be glad to put you up, but we don't.'

Alan looked at his watch. 'They're going to turf us out of here in another ten minutes. I'll speak to the staff about your housing problem on the way out, but meanwhile I want you to tell us anything you remember about your collision yesterday. First, was there a passenger in the Rolls?'

'No. I'd made my last run for the day and was headed back to the hotel.'

'And that run was?'

'A regular one. One of the hotel guests stays every other month for at least three weeks at a time. He works for a multinational and spends all day at their corporate headquarters out Batheaston way. Nice chap, but he doesn't like to drive, so I drive him there every morning and pick him up every evening.'

'Always at the same time, or do his hours vary?'

'He's one of the managers, so he calls the shots and leaves on the dot of six, every day.'

'And always comes back to the hotel, or do you sometimes take him to a restaurant or elsewhere?'

'Always the hotel. So yes, anyone observant could know exactly where I'd be in the early evening when he's in town. In case he wanted to stage an "accident".'

'Yes, that was one point. And the other, quickly, is this: do you recall anything at all about the driver of the car that hit you?'

He grinned wryly. 'Very little. I'm afraid I'm not at my best when I'm about to be smashed to a jelly. I saw the car coming like a bat out of hell. I couldn't hope to get out of its way, so I did the only thing I could: sped up, hard, and turned farther to the right to try to save myself and perhaps the bonnet. All I remember of the driver is his hands, clutching the steering wheel, and something white, a hat, I suppose. And then everything disappeared until I woke up here.'

'And here is where you're going back to sleep, young man.' The nurse had appeared at Alan's shoulder, looking at her watch and tapping her foot.

'One more moment, sister.' Alan diplomatically elevated her probable rank. 'Andrew, you said "his hands". Was there something distinctively male about the hands?'

Andrew thought about that. 'No, I don't think so. Only the attitude, the hands clenched in fury. And even that may be something I'm editing in.'

'All right, don't worry about it. Get some rest, and we'll hope you're out of here soon.'

'But where are they going to put him?' I asked anxiously as we walked toward the nurses' station. 'He absolutely must not go home alone.'

'No. It's a pity he can't stay with a friend.'

'I don't understand why such a pleasant, intelligent man doesn't have close friends.'

'I suspect he hasn't had time to get to know many people. Remember he's working most of the time, and studying the rest. And he's a somewhat reserved man. At any rate, we can't deal with it right now, love. We have to try to find the man a temporary home.'

The nurses directed him to one of the hospital offices, where an unprepossessing young man was slumped in front of a computer screen, scanning a list of names and addresses. 'Yes?' he said in an unwelcoming voice.

'I believe you're trying to find a place for Andrew Williams to stay when he is discharged,' said Alan.

'Among other things.'

'I have a suggestion,' I said, surprising Alan and even myself. 'I thought of it just now.' I looked at the nametag pinned crookedly to his shirt pocket. 'Everett, there is another patient in this hospital, a man named Sammy Campbell. Well, Samuel, I suppose. He's still in ICU, I think – the trauma unit, I mean. He lives with his grandmother. He's probably going to be in the hospital for quite some time. How would it be if I ask Mrs Campbell if Andrew could stay with her until Sammy comes home?' If he ever does, I added mentally. Please, God!

He shrugged. 'Doesn't hurt to ask.'

'They won't let me in down there, though. It's past visiting hours, and anyway, they never let anyone but family visit in the trauma unit. Do you suppose you could call and set it up for me?' You callous slug, you. I didn't say that either.

He was so bored with his job, and so resentful at being asked to do something, that he very nearly refused outright, but Alan said, 'Please do that. Now.' Something about his commanding tone of voice got through the lethargy. The man picked up the phone, made a call, mumbled something, and was about to hang up when Alan said, 'Let me talk to them, please.'

He took the phone from the limp hand. 'This is Chief Constable Alan Nesbitt. To whom am I speaking?'

Oh, my. When he went all official like that, and used his old title, I knew he was going to get what he wanted.

When he hung up, he thanked the young man, and then said, 'I'm going to give you a piece of advice. It's a mistake to carry on in a job you hate. Muster some enthusiasm for what you're doing, or find work elsewhere. The patients and staff of this hospital deserve better.'

As we went down to the ground floor, I said, 'I've never heard you sound so tart.'

'One has a responsibility not to tolerate poor service. When a person is being paid to work, it's reasonable to expect work from him. That chap has never actually worked in his life, I'll wager. Here we are.'

The waiting room for the trauma unit was like such waiting rooms anywhere: full of fear and weariness. Mrs Campbell was sitting in a corner, looking twenty years older than when we had left her earlier.

She looked up as we approached, but gave us no look of recognition.

I took a deep breath. 'Mrs Campbell, we visited you this afternoon, asking about Sammy.'

'Oh. Yes.'

'How . . . how is he?' I was almost afraid to ask.

'Not good. He's still unconscious. They're keeping him in a coma to give him a better chance.' She took a deep breath. 'I'm sorry. I do remember now who you are. You care about Sammy.'

'Deeply, Mrs Campbell. So can you tell me: did he inhale a good deal of water?'

'He did. They say he would have drowned if he had not been pulled out so quickly. He panicked, you see. He can't swim.'

'Yes, the police officer at the scene told us that.'

'Did they tell you he still might . . . might not recover? The water itself is terribly dangerous, and he swallowed a lot of it. They won't know for a day or two how it might affect him. They're giving him antibiotics, of course, but even if he doesn't develop something serious, he may be in hospital for quite some time.' She forced her voice to stop trembling. 'The house is going to seem empty without him.'

'Mrs Campbell, you'll think me terribly presumptuous, but I have an idea about that. There is another young man in this hospital right now. He was in a car smash yesterday, but he's not badly hurt except for a broken right arm. He's ready to go home. However, he lives alone, and the hospital fears he will not be able to cope well with only one hand. He knows and loves Sammy, as does almost everyone in Bath. So I'm wondering . . .' I swallowed and continued. 'Is there any chance you could let Andrew stay with you until Sammy is well enough to come home? He'd be company for you. He's an awfully nice person, polite and kind.'

She looked from one of us to the other. 'There's more to the story, isn't there?'

Alan nodded. 'There is. We, that is the police, believe that Andrew's accident was no such thing, that it was a deliberate attempt to injure or kill him. And you may know that we also believe Sammy was pushed into the pool. You might be risking some danger by taking Andrew into your home.'

'So the killer may try again. Is that the real reason you don't want him living alone?'

'Yes, it's the main reason. Though the other is true as well. Unless you've ever tried to cope with everyday living with only one hand, you may not realize how maddening it is.'

'I see.'

She was silent, considering the matter. Despite the unsettling nature of what Alan has just told her, I thought she looked better, more interested and alive, than when we'd first come into the room.

'I realize you might not want to take the risk, Mrs Campbell,' I began, but she waved that aside impatiently.

'Oh, for heaven's sake, call me Judith. I loved my husband, but I'm no more a Campbell than you're an Englishwoman. I was born right here in Bath. And in answer to your request, I'll gladly open my home to your Andrew. He's still here in the hospital, you said? Then I'll go up and meet him and give him a proper invitation. He'd be in the orthopaedic ward?'

'No, in a private room. I'll go up with you, Judith.'

And smooth the way, I thought, neatly diverting any officious nurses barring the way. 'I'll wait in the car,' I said. This interview was going to go smoothly without any help from me.

'You'll wait right here. Siamese twins, remember? I won't be long.'

Before I sat down again I stopped at the admitting desk. 'I know I can't go in to see him, but can you tell me how Sammy's doing? I'm not family, just a friend of his.'

She smiled gently. 'We don't know very much yet. He's holding his own. You can check back tomorrow.'

And with that I had to be content.

Alan came back smiling, as I was reasonably sure he would. 'Mission accomplished,' he said as we climbed into the car. 'They got on like a house afire. I stopped at the nurses' station with Judith, so she could provide the details. I was not going to subject her to that lump of indifference downstairs.'

'Good. So that's one problem solved, at least for the moment. I think he'll be good for her. But oh, Alan! What if Sammy . . .?'

'Sammy's in good hands. He's still alive. He might not have been. What do you want to do now?'

'I want to have a meal and a drink and my bed. In that order, and quickly. This has been quite a day.'

'Another one in our nice restful holiday. What sort of food?'

'Plentiful.'

TWENTY-THREE

I didn't remember any of my dreams when I woke in the morning, but I knew they hadn't been happy ones. The room was so dark when I opened my eyes that I thought I'd wakened too early, but the clock said it was after eight thirty. Almost twelve hours of sleep. And I would still have turned over and burrowed into my pillow except for a nagging sense of responsibility.

'Awake, Rip?'

'More or less.'

'Then you'd better get a move on if you want breakfast.'

I groaned. One of the worst things about staying in a hotel, or B&B or any place but home, is the breakfast schedule. At home if I want to sleep until ten I can, and the price is no more than guilt and a headache.

Good coffee put a little brighter shine on the day. Over eggs and toast I finally worked up the nerve to ask, 'How's Sammy?'

'"Doing as well as can be expected",' Alan quoted.

'Which can mean anything from much improved to barely clinging to life.'

'I think Judith would have called if there'd been any major change. We got quite chatty yesterday. I told her a little about the situation, and our suspicions, and she inferred a good deal more.'

'I'm not surprised. She's one sharp cookie. Any word from anybody else? Oh, and is Andrew settled yet?'

'I imagine. Hospitals get an early start on the day, and they were eager to get him out of there and free up a bed.'

'So what do we do now?'

He glanced around at the room, still reasonably full of breakfasters who, like us, chose to sleep late on this damp, drizzly November of the soul. 'Let's go back upstairs and decide.'

I took a cup of coffee with me, the stuff we could make in the room being decidedly inferior. Sitting by the minute table, I said, 'Okay, sounds like you have some ideas you didn't want to share with the world. Shoot.'

He ran a hand down the back of his head. 'Nothing terribly original. We've had two suspects, or near-suspects, for the thefts. One of them is now incapacitated for some time, and is under surveillance. The other, Simon Caine or whatever his name is, has not been seen for a while. I'm going to call Rob to see if they've made any progress with him.'

A moment after he'd made the connection, he put his phone on speaker. 'Rob, Dorothy is going to want to hear this, since it's her triumph. Go ahead.'

'Triumph? What—' But Alan shushed me.

'Yes, Dorothy,' said Rob's voice, 'this is very much your doing. You remember the mirror you gave me? The one with our anonymous friend's fingerprints on it?'

'Oh! You don't mean to say they're actually useful!'

'Very useful indeed. First of all, they do match some of the prints on the stolen hoard. Not all.'

'The others, I'm assuming, are Sammy's.' Alan's voice was sad.

'We've never had any occasion to have Sammy printed.' Rob's tone of voice put an end to that avenue of discussion. 'However, the match with "Simon" gave us the basis for asking for a search. We just got back the results; I would have called you if you hadn't called me.'

'All right, don't make me beg,' said Alan drily.

'The prints match those of a petty crook from London. He has used several names. No one is quite sure which is the original, so for now the Met has settled on, if you can believe it, John Smith!'

It was nice to have something to laugh about for a change.

'I don't suppose you've had any luck finding him,' said Alan.

'Not yet. I must say the Met found him very slippery. He was suspected in several smash-and-grabs and that sort of thing, and ratted on more than once. His colleagues in crime apparently didn't care for him much. But he was actually arrested and charged only twice, and convicted only once. He is a master of the quiet disappearance when the climate grows a little too hot.'

'Will you put out an APB, or whatever you call it in this country?'

'An alert, yes. Unfortunately, since we have no firm evidence to connect him with anything more than petty theft, the various forces won't take much notice. We've too much serious crime on our plates to worry about a minnow like Smith.'

'And what about attempted murder? Is that also petty?'

'Dorothy.' Alan was not happy with me. 'Remember the words "firm evidence"? There is no evidence whatever to link Smith with either the attack on Andrew or Sammy's fall. We have assumed a number of connections, but theories and assumptions carry no weight in police investigations.'

'Okay, okay, I know all that, and I'm sorry, Rob, for being snarky. I'm just frustrated. We have all these loose ends and no way to tie them together.'

'We're all frustrated, Dorothy. And there are two domestic
violence cases in my inbox right now, and a stolen identity,
along with one tourist assaulted in a park and a little boy's
bike stolen. So you see . . .'

'Yes, I see. Again I apologize. Is there anything we can do
to help matters along?'

Rob's laugh sounded weary. 'Stay out of trouble. If Andrew's
instincts are right, that may be a full-time job for you. Let us
deal with crime, even if we are a bit slow about it.'

'Don't worry about Dorothy and me,' Alan added. 'We can
look after ourselves. Keep us posted, and try not to work too
hard. And say hello to Sylvie for us.'

'Well.' I sat on the bed debating about whether to climb
back in. 'Alan, I hate to say it, but maybe we should just go
home and forget about the whole thing.'

'We could certainly go home. How well do you think you'd
get on with the forgetting?'

I sat silent.

'My love, if you really want to go home, we can do that.
I admit Bath is dreary and dismal just now, and a nice fire
and some animals to curl up with sounds very appealing. It's
just that I've never known you to abandon a project, and I
wonder if you wouldn't have regrets.'

'If there were anything productive we could do, of course
I'd want to see it through, but the only things to be done are
things the police can do better than we can. I have no idea
how to find someone who doesn't want to be found.'

'There are ways. There are always ways. But for now, since
Rob wants us to stay out of his hair, why don't we find out
if Sammy can be visited?'

I made a doubtful face. 'I don't know, Alan. What if he's
still afraid of me? Breaking down in tears wouldn't do him
any good at all.'

'Hmm. Good point. And the only way to know would
be to present yourself to him. Risky. All right, how about
going to see Judith?'

'If she's home. She might be at the hospital.'

I was in the sort of negative mood that finds objections to
everything.

'That's easy to find out, isn't it?' He consulted his phone and poked it a couple of times. 'Ah, Judith, good morning. Alan Nesbitt here. Do you have a moment, or are you at the hospital?' Pause. 'Oh, good. Dorothy and I have been wondering how Sammy is getting on.' Pause. 'That's good news. Would they let us visit, do you think?' Pause. 'Right. In about an hour, then? Good.' He ended the call.

'Right, you heard. There's good news about Sammy. So far, at least, he doesn't seem to be developing any serious infection from the water. I was told earlier that the doctors know what pathogens are in the water, so they can administer the specific antibiotics to deal with them.'

'Well, then, fingers crossed, but so far, so good. And how is he generally?'

'Judith wants to talk to us about that. She invited us over for coffee.'

'Oh, good! Then we'll get to see Andrew, too.'

We passed the hour in making lists and reviewing the information we already had. We made no progress at all. I was glad to abandon the unprofitable exercise and leave for Judith's house.

It was Andrew who let us in. Apart from the cast on his arm, which was hanging in a sling, he looked reasonably normal.

'Andrew, you are the most amazing man! Two days ago you were in a crash that might have killed you. Now here you are, walking around as if nothing had happened.'

'I try to keep fit. That helped, I think.'

'Pain?' asked Alan.

Andrew shrugged. 'Some.' He gestured us to chairs in the sitting room and left the room, presumably to help Judith with coffee.

'That man is headed for a great career,' I murmured to Alan. 'Head of Scotland Yard in twenty years, want to bet?'

'No bet. I agree. If that's what he wants. Ah, Judith!'

She had come in with a tray of cups and saucers and a plate of scones, Andrew following with a coffee pot. 'I'm afraid I'd best not pour out for you,' he said, laughing a little. 'The coffee would end up in your lap. My left arm still refuses to do as it's told.'

He went back to the kitchen for a bowl of sugar, and then again with cream. 'I cannot carry a tray yet,' he explained.

We sat with our coffee and treats and waited for Judith to begin. She looked awful, grey and weary and old.

'I'm concerned about Sammy,' she said without preliminaries. 'You all know him. Perhaps you can help me work out what's wrong.' She took a sip of her coffee. 'He's conscious now, but he doesn't want to talk to me. He's out of the trauma unit and in a room. I insisted on a room. He's too easily distracted by an unfamiliar environment, and the bustle of a ward would be too much for him. But every time I come into the room he turns away and makes little whimpering noises. He's never acted like that before, not with me. Do you, any of you, have any ideas about what might be wrong?'

'He has had a severe shock,' said Andrew, with the patient air of having said the same thing several times before. 'To the body and the mind. It takes time to recover from such things, and his mind will be slower to recover than some.'

'Yes, you keep saying that, and it's true. But I have watched when a nurse or doctor approaches him, and he says very little to them, but he doesn't cringe as he does with me.'

It was plainly hard for her to talk about this. She was deeply hurt that Sammy, whom she loved so devotedly, was quite literally turning away from her.

Alan looked thoughtfully at her. 'I'm looking at this like a parent, not a policeman. I remember when one of my children was young and had done something wrong, something for which he knew he should be punished, he would turn away from me in tears when I went to talk to him about it. He wasn't afraid of me – we had an excellent relationship and still have – but just apprehensive about what was to come, even though it was never very terrible.

'Now Sammy is in many ways still a young child. He could be afraid to tell you what happened at the Baths, lest you think it was his fault.'

'Or, of course, he could be worrying about whatever was bothering him before all this happened, the thing he was afraid of telling you.' I looked at Alan.

He cleared his throat and said, 'Judith, Dorothy and I think we may know what that is, Sammy's secret.' He told the story about the stolen objects found in our car and our attempts, along with Rob and the police, to identify the thief. 'We believe that there were two people involved, one who instigated the thefts and one who actually performed them. We have identified one of them, a man we knew as Simon Caine, which is not his real name. His fingerprints were found on some of the stolen objects. He has apparently left Bath and has not yet been found, though the police are actively looking for him.

'We think that he, Caine, was the instigator, and I'm sorry, Judith, but we believe that he persuaded Sammy to actually steal the things.'

'Of course,' I added, 'as Alan would be the first to point out, there is no actual evidence pointing to Sammy. It's all a question of inference. He works at almost all the places the stolen objects came from. He would have had the opportunity to take them. In a way, he had the best opportunity, because everyone likes and trusts him. And he in turn is a trusting soul. It would have been easy for an unscrupulous person to make use of him, in return for . . . what? Treats of some sort?'

Judith sat silent for a full minute, which can seem a very long time. A tear slipped down her cheek. She made no move to brush it away. At last she sighed heavily. 'Yes, that would explain his behaviour. His "secret", that so delighted him at first and then began to trouble him.' She thought about it for another minute or two, while we waited. 'What do we do now?'

'That's not easy to decide,' said Alan. 'It would be impossible to question Sammy in his present condition, and I'm not sure questioning would be productive at any time. The person we need to question is Caine, and at the moment he can't be found.'

'You won't . . . the police won't—'

'No,' said Alan firmly. 'No one will make any attempt to charge Sammy, or take any legal action against him. The term is "diminished responsibility". If Sammy was lured into illegal actions, it is the person who persuaded him who must answer for it.'

Judith looked a little less grey. 'What shall I tell him when I see him next?'

'Anything you think might reassure him,' I suggested. 'Would it help to say that you have learned his secret and it's all right? That you love him and everything will be all right?'

She sighed. 'It's worth a try. It's hard, sometimes, to know what he's thinking and feeling. Even after all these years.'

Alan smiled. 'It was often hard for me to know what my children were thinking and feeling, and they had no developmental difficulties. It's part of being a parent.' He stood. 'Thank you for the excellent coffee, and you make admirable scones. We'll leave you now to get on with your day. And good luck with Sammy.'

Andrew stood too, a little awkwardly. 'Drat. Even getting out of a plushy chair needs two arms. Judith, don't worry about the tea things. I can put them away, if slowly.' Judith ignored him, of course, and took the tray to the kitchen.

He walked with us to the door and said quietly, 'Are there any leads yet to our villain, whatever his name is?'

'Not that I've heard. I'm going to call Rob in a bit.'

'Judith is more upset about this than she shows.'

'Yes, we know,' I said. 'She's a strong woman and doesn't like to show weakness. Look after her, Andrew.'

TWENTY-FOUR

A nd soothing words were all very well, I thought as we drove off, but as my grandmother might have said, fine words butter no parsnips. What we needed was action.

A beautiful sunny day would have helped. I tried hard to overcome my black mood, but if coffee and scones and friends hadn't helped, I thought I was stuck.

Alan surprised me. Back in our room, the room I was beginning to detest because it represented inactivity and frustration, he said down on the bed and said, 'Still got a clean page in your notebook?'

I pulled it out of my purse and handed it over. 'Lots of them. We haven't had enough ideas to use up much paper.'

'Well, I have one now. I'll call Rob for an okay, but I propose to cast a lure.'

I just looked at him.

'We're going to draw in our fish, my dear. With a big and gaudy lure. And you're going to help me write it.'

I got it, suddenly. 'Oh! An ad?'

'No. A small news item, if Rob will allow it. I propose to concoct a fiction that will draw Caine like a magnet.'

'Something about a new source of goodies, maybe?'

'Something like that.' He wrote busily for a few minutes and then handed the notebook to me. 'How's this?'

I read:

> Police in Bath today declined to investigate the matter of a cache of objects, possibly stolen from local shops, found in the cellar of a house in [insert street here]. It was apparent that the owner of the house, which is let out as flats, had no knowledge of the matter, nor did any of her tenants admit to knowing anything about it. 'In any case,' said [insert police name here], 'the objects are of little or no intrinsic value. They might just possibly be of interest to a collector of ephemera, but there is no case here for the police.' He suggested that the owner of the house might make an attempt to return the objects to the shops where they belonged, although, he said, 'They're very dusty and appear to have been in the cellar for quite some time. Truth be told, the shops may not want them returned.' The homeowner said that she would consider the matter, but would probably simply consign them to the rubbish bin.

I put the notebook down. 'Very good indeed! I assume Rob will supply a likely address and the name of some innocent policeman.'

'Yes, and vet the whole idea. But do you think it will work?'

'Where do you plan to trail your bait?'

'Regional newspapers and TV. The national dailies wouldn't take it, and in any case, it would get lost amidst all the other news. The techy people will be able to put this up on Facebook and a few other local news sites – and I'm sure our villain will see the news piece somehow. It's amazing how news travels via social media these days . . . My biggest hope, though, is television news. It's odd enough to get a bit of play.'

'Hmmm. And you know somebody at ITV, don't you?'

'I do. Saved his bacon once. A very long time ago, but he hasn't forgotten. He'll do what he can. You never answered my question, though. Will it work? Will it catch our wily fish?'

'I think you might need to be a little more specific about the objects. Make up something, or a couple of somethings, that might appeal.'

'The trouble is, since we haven't been able to find a common denominator, we don't know what might appeal.'

'No, but we have some ideas. Everything that was stolen, everything in our cache anyway, had to do with local history in some way. So let's see.' I doodled on the notebook while I thought. 'Let's say the Roman Baths put out a glossy booklet about the most recent renovations in . . . when was it?'

'The mid-nineties, I believe.'

'Okay, good. That's long enough back that the booklet might well be dusty and dogeared. So that's one. And then there was the half-finished novel by Jane Austen that turned up in – say – 2002. That would have generated newspaper articles by the dozen. So one of those could turn up, too.'

'Dorothy, there has been no such discovery.'

'I know that, and you know that, but does our crook know that? How many people would know, one way or the other, unless they're fanatic readers of Austen and/or live in Bath? And oh, we could hint that it's just slightly salacious. That would make the TV people happy!' I scribbled for a moment and handed the notebook back to Alan. 'Add this to the cop's quote, and see what you think.

I had written: 'They include such things as a booklet describing discoveries at the Roman Baths of twenty years ago and more, an old newspaper clipping about the rather racy fragment purporting to be by Jane Austen, and other objects of similar vintage.'

'Hmm. Makes it rather long, but more interesting, I agree.

I'll turn it over to Rob for his approval, and meanwhile I'll call the chap at ITV.'

Rob approved the scheme. The 'news' item, with a little editing, was sent to the newspapers that were most read locally, a few websites, and a couple of the national tabloids, the latter on the theory that a racy Jane Austen might appeal to them. Alan's friend at ITV agreed to air it on one morning and one evening newscast, as a feature item, and asked for a picture or two. 'We are talking about television, mate.'

'Hmm. That's a bit difficult, since the objects are all fictitious. Could your people take a picture of Jane Austen and give her a semblance of a leer?'

'Have to check with legal, but doable, I think. Later, Alan!'

After that things moved rapidly. Alan and Rob decided to use radio, as well, and sent several stations the notice. To none of them except ITV did they explain that the item was untrue. 'It's protection for them,' Alan explained. 'In case there are complaints, the media can honestly claim that they had no idea they were publishing fictitious information.'

Rob set up surveillance in the street he had named, a short one with only a few houses. 'If he comes at all, he'll come openly,' Rob predicted when we met for a conference, 'with an offer to take the things off her hands for a few pounds. A pro would send someone out in advance to scope out which was the house, but this chap is a rank amateur. He won't be surprised when the first landlady he approaches claims not to know what he's talking about.'

'And the first house will be the last, because your man will stop him,' I said with satisfaction. 'He does know what Simon looks like?'

'He has Alan's description,' said Rob without cracking a smile, 'for what that's worth.'

'You know perfectly well it's accurate!' I protested. 'Alan's a policeman . . . oh.'

Rob couldn't keep his face straight.

'Darn it, I still haven't learned to recognize when an Englishman is joking! Okay, so everything's in place. Have the householders been told?'

'No, because we want their reactions to be perfectly genuine.

Some people can play a part; some can't. We can't take a chance.'

So we went out in the rain to pick up some sandwiches for lunch, and then we waited. I am not a patient person; waiting is not my best thing. I tried to read the book I'd brought with me. When Alan saw me sit for ten minutes without turning a page, he escorted me down to the common room, where there was a small library of books guests had left behind. There were a couple of Agatha Christies I'd read before (I've read them all), but always enjoyed. Not this time.

'All right,' said Alan finally. 'We'll go mad just sitting here, and there's nothing worthwhile on the tube. We need something to keep us occupied. Let's go out and find some sort of game we can play together. Do you play chess?'

'Badly. And I don't find board games very interesting. And it's pouring. Again. Still.'

'Come. We'll find something. But we'll have to walk, I fear. No hope of finding a place for the car anywhere near the shops.'

'No. I refuse. The time of my life when I enjoyed walking in the rain is *long* past. You can go and find us something if you want. I'm going to stay here and pout!'

Alan thought about that. I knew he was considering his 'whither thou goest' order. I let him chew on it. It was his rule.

'Very well. But mind you *do* stay here. Don't go out. Keep the door locked and don't open it to anyone. I'm taking my key, and I'll be back as soon as I can.'

I didn't even reply to that.

It would have been a perfect afternoon to nap, but I was too keyed up; my eyelids wouldn't stay closed. I went to my laptop and played a couple of games of FreeCell, losing both of them. I found a jigsaw puzzle site. None of the pictures appealed to me. Crosswords? Did two; both were so simple they irritated me. I was very close to throwing the poor innocent computer across the room when my phone rang. I seized it like a drowning woman reaching for a life buoy. 'Rob? Any news?'

'Yes, and I'm sorry to say it isn't good. Your husband has

been in an accident. If you'll come down, Mrs Martin, I'll meet you at the door in a few minutes and take you to the hospital.'

He rang off. I ran to the wardrobe and was struggling into my raincoat when something set off a tiny siren in my brain. Wait a minute. Since when did Rob call me Mrs Martin? And was that really his voice? I had assumed . . . but . . .

I looked at the number that had called. I looked up Rob's number. They were not the same. With fingers that shook a little I punched in a call to Rob.

'Hi, Dorothy.'

'Rob, did you call me just now?'

'No. Why?'

I dropped down on the bed. 'Someone did, telling me Alan had been in an accident. He – the caller – told me to come downstairs, and he'd take me to the hospital.'

'Alan is out?'

'Yes. He went to find us something to occupy ourselves while we wait.'

'Don't move. I'll be there in five minutes.'

TWENTY-FIVE

I was scared, a residual fear about what had so nearly happened. Our villain had set a trap for me, and how very close I'd come to getting caught in it! But I'd learned a few things from all those detective stories I'd read through the years, and from a nasty experience in Canada not so long ago.

And mixed with the fear, and beginning to overcome it, was jubilation. We were going to win! The trap would be sprung, but by Rob and his buddies. They would be waiting for the crook, and we'd finally have him!

It was a long five minutes, but at last I heard a car approach. Our window looked out on the back garden, so I couldn't see the car unless I went partway down the stairs and peered out the front door. That was probably not a good idea, though.

If I could see him he could see me, and could see that I wasn't doing as he expected. He'd already know that, though. He'd expected me to be waiting at the door, trembling with fear, frantic to see Alan and learn the worst. Should I go and show myself, acting the part, or was that too taxing a role for me?

I dithered just a moment too long. Another car was coming, one whose sound I would have known in any crowded street. Alan! Alan just a few minutes too soon! I heard the other car drive away, with a roar and a clash of gears.

I ran down the stairs, straight into Alan's arms.

'It's all right, love, you're safe, hush, now. What's this all about?' He disentangled one arm to pick up the carrier bag he'd dropped when I tackled him.

I was halfway between laughing and crying. 'Oh, we might have caught him, only you scared him away, but I'm so glad to see you!'

'I'd have been happier to see you ten minutes from now,' said Rob, who had walked in unnoticed.

Both men were dripping on the hall floor, and rain was blowing in through the open door. My housewifely instincts came to the fore. I closed the door. 'Look, take off your coats and let's go upstairs. Better leave your shoes down here, too.'

They still squished as they walked up the stairs, leaving damp spots on the carpet. Once we got to the room, I insisted on providing dry socks for Rob as well as Alan.

'All right, woman, stop fussing and tell me why you went into hysterics just now.'

'That was not hysterics. I am never hysterical,' I said, very much on my dignity. 'I was so furious with you for coming home too soon, and so relieved and happy that you were back, that everything got mixed.'

'Perhaps I'd better explain,' said Rob.

We arranged ourselves on the various places to sit, and Rob explained, clearly, succinctly. 'My men and I,' he concluded, 'were stationed where we could see, but not be seen, ready to move the moment the car appeared. Unfortunately you moved in first, parked just behind, and blew the operation.'

Alan put his head in his hands, but then looked up. 'Why

did no one tell me? If either of you had called, I'd have stayed away.'

'Would you?' asked Rob. 'With Dorothy in possible danger?'

He gave me a long look and then shook his head. 'No. I know, love, that I can count on you to behave with courage and good sense in a crisis, but no, I would have had to be here.' He was sitting next to me on the bed; he reached over and took my hand.

I smiled. 'My knight in shining armour. Even though I didn't actually need rescuing from the bad guy.'

'Rob, did you get his licence number? Or get a glimpse of him.'

'The licence, yes. But it's a hired car, so that may be no help at all. As for a glimpse, yes, only a brief one before the car was out of sight.'

'And? Was it Caine?'

'It was no one any of us recognized from that one quick glance. But one thing was certain. The driver was a woman.'

'So we're back to square one,' I said when we had recovered from that blow. 'Not Simon Caine. And we don't have one single other suspect. We're done.' I took a tiny sip of the bourbon Alan had poured for me; the rest were having Scotch. 'Unless we have some luck with our lure.'

'I'm losing hope,' said Alan. 'Maybe our crook is illiterate, or doesn't watch the telly or listen to the radio or surf the Net.'

'Or maybe she's been too busy trying to abduct me,' I said bitterly. 'If only that had worked!'

'"Of all sad words of tongue or pen . . ."' Alan began a favourite quotation.

'"The saddest are these: It might have been." And the most unproductive. I'm sorry I brought it up. But the thing is, now she's been scared off, do you really think she might bite on our news item?'

'She wasn't scared off by the police, remember,' Rob pointed out. 'I'll stake my job that she didn't know we were there. She may not even know who it was who showed up. And even if she did recognize Alan, it would just have put paid to that particular attempt. The lure could still pull her in.' But he didn't sound hopeful, and I agreed.

'One thing at least we now know for certain,' said Alan, putting down his half-full glass with finality, 'is that the threat against Dorothy is real. I trust, madam, that you will now observe all due precautions?'

'I intend to stick to you like glue, dear heart.' *I've never been so scared in my life, never wanted you more,* I wanted to say, but Rob was there. I've picked up a little British reserve in my years here. 'Rob, what do you suggest we do now?'

He looked at his watch. 'It's close to dinner time, and you've missed your tea. I'm going to strongly suggest that you eat here in your room. I know Sylvie would be happy to fetch some take-away for you. I don't mean to order you about, but I'd much rather you didn't go out this evening. It's been dark all day, and soon it will be "a dark and stormy night". A night of the sort that crooks love. I would offer, but I must get back to the office.'

'I take your point, but we can't put your wife to all that trouble,' said Alan. 'I can easily—'

'No!' Rob and I said, in chorus. The only difference was that I fear I sounded panicky; Rob only authoritative. 'That is really not a good idea, Alan,' he continued. 'Nor is ordering in a pizza or something of that sort. Oh, I saw what you were thinking! At home in Sherebury you might well know your delivery boy. Here you have no idea who might be knocking on your door.'

'But aren't you worried about Sylvie being out alone?' I asked timidly.

'Sylvie is not on someone's hit list, to put it in your American phrase.' He took his phone out of his pocket. 'Indian, Chinese, or Italian?'

Alan gave in. 'Whichever might be done best. We like them all. And thank you.' He pulled some money out of his wallet.

Rob waved it away. 'It's your treat next time. You can take us to the Royal Crescent Hotel.'

He talked to Sylvie, told us the code sequence she would use when knocking on the door, and then hurried off.

Alan lifted my glass with a raised eyebrow. I shook my

head. There was no liquid cure for my combination of frustration and anxiety. He shrugged, opened his laden carrier bag, and without consulting me opened the jigsaw puzzle box, dumped the 750 pieces out on the little table, and began methodically turning them right side up.

We didn't talk as we worked at our boring task. What was there to say? We were forced into inactivity, which suited neither of us. I tried and failed to find some good music on the radio, so we sat in silence except for the tiny sounds of bits of cardboard hitting the table and an occasional 'Oh, here's an edge piece.'

My phone rang, startling both of us. 'Dorothy, it's Sylvie. Just so you know for sure it's me, I'm Rob's wife, and his real name is Cedric, poor man. I'm leaving for your digs and should be there in about ten minutes. Rob said to tell you to watch for me and then wait for my knock. See you soon.'

'Wait! Sylvie, can you come in and join us? We're going mad by ourselves.'

There was a chuckle at the other end. 'Rob said you'd ask. I bought ample food, and I'd love to join you. Ta-ta.'

I spread a towel over the puzzle, what little of it we'd assembled, although I honestly didn't care much about it. Something to do while we waited, that was all.

Sylvie arrived without incident, thanks be. After my own experience, I'd been less certain than Rob that she'd be safe.

'I brought Indian and Italian. The really good Chinese place has closed, sadly.'

'Oh, dear. I fear we'll go hungry, then.' I tried to say it with an English-style straight face, and Sylvie reacted with an equally straight face. 'Good. If you can't eat any of this lot, the more for Alan and me.'

That broke the tension, and so did the lovely wine she'd brought. 'I know lager is the thing for Indian,' she said, 'but I forgot about it until I was almost here, so we'll have to make do.' She'd bought some plastic wine glasses, and the first thing we did was drink a toast: 'To the success of our mission.'

Well, I had very little confidence in its success after the afternoon's fiasco, but there was no point in saying so.

We heaped our plates and dug in, washing down lamb korma

and shrimp alfredo with red wine, and thumbing our noses at convention. The phone didn't ring. We didn't talk about the lure which, apparently, had failed. Sylvie had brought a lovely gâteau for dessert. It was layered with a caramel mousse and poached pears and looked sinfully delicious. Unfortunately, we were all too full to do more than look at it.

'Never mind, I'll leave it for you. That is, do you have a fridge?'

'A shared one, in the common room. We can have some for a lovely unhealthy breakfast. You take half, though, and you and Rob can enjoy it when he gets home. I'm sure he'll be tired and hungry.'

She was just packaging up the other food (of which we'd eaten less than half) and trying to persuade us to keep it, when Alan's phone rang.

'Any news, Rob?' he asked. 'Have— yes, but— yes. Right.'

He punched off. 'Sylvie, we might try some of that gâteau after all. Rob is very anxious that you not go home just now.'

'Why, for heaven's sake?'

'I don't know. He was most insistent, and sounded . . . no, frantic isn't quite the word, but certainly agitated.'

'He's all right?' Her placid demeanour was gone; the protective wife was all to the fore.

'I got no impression,' said Alan carefully, 'that he was in any danger himself.'

I looked from one to the other. 'Coffee, I think. Laced with a bit of whatever you fancy. Sylvie, why don't you cut that lovely cake while I heat water? Just the barest sliver for me, please. And then you can help us put that puzzle together. We haven't made much progress, I'm afraid.'

Sylvie had been a policeman's wife for a long time. She didn't waste her mental energy fretting, or asking pointless questions to which none of us knew the answers. She sat on the bed, on a couple of pillows to get her to the right height for the table, which we shoved over to her. With every appearance of enjoyment, she set to work on the puzzle.

It was one of those trying ones with both water and sky, so a blue bit could belong almost anywhere. There were trees, too, which were reflected in the water, alongside the grass; the greens were even worse. The central image was a castle, great expanses of grey stone and black shadows. It was a challenging puzzle, requiring concentration. I had none to spare for the task. The coffee didn't help. I'd made the fully leaded variety, thinking that none of us would get much sleep that night anyway and it would help clear our brains. It didn't clear mine.

I wasn't a policeman's wife in my early adulthood. I was the wife of a college professor in Indiana. The only time he was ever late to dinner was when some annoying meeting ran late, and he always called me. He was a good driver and had no health problems, so I never worried about him. That horrible day when he suddenly had a heart attack no one had predicted was the first time I ever had reason to be afraid on his account. That was bad enough, but it wasn't the day in, day out knowledge Sylvie had to cope with, the knowledge that any morning when she kissed Rob heading out the door might be the last time she would ever see him.

And she could sit there calmly placing a piece of blue into a nicely forming sky, while I fretted about what Rob was doing and why he was so worried for Sylvie. There's no doubt about it. It's a good thing I married Alan when his police career was nearly over and he was as far up the administrative ladder as one could go, no longer actively dealing with crooks. I'd have been a nervous wreck if I'd known him in his days as a working cop.

'Helen must have been a remarkable woman,' I said. No one had spoken for several minutes, and Sylvie looked up in surprise. Alan knew exactly what was on my mind. He always does.

'She was that. And so are you, love. You just haven't had the practice. Is that brown bit you're clutching this missing piece of drawbridge, by any chance?'

I could have used a nice cuddly cat at that point, but a nice calm husband is a reasonably good substitute. I started organizing the green pieces into light and dark, sharply focussed and wavery.

When Alan's phone rang I jumped, sending quite a few

pieces to the floor. All he said before he pocketed the phone was, 'Right. I'll be down.' He stood. 'Rob is downstairs. We'll be right back.'

Sylvie stayed where she was, and only her gaze, fixed on the door, told me how severely she was holding herself in.

Rob looked ready to drop. I stood up, and drop he did, on the bed, with a long sigh. Alan handed him a glass of amber fluid, which he downed like a man dying of thirst. 'Right,' said Alan. 'Have you eaten anything?'

When he shook his head, I moved into action. We hadn't gotten around to refrigerating the eclectic leftovers. I picked up the bag and headed downstairs to the microwave. 'And don't you dare,' I said as I left the room, 'even think about telling the story until I'm back.'

It doesn't take long to heat a plate full of food that's already at room temperature. I'd given Rob a little of everything, hoping he wasn't a food purist. It was a strange sort of meal, but a lot better than he'd have gotten at the headquarters canteen.

I held up the bottle of wine, nearly empty now, but Rob pointed to his whisky and shook his head.

We let him eat and drink and recover while we pretended to occupy ourselves with the puzzle, but the moment he put down his fork, I said, 'Okay. Now.'

He wasn't quite too tired to grin, though it was rather a weak effort. 'Yes. In the abridged form, we had him and we lost him.'

'Who? Or do I mean whom?'

'Our old friend Caine, or Smith, or whatever name you like. He went up to the door, rang the bell, and started to ask about the box of lollies, when something tipped him off. We were watching, of course, with a telescope, but it was dark and raining hard, and he was carrying an umbrella, so we couldn't see well. But we were using a directional mike; we could hear him quite clearly. He couldn't have seen us, so God knows how he knew we were there, but he suddenly went flying down the steps and was at his car and gone before we could stop him.'

We heaved a collective sigh of frustration, but Sylvie said, after a moment, 'I don't understand, darling, why you were alarmed about me.'

'The man was screaming threats as he drove away. Our mike picked them up. I won't repeat them, but they suggested that we'd best watch out for ourselves and those we cared about. The man has demonstrated that he doesn't stick at attacking anyone who gets in his way, including women. We didn't know where he had gone, and I wanted you out of harm's way, that's all.'

She and I exchanged a glance, eyebrows raised. This, at least, was familiar ground for me as well. The chivalrous English male. Oh, well, it was sweet, if a bit stifling at times.

'But I thought,' I said, bringing the conversation back to the issue at hand, 'you said the person who high-tailed it out of here earlier was a woman. I'm confused.'

'So are we,' said Rob, polishing off his whisky.

'And anyway, how can you be sure it was Caine, if you couldn't see him?'

'One of our men knows him, or at least has met him. We watched him climbing the stairs up to the door of the house. I'm sure you know that the way a person moves can be very distinctive, and a back view is almost always revealing. He's sure. In any case, we had a good view of his car as he drove away. And of the licence plate.'

'You had time to run it?'

'It's quick now, Alan, quicker than even a year or two ago. There was no trouble. It came up almost at once with the many-named Mr Caine.'

Alan shook his head. 'Dorothy and I have said all along that he was an amateur at crime. A crook who knew what he was doing would never have used his own car.'

'Well, he did,' I said with satisfaction, 'and with all that – licence number, fingerprints, and all – surely they won't have too much trouble finding him.'

'You'd think so, wouldn't you? But he's managed to slip through a lot of fingers up to now. The Met people I know say he's a chameleon, can assume a new appearance and even a new personality in minutes when necessary.'

'He can't change his fingerprints!' I retorted.

'No, love. But they have to catch him before they can print him.'

I was discouraged again. 'So what do we do now?' It seemed I'd been saying that a lot lately, and every new idea we came up with fizzled out.

'We go home to bed and leave you two to do the same. Who knows? By morning they may have caught him. The word is out, you may be sure of that. And even if not, we'll be a lot brighter when we've had some sleep.' Rob yawned so widely I feared he might crack his jaw. 'Sorry. I couldn't help . . .' Another yawn.

'Sylvie, take him home. We'll talk in the morning.'

TWENTY-SIX

I slept like I'd been hit on the head, and woke to lots of light.

'Good grief, did I sleep till noon?' I said, sitting up.

'No, love, only half-seven. That bright light is because the sun decided to show itself. Remember the sun?'

'Vaguely. I'm sure I must have seen it before.' I yawned. 'Maybe it's a good omen. Maybe something nice will happen today. What day is it?'

'Friday, the thirtieth October.' He held up a newspaper. 'I'd rather lost track myself, but here's proof.'

I yawned again. 'Anything interesting in the paper? Besides the correct date?'

'Nothing much. The planet is on the brink of destruction.'

'Oh, that. For how many decades now?' I stretched and pried myself out of bed. 'What do you say we go out for breakfast? The coffee here is very good, but I've got a hankering for a Starbucks latte. With whipped cream. And something like a cheese Danish.'

'And to hell with healthy, eh? I'm on. I've showered; it's all yours.'

We set out on foot. Neither of us could quite remember

where we'd seen a Starbucks, but there was bound to be one not far away. 'And it's the kind of morning I feel I could walk for miles.'

'Amazing what a change fair weather makes.' Alan was stepping along briskly himself.

'I can believe in anything in this kind of weather, even that we'll solve our problem. I don't suppose you've heard from Rob?'

'You'll be the first to know, my love.'

When we'd devoured our delicious empty calories – without a single pang of conscience – I saw that we were quite near the abbey. 'Let's go in, just for a moment,' I suggested.

'Yes, it certainly is the sort of day for a little thanksgiving, isn't it?'

Alan almost always knows what I'm thinking.

The abbey was crowded with tourists on this beautiful day, perhaps the last one before November descended. It was peaceful, all the same. Sound in these great Gothic temples tends to go upward, and though there are reverberations every- where, somehow the essential stillness is not disturbed. We said our prayers and then wandered idly, appreciating details we hadn't noticed before.

For once I didn't want to visit the gift shop. With Sammy in trouble, it didn't feel right. We were exploring some of the lovely carvings in the choir when Alan's phone rang.

'Blast! I forgot to mute it! Sorry,' he added, presumably apologizing to the abbey. He silenced the ring and looked at the display. 'It's Rob. I'd better take it.'

We left by the nearest door, and Alan called back, listened for a moment, and then turned a smiling face to me. 'They've got him!'

'See! I knew something good would happen today. Tell me everything.'

'I don't know much, Rob said only that the Bristol police spotted his car and stopped him.' He shook his head. 'They always think they're safer in big cities. They forget that the police there are highly trained and can act fast.'

'The Met had a hard time finding him,' I pointed out.

'Yes, well, London is a special case. Far higher population

than Bristol, for one thing, and *far* more tourists. Caine would have done better to try to hide there, where he has boltholes. But Bristol is so much closer, and I suppose he thought he could then head north a few miles and slip into Wales. A mistake, again. He couldn't hide there; he's too obviously a Londoner.'

'Unless that's part of the act he knows how to put on.'

'Perhaps. The great thing is that they've got him in custody.'

'Where? Here or in Bristol?'

'I didn't ask. I'd imagine Bristol for now. Look, I'm getting hungry. That sweet binge we indulged in for breakfast was all very well, but it doesn't have much staying power. Let's find some lunch.'

'Nearby. I'm just about walked out.'

There was a pleasant-looking pub just across the square, or plaza, or whatever they called it, and we were settled with our beer, waiting for our ploughman's lunches, when Alan's phone buzzed. If the pub had been just a little noisier he'd have missed it.

'Drat! Now I forgot to un-mute it. I'm getting old, Dorothy.' He looked at the screen. 'Rob again.' He listened, spoke, punched off. 'He's going to join us here in a few minutes.'

'Good! I'm dying to hear all about it.'

Alan ordered another ploughman's for Rob, and they all arrived the same time he did.

Alan and I were both hungry, but Rob was ravenous. He devoured half his lunch before taking a deep breath and finally really looking at us.

'Sorry,' he said. 'No manners at all.'

'Rob, when did you last eat? Or sleep?'

'Can't remember. Or no, I had supper last night, with you. Then Sylvie and I left for home, but my people called before we got there. So I dropped her off and went back to work. And I was busy all night.' He took a hearty swig of his beer and another bite of bread and cheese. 'Reports kept coming in. Our crook had been spotted all over England and Wales. London, of course. Swansea, Cardiff, Lincoln, York, Durham. No sightings in Scotland, but it would have been just a matter of time. And every one of them had to be followed up, even those that seemed impossible. I was just about to call it a night – or morning – and leave the mess to the rest of the crew when the call came in from Bristol, the real thing this time. That woke me up. We drove over and found our boy sitting in jail, very unhappy.'

'What did he say? Did he admit anything?'

'He said exactly one word, when he was first arrested. He was read the usual caution and told that he had a right to free legal advice. He said, and I quote, "Yes." That was at about six this morning. From then until I left an hour or so ago, he has said nothing at all.'

'Has he been questioned?' I asked.

Both men shook their heads. 'Once he's asked for legal representation, we can ask nothing without a solicitor present,' Rob said. 'No one from the DSCC was immediately available, and no one had got there before I left.'

'DSCC: Defence Solicitor Call Centre,' Alan explained, and I nodded. 'He doesn't have his own solicitor, then?'

Rob shrugged. 'Don't know. He won't even acknowledge his name. Not surprising, that, since he has so many. We don't know his current address, his real name, or anything except what's in his record, and that's sparse enough.'

'His passport?' I suggested.

A wry laugh. 'Which one? He was carrying three, different names, different addresses, different birth dates. Same picture for all. That does tell us one thing; he has at least one good contact in the criminal fraternity. First-class forged passports can't be bought at Harrod's.'

'And I don't suppose they come cheap, do they?'

'No. This little lot would have cost him several thousand pounds.'

I whistled. 'Good grief, crime must be paying well these days.'

'Well, that's the thing, you see. If he'd sold every one of the trinkets he lost when they turned up in your boot, and sold them at the highest possible rate, it wouldn't pay for even one of those passports. So he must have some other source of income, legal or otherwise, that we don't know about.'

'But if he won't talk . . .'

'Exactly.'

I sighed. 'We'd all decided he was a pretty stupid and inept crook, but he's acting smart now.'

'In some ways. It was stupid to keep his car, when he knew we'd identified it. It was stupid to carry all those passports with him. One would have confused us about his real identity. Three just affirms our confidence that he's a criminal. The only smart thing he's actually done is to keep his mouth shut.'

'Smart for him. Frustrating for us!' Alan put his beer glass down with a thump. 'I assume the usual enquiries are going forward?'

'Oh, yes. Questioning everyone he is known to have known, searching every known residence – and there have been a lot of them. Talking to every known employer – very few of them! He's not the sort to enjoy working for a living.'

'Women?'

'The Met has tracked down a few. They are apparently not his chief interest in life. His lusts, so far as we know anything about them, are for filthy lucre and excitement. And not necessarily in that order. He seems to enjoy the thrill of the chase, the delight in outsmarting us bone-headed coppers, almost as much as the money his dubious activities bring in.' He put down his beer glass and shook his head at Alan's gesture. 'If I have any more, I'll fall asleep right here and someone will have to carry me out.'

He stood. 'I'm going home. If the abbey is carried off, stone by stone, while I'm asleep, leave me a note.'

We sat and watched him out the door, drooping with weariness. 'He surely isn't driving, is he?'

'No, he'll have a driver. I almost always did, as you'll recall. One of the perks of higher rank. Do you want me to find a cab to take us home?'

'Yes, when the time comes. Right now I want some coffee and something sweet. I don't care what.'

He came back with two coffees and a piece of apple-walnut cake. 'Nothing for you?' I said as I took the first luscious bite.

'I'll finish yours.'

'Don't you wish!'

He did, though. I'd had enough to eat, though that seldom

stops me in the middle of something delicious. But I suddenly had a vision of Sammy lying in a hospital bed, confused and afraid, and perhaps suffering in his muddled conscience over sins he wasn't responsible for. I saw his grandmother, torn with worry about her beloved boy, mind and body. I saw Andrew, trying to help her with only one arm, trying not to worry about his lost job and his ambitions put on hold.

I put down my fork. 'Alan, we have to know what happened. If he won't talk, and they don't have enough evidence to charge him, they'll have to let him go, won't they?'

'No. His fingerprints on the stolen goods are enough for a minor charge. But you're right. They can't keep him there forever. They don't want him convicted for petty larceny, but for attempted murder, among other things. For that they need real evidence.'

'And all our suppositions, all our scenarios, don't constitute evidence.'

'No.'

We were silent in the cab.

'Love,' said Alan, when we'd got back to our room, 'we've accomplished just about all we can here.'

'Little enough!' I said with some bitterness.

'We led Rob to Caine. I think I'm going to keep that name for him. It's apt.'

'Yes, and now they've got him, it isn't going to do a bit of good unless he talks. Which he's smart enough not to do.'

'Rob and his force are working hard to find real evidence. Even the Met is on the case; they don't like being made fools of by a small-time crook. This is the sort of thing the police are very, very good at: sifting details, comparing statements, searching backgrounds. Which leads me to my point. I'm not sure we can be of any more use to Rob. Shall we fold our tents and steal away?'

I sat down on the bed and looked away. 'I don't know, Alan. I suppose you're right. We've been away nearly two weeks. The kids are missing us, I know.'

'Hah! Don't forget two of them are feline. They'll never admit they need us.'

'I know. They do, though, and they love us in their own

cat-like way. As for Watson, he misses us when we go out for
dinner. Two weeks must be an eternity to him. But—'

'But you don't want to go.'

'I do and I don't. It would be lovely to see the beasts again,
ornery as they are. But . . . oh, you know. If we go home I'll
spend all my time worrying about Sammy and Andrew and
the whole mess, and wanting to call Rob every five minutes
to find out what's happening. Which wouldn't help a bit. I
know.'

'I agree. But I don't honestly see that there's anything
productive for us to do here.'

'Me, neither.' I ran my fingers through my hair. 'I keep
thinking there must be something. I have that irritating itch
that an idea is lurking somewhere but won't come to the
surface. I need to take a walk and think of something else,
but I've walked too much today.'

'Hmm. A nap?'

'I know I wouldn't sleep. I'm too keyed up.'

'A nice relaxing bath?'

I thought about that. 'You know, that might just work.
Especially if you could find some good music on the radio.'

He came up with something lovely and dreamy on
BBC Radio 6. I didn't recognize the composer. So much the
better. I would be mentally humming along or criticizing
the performance. I could just relax into it.

Most English bathtubs don't have a nice flat rim that you
can sit on or put a glass on. But there are plastic trays
you can put across the tub, one end resting on each rim, that
are handy for setting down anything you like. The soap, the
washcloth, the book you're reading, or a friendly glass of wine.
Alan brought me one, saying, 'Now don't relax so much you
fall asleep and drown in the tub. I'd hate to have to explain
my dead bride in the bath.'

'Good thing your name isn't Smith. Go away, love. I want
to empty my mind. I'll call when I need your help getting
out.' My two artificial knees make getting into a tub, especially
the long narrow English variety, difficult. Getting out by myself
is impossible.

The water was just the right temperature. The music was

at just the right volume. The wine was delightful. I had rolled up a towel to support my neck, so I could lie back, stretch out, and relax into what I think Buddhists call nirvana. I'm probably wrong about that, but mindless bliss is just as good a term. I let the music carry me.

After a while, thoughts came drifting back in. Peaceful thoughts. Happy thoughts. No responsibilities, no worries, just living life. Floating. Like Sammy, I thought. Sammy before all this awful stuff happened.

And there I was back in the problem, but so comfortable physically that it didn't upset me. Sammy needs to get his innocence back. Most of us can't, once we're past childhood, but Sammy is special.

Suddenly the thought became so insistent that I sat bolt upright, or tried to. The result was a lot of splashing that brought Alan into the room in an instant.

'All right, love?'

He wasn't able entirely to keep the panic out of his voice.

'It's all right, dear heart. Sorry I scared you. I just had an idea. I think it's the one that's been driving me crazy. Help me out, will you, and I'll dry off and tell you about it.'

He got almost as wet as I was in the rather exhausting process of extricating me from my wet, slippery prison.

'Whew! That's why I almost always take showers. Not as soothing, but a lot quicker and easier. Now. Make us some tea, will you, while I dress, and then we can talk.'

TWENTY-SEVEN

'My idea doesn't seem quite as brilliant now as it did when I was in that semi-coma, but it's an idea, anyway, something to go on with.' I took a sip of tea. Still too hot to drink. 'It occurred to me that the only person who knows the truth of this, besides Caine, is Sammy. And if we can figure out the right way to approach him, he might be able to tell us quite a lot.'

Alan looked dubious.

'Okay, I know Sammy's mind doesn't work quite the way ours does. But he's not an imbecile. He can read and write a little. He's held down several part-time jobs, to the entire satisfaction of his employers. His association with Caine has been important to him; I think he'll remember a lot about it.'

'Dorothy, given all you say – and I don't dispute it – his evidence would be useless in court. Any barrister worth his title would tear him to shreds.'

'I know that. And anyway, I wouldn't want him ever to have to appear in court. It would terrify him. No, what I'm hoping is that he might tell us something to lead us to other people who might tell us more. If he was meeting Caine at one of the shops, for example, other people would have seen them together. Even if they met somewhere else, there would have been people around. This is a tourist town. There are crowds of people everywhere.'

'A tourist or two wouldn't do us any good. They'd be long gone, gone even to other countries.' Alan was determined to find all the flaws he could.

I understood. He didn't want me to launch hopefully into a project that was doomed from the start. 'You're right. But the people who serve the tourists – the waiters and shop clerks and guides – they're still around. And before you say it, no, they wouldn't remember one person out of the hundreds they see every day. But Sammy is different. He stands out in a crowd. And even in a city as big as Bath, he's pretty well known, at least in the museum and abbey circles. I think someone might remember. If Sammy can give us a nudge, I think it's worth a try.'

Alan spread his hands in surrender. 'Very well. I concede. Provisionally. But the first job is to get Sammy to talk, and that seems to be the hardest job.'

'Yes. That's why our first visit will be to Judith. If anyone can approach Sammy, it's her. He loves and trusts her. He's been afraid to talk to her lately, because he has feared that she might be angry with him, but I think – I hope – she's defused that now. So let's call her and invite ourselves over for tea.'

Andrew answered. Judith was at the hospital visiting Sammy. Yes, he was doing well, and he was sure Judith would be delighted to see us. 'She'll be home soon. I'll get out the tea things and make some cinnamon toast for you. I can't manage baking yet, not with one hand, but cinnamon toast is a piece of cake. So to speak. See you in about an hour?'

We spent that hour working out what we wanted to know from Sammy. It was tricky. We didn't want to say anything that might upset Sammy, but the whole subject was potentially upsetting. Sammy, a gentle, honest soul, ready to love everybody, had, we thought, become embroiled in a scheme of thievery, had been set up as a patsy. And no matter how tactfully he was questioned, he would be reminded of what he had done and how shamefully he had been used.

'All right,' I finally said, closing my notebook. 'We need to know when and how they met, both the first time and later. We need to know exactly what Caine told him, and what he was asked to do.'

'And we must make sure it was in fact Caine. We have no proof yet of that,' said Alan, the policeman.

'Would Rob have a picture of him?'

'I don't know. A mugshot, perhaps.'

'If not, do you suppose he could take one? Just a simple one, with his phone. Is there any law against that, do you know?'

'I'm sure Caine's solicitor will know! We can ask. But aren't you getting a little ahead of yourself? A photo is no use unless we can talk to Sammy.'

'Right.' I glanced at the alarm clock. 'It's about time. Let's go. Oh, and let's stop at a bakery and get something to augment the cinnamon toast.'

There was a small bakery on the way where we picked up some Bath buns, which made us a little late for our tea. Judith was home and was busy making the tea, while a faint smell of burning from the kitchen suggested Andrew was having trouble with the cinnamon toast.

'How is Sammy?' I asked before even sitting down.

'He's doing very well. No sign of infection yet, and they may let him come home much sooner than they thought at first. Here, let me take your cardi.'

I was glad I'd brought my Irish fisherman's cardigan, just the right weight for a day like this. I handed it to her and went on: 'Is he still upset about falling into the Great Bath?'

'I think he's forgotten about it. I'm told that people with his condition do sometimes forget unpleasant events quickly.'

'Oh, what a blessing! I wish I could do that.'

'So do I.'

There was such a weight of unhappy memories behind her words, I couldn't think what to say.

Alan rescued me, as he often does. 'I must apologize for inviting ourselves, but we have a favour to ask of you, and it's rather urgent. We think Sammy can help us, or rather can help the police, with the investigation into the thefts, and probably the attacks on him and Andrew as well, but we need your advice about how to approach him.'

Judith nodded. 'I knew this was coming, of course. He could tell us a lot about this Simon Caine, if he would, but it won't be easy. He has shied away from talking about it. He doesn't lie. Sammy never lies. He just turns his head to the wall and won't say a word.'

'The thing is, Judith,' I said, 'that Caine isn't talking either. He has a good reason for his silence, of course. If the police can't get anything out of him, they won't have enough evidence to convict him of anything much. And there are rules about how long the police can keep someone in custody. Even when they charge him with petty theft – they have the evidence for that – it's a minor crime and a good lawyer will have him out of there in no time. And then he might well disappear into the blue again. So you see, we need Sammy's evidence as soon as possible.

'And I have an idea that might work with Sammy. Will they allow more than one person at a time in his room?'

'Yes, Andrew came with me once.'

'Well, then. Suppose I visit with you. Sammy might be afraid of me at first, if he remembers seeing me with Caine. I think that's what set him off the last time. But since that was unpleasant for him, he might have forgotten. And even if he hasn't, seeing me with you, whom he loves and trusts, might set him at ease.'

'Might do. No way to know, really, unless we try it. Did you plan to ask him questions? I warn you, he won't answer.'

'No, my plan was this. I go in with you. I chat with Sammy a little, if he doesn't panic at the sight of me. If he does, I'll get out of his sight, in the hallway or the bathroom. But I hope he doesn't. However he reacts, you and I then get into a conversation about what has happened. The basic theme will be how much everyone misses Sammy and hopes for his quick recovery, how much they need him in the shops, and so on. Laying it on pretty thick.

'And then, little by little, we can work our way around to having the bad guy in jail and how he won't talk about what happened, about how he trapped Sammy into bringing him things. I think we won't use the word steal or stealing or theft. Stay neutral. And how much we all wish we knew more about what actually happened.'

Judith considered. 'That might work. You'd have to guide me to say the right things.'

'I have another idea,' said Andrew. 'What if you tried a different approach? You could say that Caine was in jail and was blaming Sammy for everything. Judith has told me he gets really upset by bullying and injustice. You could say you knew it was all lies, but since you didn't know the truth . . .'

'That might be an excellent ploy,' said Alan. 'Unfortunately none of the information gained could be used as evidence in court.'

'Of course not,' I said impatiently. 'Hearsay.'

I was about to go on, but Alan interrupted me. 'Even if Sammy could be prevailed upon to repeat what he said as a formal statement, it would still be suspect, because it was initially stated under coercion.'

'Alan Nesbitt! We wouldn't be bribing him or threatening him or anything like that!'

'You would be threatening him, though. Think about it. Saying that Caine is telling lies about him, lies that might get him into trouble, is certainly a threat. Furthermore, it isn't true. And that could cause problems in court, too. I'm sorry, Andrew. It's a good idea, really, except that it won't advance our cause much.'

I must have looked as crestfallen as I felt, for Andrew spoke up. 'I realize that, sir. What I was thinking was that if Sammy could tell us where he'd been with Caine, and who might have seen them, we'd have a head start on collecting witnesses.'

'But will he know anyone's name? Oh, I agree that places to look will help a little, but it's still an uphill battle.' I was getting more discouraged by the moment.

Judith reached over and patted my hand. 'Maybe not as hard as you think. Sammy's visual memory is excellent, you see, and he's remarkably good at drawing faces. He might be able to draw us pictures of some of the people who were around when he met with Caine. He wouldn't know their names, probably, but surely pictures would help the police find them, and get *their* stories about what they saw and heard.'

We all sat there, stunned.

'You mustn't expect them to be photographic images,' Judith went on. 'They're quite abstract really, and they reflect Sammy's feelings about the subject. But they're always easily recognizable. Wait, I'll find you some. You'll see.'

'Pictures,' I said after a moment. 'Who would have thought? I didn't know people like Sammy could draw.'

'I did,' said Alan, 'and I should have made the connection. There's one young woman with the same condition who's had quite a successful exhibition at the Tate Modern.'

Judith came back holding two framed pictures, each about twelve by eighteen inches. 'All right,' she said, 'who's this?'

It was a work in crayon, soft pastel colours, a picture of a woman. Her face was pink, the colour of a baby girl's first blanket. Her eyes were a soft green, and her lips lavender. The crayons had been used lightly, just brushing the paper, with no hard edges anywhere. It was a child's drawing. And yet . . .

'I don't know her name,' I said without hesitation, 'but it's the woman who runs the abbey giftshop.'

Alan nodded. 'Sammy likes her, doesn't he? It's a sweet, loving portrait.'

'What about this one?'

The technique here was very different. Still crayon, but applied with such force that small bits of wax clung to the paper here and there. Strong dark colours and a lot of black lines formed a full-length picture of a man, instantly recognizable to us all.

I began to laugh. 'Oh, dear, Sammy doesn't like him much, does he?'

Judith smiled, too. 'Sammy was only a boy when Diana died, but he had flat fallen in love with her. He considers that Charles treated her very badly, and still holds the grudge. Now do you believe that his drawings might help you?'

'No question,' said Alan. 'Again, probably not admissible in court, but certainly a guide to where to go, whom to interview. Judith, when might be a good time to see him?'

We made arrangements to go as early in the morning as they'd let us in. Alan insisted on accompanying me to the hospital, but said he'd stay in the waiting room. I was getting a bit tired of the guard-dog set-up, and said so. 'Alan, Caine is in jail. He can't possible do me any harm now.'

'The car at the B&B door was driven by a woman. Until we find out who that was, and what her part is in all this, I'm sticking to you like a burr.'

His voice and expression brooked no argument. I know when I'm bested. I made a face, but shut up.

I was up early the next morning. The fine weather had departed; November was shaking its fist again, even though the calendar said it was still October. I didn't care. Today Judith and I were going to talk to Sammy, and maybe we'd finally figure out a few things about this miserable mess.

Alan and I hit the breakfast room the moment it opened. We were the only guests there on this uninviting morning. 'You're early birds today,' said Amy, our hostess, as she put out a plate of pastries and made sure the cereal cannisters were full. 'Not a very nice day, is it?'

'Not outside, I suppose,' I responded, with a sunny smile that must have confused her, 'but it's lovely from where I sit.'

'Something nice planned, then?' she said as she poured coffee for both of us.

'Oh, thank you. That smells so good! Yes, we're looking forward to our day. We think we're going to . . .' I paused.

'Track down a nasty crook,' would sound very odd. 'Visit a friend in the hospital' didn't sound very inviting, either.

Alan rescued me. Again. 'We hope to wrap up a problem that's been bothering us,' he said with a smile. 'Now, let's see,' he went on, 'perhaps scrambled eggs and bacon this morning? And what about you, love?'

I didn't actually want anything cooked. I was impatient to be on our way. But I appreciated Alan's ploy to divert any further questions Amy might have had. She wasn't snoopy by nature, but she did enjoy talking to her guests. Perfectly natural, but today we didn't want to talk about our plans, and as we were the only guests in the room, her sociable habit would have to go unsatisfied. I asked for sausage and one fried egg, just to keep her busy.

'She's such a dear,' I said when she had left. 'I wish we didn't have to . . .'

'Yes. Pity.'

One of the nicest things about a good marriage is the ability to communicate without words.

When she came back into the room with our food, her dog Jupiter sneaked in with her. He was a sweet little white dog of no particular ancestry, who loved people. He wasn't supposed to be in the breakfast room, and knew it, so he looked up at us with melting eyes that clearly said, 'I know I'm being bad, but won't you forgive me?' There may be people who can resist that look, but Alan and I are not among them. We were grateful for his intrusion this time, anyway, because it gave us a subject for conversation that took us away from the plans we didn't want to discuss.

So by the time we'd finished our meal and talked about our animals, past and present, another couple had come in seeking breakfast and it was time to leave for the hospital.

'We'll have to tell her about it when we can,' I said as I got into a warm jacket.

'A suitably edited version.'

'Of course.'

The hospital's car park on this raw, gloomy day wasn't more than half full, but we still had to park quite a ways from the entrance. I was grateful for Alan's arm as we walked to the door; unpredictable wind gusts were enough to put me off my balance and knock me down without his help. 'My tower of strength,' I murmured as we went inside.

Judith was waiting for us, along with Andrew. 'I brought him a present,' she said, holding up a carrier bag. 'New art materials. If anything will get him busy drawing, these will.'

I laughed. 'When I was a kid, my favourite present was a new box of Crayolas. If it was the box of sixty-four colours, with the silver and gold ones and the crayon sharpener, I felt like a princess! But don't most kids nowadays prefer markers?'

Then I realized what I'd said. Sammy was, after all, not a kid, not in terms of age, anyway.

But Judith didn't seem to notice. 'Not Sammy. I gave him some once and he didn't like them at all. He couldn't tell me why, but I think he prefers the shading, the nuances you can get with crayons. I brought both kinds of paper, too, smooth and textured. He's as particular about his materials as any other artist. And I've had an idea about the gift. Why don't you give it to him? It will help to make sure he believes you are a friend.'

'That's generous of you, Judith, and a good idea. We'll do it.' I took the bag.

'Well, shall we go up? Andrew, are you coming? He'd love to see you.'

'No, I'll stay and keep Mr Nesbitt company.'

Alan lowered his head and looked over his glasses at the young man, who laughed and said, 'Sorry, keep *Alan* company,' and Judith and I headed for the lift.

TWENTY-EIGHT

Sammy was sitting up in bed, watching something on television and looking very bored. He broke into a big smile when he saw Judith. Then he saw me, and the smile disappeared.

'Sammy, I think you know my friend Mrs Martin, don't

you? She met you a few days ago, and when I told her you like to draw, she got you a present.'

'What is it?' His tone was neutral.

I handed him the bag, saying not a word.

He was suspicious, but took the bag and, after a moment of uncertainty, dumped it upside down on his bed.

That did the trick. He looked at the box of crayons with sheer joy on his face. 'Crayons! My favourites! New ones, nice and pointy.' One of the pads of paper threatened to slide off the bed; Judith rescued it.

'Those crayons are my favourites, too.' It was true. I don't often use crayons anymore, except to touch up worn spots on oddly coloured shoes when no shoe polish will work, but I still love them. I love the smell. Blindfold me and put a box of Crayolas in front of my nose, and I'm instantly eight years old again, lying blissfully on my stomach with a colouring book in front of me, carefully outlining the cat's body before filling it in with a soft grey. 'I hoped you would like them.'

'Yes, yes, yes! You are a nice lady! I'm going to draw now. I'm going to draw you.'

He picked up the two pads and instantly dismissed the smooth-surfaced paper in favour of the textured. I let out the breath I hadn't known I'd been holding.

Sammy scooched himself up in the bed. Judith raised the bed so he was sitting nearly upright, stuffed a pillow in the right place for back support, and moved the tray table closer. It was the hinged kind, with storage space under the tray, so she raised it and looked around for something to keep it open. I offered my purse.

Judith hefted it. 'Goodness, what *do* you keep in there?'

'Anything I think might come in handy someday. I could probably survive on a desert island for quite a while.'

Sammy found that excruciatingly funny and roared with laughter. I smiled in sympathy. Whatever Sammy did, he did with all his might. Right now he was enjoying his visit with his gran and me.

As soon as his workstation was set up to his satisfaction, though, he dismissed us from his mind as completely as if we had left the room. His concentration was fixed entirely on the picture he was creating. He glanced at me from time to time, but it was apparent that he regarded me simply as a model, not as a fellow human being. He worked quickly and intently, his tongue sticking out of one corner of his mouth, his hand pausing only to select another crayon.

It was only about twenty minutes before he put the crayons neatly away in their box and handed me my portrait. My eyes were lavender, my hair a pale pink, my (deep red) shirt the palest of greens with thin white stripes here and there. It was all very abstract, but it was in his most loving style. And it was, somehow, the face I saw in the mirror every morning.

'Sammy, it's beautiful,' I said, my voice breaking. 'I'm nothing like that beautiful.'

'You are, too! Are you crying? Don't cry!'

'I'm crying because I'm happy, Sammy. Women do that. I'm happy because you made such a beautiful drawing of me. You're really, really good at drawing people.'

Judith recognized her cue. 'Oh, he can draw anybody. Sammy, can you draw us some of the people you see in the shops where you work?'

His face instantly lost its smile. 'I can't go back to work. They won't let me. I feel good, but they won't let me get out of here.'

'Soon they will. I promise, Sammy. They told me today that in two more days, maybe three, they'll let you go home. And as soon as we're sure you're really well, you can go back to work. Why don't you show Mrs Martin some of the people you like where you work? You can draw them from memory, I know.'

We were getting away from our mission, but we might be able to get Sammy around to it. Meanwhile he was happy, and that was part of the goal.

Rapidly he drew a few faces, all of them in the bright, happy style. Some men, some women. I recognized some of them and was able to identify them for Sammy. 'That's the man at the Jane Austen Centre, isn't it? And this must be the manager at the Baths shop.' And so on. He beamed every time I could tell him who the original was.

'And wasn't there another man you met at one of the shops?'

Judith ventured into dangerous territory. 'I think you thought he was your friend, but he wasn't, really, was he?'

Sammy swept his drawings onto the floor. 'Bad man! Don't like him.'

'No, we don't either.' I took up the thread. 'Nobody likes him, Sammy. Even the police don't like him. They've arrested him, Sammy, and he's in jail.'

'Good! He's a bad man.'

'He's so bad, Sammy, that he's telling lies to the police. They think he stole a lot of things, but he's lying and telling them you did it. We know that's not true, but it would help them if you could tell us what really did happen.'

'You like stories, Sammy,' said Judith in a nursery sort of voice. 'Why don't you tell us this story? Once upon a time there was a very bad man . . .'

'He made me do bad things! He told me to take things and then he would pay the shops for the ones he wanted to keep and give the others back, but he never did. He made me put things away in a car, and then he got mad at me because it wasn't his car. He made me cry!'

'You took a trip with him once, didn't you, love? I remember you told me he was taking you out for a treat, but I don't remember where.'

This was the first I'd heard of any such outing. I listened carefully to Sammy's answer.

'It was just a place where there were lots of rocks. Not very nice. No ice cream or anything. There were lots of people there. I don't know why. It wasn't fun. Gran, can I have some ice cream?'

'I don't know if they have any here. This place isn't very much fun either, is it? I have a Mars bar, if you would like that.'

'Do you have one for my friend?' He smiled at me, his good nature restored. For the moment.

'Oh, Sammy, thank you, but it's a funny thing, I've never cared for Mars bars. You have it.' I love them, but there are times, I firmly believe, when white lies are not only forgiven, but approved.

I waited for him to finish his candy bar, which he did

surprisingly neatly. He wiped his hands carefully on the napkin Judith gave him. 'Don't want to get chocolate on my drawings,' he explained. 'Got to keep my hands clean.'

'Right,' I agreed. 'Sammy, I'm interested in that trip to the place with rocks. I sort of like rocks. Were these the pretty kind you can take home and polish?'

He shook his head emphatically. 'Not pretty. All alike. Boring. The bad man made me take one, though. It was heavy. He said he was going to give it to a friend.'

'Did you ever see him talking to a friend?'

'No. I want to go to sleep now.'

'Oh, but you haven't drawn us any pictures of the people at the rock place,' urged Judith.

Sammy shrugged. 'Nobody interesting. Well, just one. The bad man talked to her for a little while. He told me she was an old friend, but I think he was lying. They didn't look like they were friends. She went away. And then he told me to get that rock and then we left. She was funny-looking. I didn't like her.'

He reached for his other pad, the smooth finish he preferred for his hostile portraits. Bearing down hard on the crayons, he produced a picture of a man and a woman in his same semi-abstract style. In essence it was a picture of hatred slashed onto the page. It was also a picture of the man I knew as Simon Caine, and a woman I couldn't identify.

'Sammy, may I keep this one, please? And the picture of me?'

'All of them,' he said, spreading his arms wide. 'I can make lots more. Goodbye.'

He crunched down in his bed and closed his eyes. Judith lowered the bed back to almost flat and took away the tray table. Sammy was asleep before she had finished putting away the drawing materials.

We picked up all the pictures, including the ones that had been swept to the floor, and carried them down to the waiting room, where Alan and Andrew were intent on a game of chess, playing with a set of miniature men and a board about the size of a fancy Christmas card. From the look of the piles of captured men, they were just about evenly matched.

'Come back, you two,' I said in a voice a little too loud for a hospital. Alan looked up, plainly not quite sure for a moment who I was and why I was interrupting something important.

'It's the only way,' I said to Judith, 'short of tipping up the board and spilling everything to the floor. When he gets involved in chess, a whirlwind could take the house away and he wouldn't notice, provided the game was still intact.' I moved closer to Alan and looked him straight in the face. 'I don't suppose you'd have any interest in how our talk with Sammy turned out.'

'Oh. Oh! Good heavens, I'd actually forgotten. Andrew's very good, and I was working out what, if anything, I can do to evade his clutches.'

'Yes, I could see that. It's a miracle you are able even to see the pieces. I'd have to hold them up to my nose to tell which were bishops and which were knights, and the king and queen look exactly alike to me. That's a reflection on my eyesight, Andrew, not on your men.'

He grinned. 'It is rather small, isn't it? My father gave it to me just before we left Jamaica, so we could play on the ship. I almost always keep it in my pocket.'

'And a good idea, too. But may I request that you memorize the positions, or take a picture or something, and put it away for now? There's lots we want to tell you and show you, and I'm starving. Let's all go find lunch some nice place where we can talk.'

Judith and Andrew bickered amiably about pubs while we walked to the car park, and finally chose one which, they said, would be crowded enough to mask conversation but not uncomfortably full. 'And they have excellent beer.' That from Andrew. 'And decent food,' added Judith, smiling at me.

What I really wanted at that point was some meatloaf from my own freezer, along with my own mashed potatoes and gravy. However, failing that, an excellent fish pie would be welcome.

'So,' I said when we were settled in a quiet corner, 'we have some things to show you.' Judith pulled out the stack of pictures, with my portrait on top.

The men looked from me to the picture and back at me again.

'It's . . . astounding,' said Alan. 'How does he do it? The colouring is wrong, the drawing is crude – but it's you. He's got your soul down on paper.'

'I know. And he did it in about twenty minutes. It's a little scary, actually. Now look at this one.' I pulled out the picture of Caine and the woman he talked to at the 'rock place' – presumably the quarry in Wales where the bluestone came from.

'Caine, of course. Did Sammy name him?'

'He calls him the "bad man". He told us a little of what happened between them, all corroborating what we'd already guessed.'

'Hmm. But who's the woman?'

'I don't know. I have the feeling I've maybe seen her before, but I can't place her. Sammy says she was at the quarry and talked to Caine for a while. Or no, he said he – Caine – talked to her. I'm not sure that makes a difference, but to me it implies that Caine initiated the conversation.'

'Would he be that precise?' Alan asked dubiously.

'I think so,' said Judith. 'As you see, he's good at drawing people, even their characters. He's also good at understanding relationships. For instance, when he was small and at school, he would tell me about the other kids bullying him. Sometimes others would stand up for him and there would be a fight, or at least a hot argument, which he would describe to me in detail. If I checked with the teacher afterward, his account would always be accurate in every detail. So when he says this man talked to this woman, I think we can assume that's the way it happened.'

Alan let that drop for the moment. 'And these other pictures?' he asked, riffling through the stack.

'We asked him to draw some of the people at the shops. You can see he drew only people he likes.'

'Which includes almost everyone,' said Judith. 'This Caine person with the woman, and the Prince of Wales one, are the only drawings I've seen in that hard, angry style.'

'Which is interesting, if you think about it,' I said slowly. 'It must mean he doesn't like her, either. In fact, he said so, I remember now. And why would he dislike her, from only that one encounter? He didn't even talk to her.'

'I would imagine,' said Judith, 'that she looked at him in a way he's come to mistrust. A combination of scorn and pity, with scorn predominating. He still gets it a lot, from people who don't know him.'

Our food arrived, hot and fragrant, and we fell to with a will, and dropped the subject while we ate. When we got to dessert, we all chose a lovely apple crumble, and while we waited for it, Alan made a proposal. 'Judith, I'm not a connoisseur, but I do love art, and I've been visiting museums and galleries for most of a long life, so I have something of an eye. I believe Sammy's talent to be exceptional. Would you allow me to take these pictures to a friend of mine who has a gallery in London? I think he might be interested in doing an exhibition.'

'I . . . goodness, I hardly know what to say. Of course we think he's wonderful, my friends and I, but then we love him. And we know the people he draws, so we can see how marvellously he captures them. To someone who didn't know them . . . I don't know, maybe they would just look like crude children's drawings.'

'I don't think so. You'll recall that I've never actually met him, and I could see the genius in his drawings instantly. I can't make any promises, of course, but if you'll let me show these to my friends, we'll see.'

'I'm not sure, Alan. Suppose the man did like them, and wanted to do a show? Would it mean Sammy would have to do a lot of drawing quickly? He isn't always in the mood, and he can be very stubborn if he doesn't want to do something. And then, would he have to go to London? He's lived here always, with me. I think London would terrify him.'

'I don't know the answers to those questions, but we could take it one step at a time. It's just that I hate the idea of his hiding that great light under a bushel.'

'And maybe,' I offered, 'knowing that people really liked his work and wanted to hang it up in a shop in London, maybe that would help make up for the betrayal by the man he thought was a friend.'

'Yes, I see that it might. Very well, Alan. Take them and

do whatever you like with them. I won't mention any of this to Sammy. Not yet.'

'Quite right. Much too speculative as yet. Meanwhile I think Dorothy and I will stay in Bath for another few days. I want to tell Inspector Roberts what Sammy told you two, and I want to show him this picture. It may get Caine to open up, that and Sammy's story.'

He wasn't, however, very hopeful, he told me on the way back to our home from home. 'If he says anything at all, he'll just pooh-pooh Sammy's story, claiming he's too stupid to remember anything or get it right.'

'Yes, I can hear the nasty language now.'

'As for the drawing, he'll make fun of it, claim it's nothing more than a crude piece of rubbish, all Sammy's imagination.'

'All the same, Alan, I'm sure I've seen that woman some-where, and not long ago. I wish I could remember where.'

TWENTY-NINE

The answer came to me just as I was dropping off for my nap, and woke me with no hope of getting back to sleep.

Alan had just put down the newspaper before succumbing to sleep. He sighed when I sat straight up. 'Now what?'

'I remember her!'

'Remember who, dear heart?' He sounded drowsy.

'Whom. The woman in Sammy's drawing. The one with Caine.'

That woke him right up. 'Who is she?'

'I don't know, but I know where we saw her. Twice. The first time was at Stonehenge. Do you remember that woman who was making a fuss in the gift shop? I didn't catch much of what she said, but she was very upset about something, and kept arguing with the clerk. She finally stormed out in a huff, and we could buy what we wanted.'

'I think I remember. Vaguely. The chain of events that happened shortly after that wiped it out of my mind. And you say there was another time?'

'I think so. I'm not so sure about this one, but I think she was in the gift shop at the Baths that day when the jewellery was stolen. Or maybe the next day, when I was trying to find out some stuff and then the chain-reaction accident made such a mess.'

'Hmm. And that was the day when Caine bumped into you.'

'Yes.'

We looked at each other, and Alan picked up the phone to call Rob.

Certain plans were made; certain actions were put in train. Then Alan stooped and put on his shoes. 'I think it's time we talked to the manager of the shop at Stonehenge.'

The day seemed to have lasted a long time, but it was still early afternoon when we set out. We expected to find few people at the monument on such a cold dark day, and we weren't disappointed. The car park was almost empty. We told the ticket-taker that we were there only to visit the gift shop, not the henge, and he let us through.

'I hope the same person is on duty,' I murmured to Alan. 'Maybe we should have called?'

'It's nearing the end of the season,' he said. 'I'm betting that the summer help will have departed and only the regular staff will be here. As I recall, she looked like a settled member of the crew.'

Whether Alan was right or not, the same woman was in fact at the desk. Middle-aged, a bit dumpy, she certainly did look settled. And bored. She looked at her watch before she saw us and then brightened a little.

'Good afternoon,' she said with a smile. 'Actually rather a frightful afternoon, though, isn't it?'

'Terrible,' I said with a shiver. 'And yesterday was so beautiful.'

'A perfect day for visitors,' she said with a nod. 'We were worked off our feet. And today look at it!'

'I don't know about you,' I said, 'but I'd always rather be busy. It's tiring, but the time goes so much faster.'

'And it's more interesting. Most people are delightful, fun to talk to. Then there are the others – but they're interesting, too.'

'Actually, we came here to talk to you about one of the other sort, the not-delightful kind. We were here early last week when you were having a good deal of trouble with one woman in particular. She was tall, with very thin hair, and oddly dressed. She looked a bit like what we would in my day have called a hippy, except she was far too old. Sixties, at least, I'd say. Do you happen to remember her?'

'Do I! I thought I was going to have to call the manager, or the police! She wittered on and on about how mistaken we all were about the henge, how we were angering the gods of the place and we would face fearful retribution. That was her phrase, fearful retribution. Can you believe, in this day and age? Of course she was dotty, but there's dotty and dotty, and she was the dangerous kind.'

'Goodness! Did she make threats, or what? Besides "fearful retribution", I mean.'

'I didn't really listen, to be honest. It was all the usual hodgepodge, Druids and that, ancient rituals we were profaning. They come now and then, you know, the Druids. Usually at the summer solstice. They think the place was theirs, originally. They're quite wrong, but they're harmless, really. But this one wasn't. She was . . . she put the wind up me proper, and I admit it.'

'I think,' said Alan, 'that we should introduce ourselves. My name is Alan Nesbitt, and this is my wife Dorothy Martin. Shortly after we witnessed that little scene between you and the unbalanced woman, we went out to our car and found some items in it that were not ours, and that we hadn't put there. When they turned out to be stolen goods, and we were temporarily under suspicion, we were naturally interested in investigating the matter. As it happens, I am a retired policeman, so I know a little about investigation.'

'I'm sure you do. I think I remember a little about that. I'm Emmy Brice, by the way. How do you do.' We all exchanged nods. 'Of course you'd want to find out who did such a thing.'

'And that,' I finished, 'is what we're doing here today. We

are beginning to think this woman might have been involved in some way in the thefts. Now, you may think *us* dotty, but we wonder if this is the woman in question.'

Alan produced an envelope from the case he'd been carrying. 'It's not your conventional sort of picture, I admit.' He pulled out Sammy's drawing of Caine and the woman.

'My word! No, not conventional. But yes, this is the woman. It doesn't even look like her, really, but it's her. I don't know the man beside her. Nasty type, isn't he?' She looked again and then looked back at us, puzzled. 'How does he *do* that? The person who drew this, I mean. It's just a mess of colour and peculiar shapes, but I knew it for that woman straightaway.'

'I think it's just pure genius,' I said. 'It was a young man who drew this, a man who suffers from Down syndrome. He's never had any art training, but somehow he can produce portraits of absolutely anybody.'

'Oh, is it Sammy?' Her face lit up.

'You know Sammy?'

'Everyone knows Sammy, at least everyone in the museum shop world. He's famous. I've never happened to meet him, but I know all about what a great person he is. I didn't know he was also an artist.' She looked again at the picture. 'I can't get over this. No technique, no attempt at realistic drawing, and yet . . .'

'Alan thinks he can paint people's souls. That's really scary, but I think it's true.'

'I also think,' said Alan quietly, 'that God often gives special gifts to people with handicaps, to make up for what they can't do.'

'Well, if Sammy really can do that, and I think maybe it's true, I feel sorry for this pair. Their souls are really ugly.'

Reluctantly she gave the picture back to Alan, who opened his mouth to say thank-you-and-goodbye. I put a hand on his arm.

'Alan, I'd like to take another look at that chess set. That's if you still have it?' I added to the clerk.

'Oh, yes. I had to put it back for a while, because we'd somehow lost one pawn. Fortunately the artist had another he could send us. In any case, it's a bit pricey for a shop like this, where people mostly want cheap souvenirs. We keep it under lock and key now.' She led us to a glass display case where the set was laid out in all its glory.

'It's quite heavy. Everything is made of local stone, and the pieces are meant to be symbols of Stonehenge.' She opened the case and picked up one of the men. 'See, this is the king. The sun. And the queen is the moon.'

'Of course, because the henge is a kind of astronomical calendar!' I exclaimed.

'Well, that's one of the theories, anyway. The bishops are meant to be Druid priests – historically inaccurate, that, but never mind. The rooks are of course bits of the henge itself, and the knights – well, they're knights, though not on horse-back as is usual. You see they have shields. That's a nod to another bit of folklore, that King Arthur, with the help of Merlin and lots of knights, brought the stones here from Ireland.'

'Fascinating,' I marvelled. 'A lot of spurious history in art. And the pawns?'

'What one might expect. Stylized stone-age labourers. Perhaps the least spurious depiction of them all, since they almost certainly did build the place.'

'Alan.' I turned a pleading eye to him. 'I know it's a lot of money, more than we can really afford. But I'd like to give it to Andrew. He's a good player if he had you almost stalemated, and he should have something better than that tiny set. And he's been through such a lot . . .'

Alan gave me the wonderful smile that I first fell in love with, and said to the clerk, 'Wrap it up, please.'

That took a while. We wandered around, looking at this and that, not intending to buy anything more. Our budget had been more than bent! As she worked, the clerk chatted. We were still the only customers in the shop, and closing time was soon. The poor woman was relieved to have something to do and someone to talk to.

'You know,' she said, wrapping the last pawn and nestling it in the box, 'it's funny, but it was this very chess set that started that woman's rantings. She claimed it was all wrong.

Well, of course it is, but it's just meant for fun, not to be historically accurate. And the thing was, she claimed only the bishops
really belonged, that the rest were . . . goodness, I think she
really used the word "blasphemy". Then she picked up one of
the knights – the display was open then – and made to throw
it across the room, and that was when I was ready to scream
for help. But someone came into the shop just then, and I was
able to get the knight away from her, and she said something
that sounded like very bad language indeed, only thank goodness it wasn't in English, and then she left. Now, there you
are, all secure. Quite heavy, though. Thank you very much
indeed, sir,' she added as he handed her a credit card. 'Would
you like some help getting the box to your car?'

Alan disclaimed all need for assistance and we left with
expressions of mutual esteem. 'Okay,' I said when we were
out of the car park, 'I'm in need of sustenance. Tea would do.
Beer would be better. What can we find on the way back?'

What we found was a nice little inn that could provide
either. The weather hadn't got any more friendly, and in view
of the roaring fire at one end of the room, I changed my mind
and opted for tea. We were directed to a parlour room, also
with a fire, and ordered a full afternoon tea, scones, sandwiches
and all.

'I'm going to weigh three hundred pounds when we get
home,' I commented.

'Call it twenty stone. It sounds better,' he said calmly. 'We'll
walk it off once we're on home ground. Ah, here we are.'

I poured the hot, fragrant tea, and Alan held up his cup in
a toast. 'Here's to a very successful afternoon!'

I sipped. 'Ouch! Too hot to drink yet. Yes, thank God for
bored, gossipy clerks! She never even wondered why we were
asking all those questions.'

'I think perhaps she's the sort of woman for whom asking
questions is the normal manner of conversation. I explained
in order to lead into the main point. And it worked, didn't it?'

'Even better than I'd hoped. She not only recognized the
woman, but told us she's a nutter.'

'With a fixation, or an obsession, or whatever one might
want to call it, about Stonehenge.'

I picked up a scone and buttered it. 'What is Rob doing, meanwhile?'

'Checking with the people at the Baths. If you're right, and you saw this woman there, they might remember her. She certainly sounds odd enough to stick out in a crowd.'

'Right, and the next thing is to get this picture duplicated and in the hands of the police. It isn't your typical ID photo, but if the woman at Stonehenge – Emmy, that's right – if she spotted it right away, other people will, too.'

'Yes, and Rob needs to know the story we picked up today, as well. We're closing in, love. We've got Caine and this woman together at the bluestone quarry. We've got her at Stonehenge, and maybe at the Baths at the time Caine was also there. The connections aren't very firm, as yet, but now we have some ideas.'

'But what on earth is the connection between Caine and Nutcase? They're not friends. At least Sammy had the impression they met for the first time at the quarry, and talked only for a little while, and then left separately.'

'And before they left,' Alan said, gesturing with a sandwich to reinforce his point, 'Caine told Sammy to get that piece of bluestone.'

'You think it was for her? But if she wanted a piece, why didn't she just take it herself?'

'I'm speculating here. But perhaps she was intimidated by the prohibitions against stealing the stone.' I opened my mouth, but he held up a hand. 'I know, I know, she doesn't seem the law-abiding sort, from what little we know of her.'

'She was about to throw that chess piece, destroying the museum's property.'

'Agreed. But there are other possibilities. Perhaps the stone was simply too heavy for her. I didn't try to lift it when it was in that box in our boot, but even a smallish rock can weigh quite a lot. Or, and this is maybe the most likely, she may have felt it would be sacrilege to take some of the material that built the henge.'

I finished the scone, washed it down with some tea, and picked up a sandwich. 'Okay.' I thought for a moment while taking a couple of bites. 'How's this? Caine spots her, for some reason, as a likely mark. Sammy doesn't give us much idea of how she was dressed, but when we saw her, she was wearing bits and pieces, looking like she had dressed out of a ragbag, a colourful one, though. So Caine approaches her, starts her talking, soon catches on to her obsession. He decides he's going to try to sell her a piece of bluestone. As soon as she leaves, he tells Sammy to get a piece, and they take it away.'

'Hmm. But he never does sell it to her, does he? Because it landed in a box in our car. And what about the stuff from all the other museums?'

'I don't know.' I polished off the sandwich, left the fruitcake for Alan, and poured myself another cup of tea. 'There's an awful lot we don't know. But I'd bet money on those two being in this mess together, somehow.'

Alan sighed. 'We're making bricks without straw again.'

'We've made some very nice ones from time to time using that very method. Let's get back to our room and call Rob. He might have some straw for us.'

THIRTY

Rob called us before we got back. Actually he called Alan, but as he was driving I picked up. 'Rob, we're in the car. We'll call you in a minute or two when Alan finds a place to stop.'

There was a lay-by not far ahead. Alan pulled in, killed the engine, and called back, putting the speaker on. 'We collected some bits of information just now that will interest you,' Alan began. 'What about you? Any successful digging?'

'A trifle or two at the Baths shops. We talked to people at both of them, the small one in the complex itself and the larger one up top. We'd have learned more if we'd had a picture of the woman in question, but we did show them Caine's picture, and several of the clerks said they had seen him in the shops more than once. One said she'd been a little uneasy about him, thought he might be up to no good, and kept a close eye on him. Of course, that might have been because it was the police who were asking.'

I groaned. 'Oh, yes, the hindsight effect. "'Ee looked shifty, officer. I told meself, 'ee'd bear watchin', 'ee would."'

Both Alan and Rob laughed at my Agatha-Christie-esque quote. 'Spot on, Dorothy! But in this case my people thought it was genuine. The clerk said Caine had been spending time near the more expensive items, particularly the jewellery, but when asked if he'd like some help, shied off. And then, of course, some of the jewellery was stolen shortly after that. But no one saw Caine actually steal anything.'

'You know,' I put in, 'I've been wondering about that. There was almost nothing extremely valuable in the loot found in our car, and some of it was literally valueless. Is it a little out of the . . . the pattern, or whatever, for Caine to steal expensive jewellery? Or to get Sammy to take it for him, which is what I, at least, believe?'

'That, of course, is one of our problems. And we have not yet been able to get a single word out of Caine, who is at present our only source of information. We've charged him with petty theft, so we can continue to hold him, but we're sure there's a lot more going on. We just can't prove it.'

'We have some information that may help,' said Alan. 'Shall we meet somewhere to talk about it?'

We ended up at the fish and chips place, and Sylvie joined us. It was too early to think about supper, but we had beer and conversation.

'All right, what do you have to tell us?'

'Oh, my. A lot. But before we even start, Alan, show them the picture.'

'A little gift from one of your grandchildren?' asked Rob with an indulgent smile when it was put into his hands. Then he took a second look. 'Good grief! It's Caine! Who drew this . . . this extraordinary picture?'

'Sammy,' I said smugly. 'He's an amazing artist, isn't he?'

'Amazing isn't the word. Sylvie, take a look at this.'

Sylvie wasn't as blown away as the rest of us had been. 'Yes, I knew Sammy liked to draw. He once showed me a picture he had drawn of a rose, and it was all the wrong colours and shapes, and yet unmistakably a rose that he loved. He somehow gets to the heart of whatever he's drawing.' She picked up the drawing. 'So this is Simon Caine. Nasty sort of man, isn't he?'

'That's exactly what the clerk at the Stonehenge shop said.'

'And who's the woman?'

'That's what we don't know,' said Alan. 'But according to Sammy, this is a picture of their first meeting – at the bluestone quarry. Sammy says Caine saw her, went over to talk to her, and shortly after she left, got Sammy to carry off that piece of stone that we later found in my car.'

'And . . . wait for it,' I chimed in, 'the clerk recognized her as a woman who came to the shop and made a scene, plainly out of her gourd, ranting about the history of Stonehenge and how they had it all wrong. She, the clerk, wrote her off as a particularly crazy latter-day Druid. She even tried to smash one of the pieces from the chess set. So isn't it interesting that she and Caine talked together? And that a pawn from that chess set was found in the loot?'

Rob finished his pint. 'Alan, if you'll let me have the picture for a few minutes, and ladies, if you'll excuse me, I need to get this circulated as soon as possible. I won't be long. When you're ready to order your meals, order one for me, too. Sylvie, you know what I like. Back soon.'

'You think this woman is a part of the problem?' Sylvie took a sip of beer.

'I think, and this may be just my own weird brain at work, but I think she might be the key to the whole thing. For one thing, the thefts haven't made much sense. She apparently doesn't have a whole lot of sense. And she's not a nice person. I have two pieces of evidence for that judgement: first, her behaviour at the Stonehenge shop, which Alan and I happened to witness, and second, Sammy's opinion of her. He said he didn't like her, and the drawing has his feelings written all over it. And I have great respect for Sammy's ability to judge character. I know, I know, Alan. None of this is evidence.'

'No. But it's suggestive. I agree with you about Sammy's reaction to the woman. We're told he likes almost everyone.

When he takes an instant dislike to someone, there's a reason. I'm inclined to think it's based on his uncanny ability to see right through people.'

'As against that, let's not forget that he liked Caine very much at first. And didn't you two think he was pleasant when you first met him?'

'I don't know that I thought much about it.' I searched my memory. 'He was just someone who talked to us for a few minutes. He was interesting. You took him for a London cabbie, didn't you, Alan?'

'As I recall, yes. I usually like London cabbies, so that must mean that my impression was favourable. Like you, I scarcely remember.'

'And even when he cannoned into me at the shop, he was pleasant and considerate. It was only later that I began to wonder whether he was up to something. And that was because other suspicious things had happened. More twenty-twenty hindsight.'

'So if you two,' persisted Sylvie, 'who are pretty good at sizing up people yourselves, if you were fooled by Caine, I think it's reasonable to suppose that Sammy could be taken in at first by someone who was nice to him, gave him presents, gave him something fun to do.'

'Yes, and . . . oh, I've just thought of something. When I was teaching, the thing that upset the Down children more than anything else was being betrayed. I told you about the sixth-grade crime wave. The child, Bert, who was the victim of those hoodlums was devastated when he worked out what they'd done to him. He never forgave them, hated them with a burning passion. And they had the sense to steer clear of him after that.'

Sylvie nodded. 'Yes, that makes sense. Sammy's a good friend, but a bad enemy. He loves the manager of the abbey shop, and I once saw him tear into a man who was giving her a hard time. He was furious! I was helping out that day, and I had to go over to the customer after he'd left the shop and give him a few words of wisdom.'

'Right,' said Alan, summing up our musings. 'So we agree that this unknown woman is probably a bad lot. But as long as we're spinning a web of possibilities, what might be her role in our imaginary gang? Is she Caine's colleague, assistant, boss – what?'

I sipped my beer and thought about that for a while. 'Caine thought she was going to be a customer,' I said at last. 'When he made Sammy steal that stone, rock, whatever you want to call it. I'll bet they talked about Stonehenge for a bit, and he found out how demented she was on the subject, and thought he could get a good price from her out of a piece of bluestone.'

'Okay, but what about the rest of the loot?' demanded Alan. 'Most of it had nothing whatever to do with Stonehenge.'

And neither Sylvie nor I could come up with an answer to that.

The restaurant was filling up, and the smell of food was making all of us hungry. 'Rob is taking longer than he thought,' I commented.

'He almost always does,' said Sylvie. 'Let's order. I won't order for him, though. Who knows how long he'll be?'

In fact we had almost finished our fish and ships (much better eaten fresh and hot) when Rob walked in. He stopped first at the bar to order his food, and looked over with lifted eyebrows to query us about beer. Sylvie and I refused, miming drinking from cups. When Rob brought over a tray with two brimming glasses and two brimming coffee cups, we made room for him and let him sit down before Sylvie said, 'Well?'

'Well, indeed. Pass, friend, and all's well.' He held up his beer glass. 'Here's to Sammy!'

'Okay,' I said when we had all toasted in our respective beverages, 'I think we all agree to that, but why, in particular?'

'Because his picture has broken the case! This is a celebration, ladies and gentlemen!'

He grinned. We waited. I finally said, 'Are you going to make us beg?'

'I thought a little suspense might be in order.'

'I have,' said Sylvie sweetly, 'a very hot cup of coffee here.' She raised it, not to her lips.

Rob grinned even more broadly. 'Which you know you want

to drink, rather than pour over my head. All right, you'll hear the whole story. It all begins with the picture. Which reminds me.' He reached inside his jacket. 'Here it is, without a scratch. Which is lucky. Because when Caine saw it, he lunged for it. I was lucky to keep it out of his hands.' He took a swig of beer. 'Aahh. That hits the spot. Now, where was I?'

'Showing Caine the picture. What is his name really, by the way?'

Rob laughed, nearly choking on his beer. 'Jack Robinson!'

'No! Not really!' we chorused.

'He swears he was christened John Robinson, and backed it up with information about when and where. We're checking it out, of course, but I think we'll find it's true. I just wish it were a little further removed from my name.'

Alan ignored that. 'So he's talking now,' he said with satisfaction.

'A blue streak. As I said, it was the picture that did it.'

'So Caine/Smith/Robinson saw it. I'd have thought he'd make fun of it, refuse to see anything except a childish scrawl.' I reached over to the next table, whose occupants had departed, leaving a tray with milk and sugar behind. I doctored my coffee and shoved the tray over to Sylvie.

'That's what he tried to do later, but his initial reaction put the lie to his disclaimer. So then he changed his tactics and blamed everything on the lady.'

'Charming,' said Sylvie. 'No, thanks, I take mine black. When in doubt,' she went on, 'say it's the woman's fault. They've been doing it since Adam.'

'What's her name?' asked Alan, ever the policeman eager for facts.

'He claims he doesn't know it, and I'm inclined to believe him. Lovely, thank you, Sue,' as the waitress put his dinner in front of him.

We paused as she cleared away our used plates and utensils, which gave poor Rob a chance at a bite or two of food before we insisted that he go on with the story.

'Claims he doesn't know her name,' I prompted.

'He says she calls herself "Priestess of Truth" and says she is the only true Druid left in the world, a direct descendent of the ones who built Stonehenge. Apparently this all came out in a series of meetings when Jack, as I guess we have to get used to calling him, was trying to work out a plan for making capital out of her obsession.' Rob ate some chips and washed them down with beer.

'Her mission in life is apparently to spread the truth about Stonehenge and destroy the blasphemers and their sacrilegious temples. I'm quoting, you understand, as he was quoting her. Jack decided that stealing from those sacrilegious temples might please her, and net him a nice tidy little sum.

'Not that he put it that way. It was all her idea, according to him. She told him she wanted to build a sort of black museum of relics of heretical history, but she didn't want to buy anything from these profane institutions. That would be supporting them and their ideas. Far better to steal it. Or get Sammy to steal it. She – the "priestess" – wanted some things from the abbey gift shop, but apparently Sammy dug in his heels at that.'

'Good for him! So Sammy stole the other things for Caine, who handed them over to the woman, who then, presumably, paid Caine. I mean Jack. Not very logical.' I poured myself some more coffee.

'Logic,' said Alan drily, 'would not seem to be an outstanding characteristic of this woman. I wish we had something to call her!'

Rob glanced at his wife and me. 'I've thought of several things to call her, actually, but not in this company. But I've saved the best for last. We may not know her name, but we know where to find her. Jack had made an appointment with her for tonight, to turn over the latest collection of loot.'

'That would be the stuff from our trunk. Boot.'

'Right. We intend to keep that appointment.'

'With an officer substituting for Jack.' I rubbed my hands with glee.

'No. With Jack himself. We're offering him a certain amount of clemency if he cooperates.'

'He'll be wired, of course.'

'Of course. And under close surveillance.'

'Rob . . . no. Forget it.'

'I wonder if I can guess what my wife was about to say.' Alan looked at me. 'You want to go along.'

'Of course I do, but I quite realize it's out of the question. You can't have a civilian horning in on a police operation, especially when it's going to be a delicate one. There might even be a certain amount of danger. And I could get in your way.'

Rob looked at Alan and then at me. 'Dorothy, you've made all my arguments for me. So there's really nothing left for me to say except, get your coat. We haven't much time.'

THIRTY-ONE

R ob's driver took us all in an unmarked police car. Rob leaned over so he could talk to us in the back seat. 'I knew you'd want to come, Dorothy, and I could see no real reason why not. You and Alan were in this from the beginning. It's only fair that you see the end. Or what I hope will be the end. These things don't always work out as planned, you know.'

'I do know. Alan's told me about some real disasters. But Rob, how did you get Jack to agree to this? I mean, there must have been something besides the gentle bribe.'

'Oh, there was, there was! That was what gave me the idea in the first place. Turns out the reason Jack reacted so violently to the picture of the Priestess is because he's furious with her. He's given her all kinds of things for her museum or whatever she calls it, and now she's refusing to pay him. They'd made arrangements for a bank transfer, and now she says she's changed her mind. Her project is to be a shrine, and objects in a shrine should be freely given.'

I couldn't help giggling. 'So he's gone to all this trouble for nothing, got himself arrested and charged, and he won't get a thing out of it except some time in jail.'

'I wouldn't feel too sorry for him,' said Sylvie. 'Don't forget what he's done to Sammy.'

'Did you ask him about that, Rob? Was he the one who pushed him in?'

'He swears not. Claims he really likes Sammy and wouldn't dream of doing him harm. I'm quoting again.'

The police car slowed, and the driver asked Rob something. He pointed, and then turned back to us and spoke very quietly. 'Here we are. Lee's going to park here; the rendezvous is round the corner. Most of the cars you see belong to us. Once we have the evidence we need on tape, we'll move in. There's no telling how it will go down. The lady has been known to lose her temper on occasion, as you observed. So I will ask you all to say nothing, and not to move out of the car. I'm giving you all earbuds so you can hear what's happening, but you are not to react in any way, even if Lee and I have to leave the car. Is that clear?'

I murmured agreement, and I meant it. I truly did. Honestly.

Rob doled out the earbuds, which I found surprisingly uncomfortable. I could hear nothing. I looked at the others, miming a question. They shook their heads. Alan pointed to his watch, which I took to mean that we were a little early, and the action wouldn't start for a little while. My nerves were taut, my muscles tense. I tried to relax them.

'Mr Smith, you are late.' The voice came so clearly in my ear that I jumped and looked around. Just us, in the dark car, on the dark street corner.

'I was busy, madam.'

'You will address me properly, sir.'

'How can I do that, when you haven't seen fit to entrust me with your name? Or indeed your address.'

That was Caine, unmistakably. That hint of London was there even when he was being formal. As for the other voice, the woman's . . . I mentally shrugged. I'd heard too little of that argument at the Stonehenge shop to be sure this was the same person.

'My worldly name is unimportant. We are wasting time. Have you brought me the blasphemous jewels?'

'No, I have not. I am waiting for you to pay me what you owe.'

'I have told you why I will not do that. This is not a matter of commerce, but of enlightening the world to their folly and sacrilege. How dare you reduce it to a base matter of filthy lucre!'

'I find that I enjoy eating and drinking, and a warm place to live. All that requires some of that filthy lucre. I've done what you asked of me, madam, and more. Now I want my money.'

'You grow tiresome, Mr Smith. I find that I have no further need of your services. You may go.'

'Not until you pay me!'

She apparently ignored that. 'I must find someone else to provide me with what I need. Perhaps that boy . . . unless he dies . . .'

'And that's another thing! If he dies you'll have murder on your conscience! You had no reason to push him into that damned pool!'

'It was necessary. He was beginning to be dangerous. I'd have thought even you would understand that. He no longer trusts you, and if he talks to the authorities about what you asked him to do, you could be in a great deal of trouble.'

'Me! What about you? You're the one behind this whole crazy plan! You're cracked, that's what you are!'

'*You will not refer to me in that way!*'

I thought her voice was going to shatter my eardrum.

'*I am the Priestess of Truth! I have powers you cannot conceive of! You will leave me, peasant!*'

'I will not leave without my money!' He was shouting, too, but his voice, a couple of octaves lower, wasn't so painful.

A very quiet male voice sounded in my ear, cutting out the other voices. 'Go in now, Rob?'

'Not quite yet. But be ready.'

The others came back, louder and shriller than before. '*You will be punished! You will be punished by the spirits of the earth!*'

'*And so will you, by the Bill! For hurting Sammy, and trying to kill that driver and that idiot woman!*'

Then no words could be distinguished, only screams and shouts and the sound of something breaking. 'Now!' said Rob, as he left the car and raced toward the corner.

He got there at exactly the same moment as a tall woman in billowing white robes. She was screaming at the top of her very powerful lungs, and looking back as she ran. She cannoned into Rob, knocking him flat.

All three of us were out of the car, against orders, almost before Rob hit the ground. Alan spoke into the radio on Rob's shoulder: 'Officer down! Need back-up immediately!' Meanwhile he was trying to restrain the woman, who was fighting him with the strength of the mad. I tried to help him, while Sylvie knelt by Rob and tried to assess the damage. A phalanx of policemen approached at a run from around the corner, but before they could get there the Priestess of Truth landed a kick on my head and I quietly left the scene.

Things were very quiet when I opened my eyes. Quiet and dark. My head seemed to be a balloon, trying to float loose. I turned it to try to see, and regretted it instantly.

'Better not try to move for a bit,' said a voice I felt I ought to recognize. A pleasant voice. 'Talk some more,' I said, but I didn't seem to make any sound.

An interval. Something cool and soothing on my head. The voice again. 'Are you with us, darling?'

'Alan?'

'The very same. They don't want you to talk, so I'll explain. You got the hell of a kick in the head from that she-devil. The paramedics did triage, decided you weren't as bad as Rob, and gave you a shot for the pain. How is it, by the way?'

'Bloody.'

'My dear! I'm shocked. It will probably get worse, but they think there's no concussion.'

'Where?'

'In the police car. Things were a bit lively there for a bit, and the ambulances were needed for Rob and the priestess.'

'Hurt?'

'Not really, but raving mad. They had to use a straitjacket, and it took three men to get her into it.'

I swallowed and licked my lips. 'Drink.'

I think he gave me some water, or ice, or something, and

that's the last I remember before waking up to bright sunlight in a comfortable bed.

'Ouch!' It was a comment about everything in general, but particularly about that bright sunlight. I tried to grab a pillow to put over my eyes, but it was too heavy. I turned my head, groaned, and saw that the pillow was weighed down by my husband's head. He hadn't even moved when I tried to take his pillow away.

Very, very gingerly I got out of bed, went to the bathroom, and stopped on the way back to draw the curtains. I crawled back into bed as quietly as I could, but I could have brought a brass band with me. Alan was out for the count.

When I next woke, it was to the smell of coffee. I sat up, carefully. Alan wordlessly handed me a cup, and I finally surfaced enough to look at him properly.

And a sorry sight it was. One eye was purple. A bandage on his cheek didn't quite cover three long scratches. The hand holding his cup of coffee had— 'Alan Nesbitt, is that a *bite*?'

'It is. The lady was not acquainted with the Marquess of Queensberry Rules. Fortunately she didn't break the skin. A human bite can be nasty to treat.'

'We look like the sole survivors of a losing battle. Oh, but this is life-saving!' I held up the coffee cup.

'I went downstairs and cajoled Amy into letting me bring up a pot of the real stuff. We got in quite late last night, and looked rather the worse for wear, so she's feeling sorry for us this morning.'

'Also dying to know what happened!'

'She's already read most of it.' He held up a paper. 'We're all over the news, my dear.'

'Hmph! The saying used to be that a lady appeared in the news only three times: when she was born, when she married, and when she died. I'm grateful that that last doesn't apply here. For a moment or two last night I thought it might. Let me see.'

I sipped coffee as I read through the news account. The reporters and photographers had apparently arrived shortly after the rush of policemen, because there was a lovely picture of me lying on the ground with Alan hovering over me, blood streaming from his face. Another photo showed the Priestess in a straitjacket being wrestled into an ambulance. The written account was almost as lurid as the pictures. They got my name wrong, and misspelled Alan's.

I set it aside. 'I hope this doesn't hit the national news. Our friends will figure out the name glitches, and they'll be appalled.'

'I'm afraid Jane has already called, and the Allenbys. I told them the reports of our deaths were highly exaggerated.'

'Thank you, Mark Twain.' I picked up the paper and turned the pages. There was nothing more about our colourful evening. 'They don't actually say much, do they? No details about the crimes those two are charged with, nor the quarrel between them that led to the violence. And, of course, they don't give her name.'

'Because nobody knows it. At least, somebody does, but not the police here. I would imagine this story has brought Rob several calls about her. Such a bizarre figure is bound to be known somewhere. Meanwhile they've booked her as Jane Doe.'

'Now. If you've finished your coffee, Rob has invited us for Sunday brunch.'

'Sunday! Oh, Alan, and it's' – I counted on my fingers – 'it's All Saints' Day! What time is it?'

'Far too late for church this morning. I think God will forgive us for once. There are extenuating circumstances, and we can go to Evensong. Can you make it to the shower, do you think? Hot water might be good for what ails you.'

It was. I felt much better once I was clean and dressed. My hair, on the other hand . . . Oh, well, I just wouldn't look in the mirror. 'Do I need a coat?'

Alan looked out the window. 'The trees are blowing about.' He opened the window a crack and quickly shut it again. 'Bright but brisk. Yes, certainly a coat. And hat or scarf.'

'Scarf, I think. A hat would blow off.'

I hobbled a bit, and when we got out into the wind I had to hold Alan's arm, but on the whole we walked into Rob's house not looking too much like the Spirit of '76.

'Congratulations!' said Sylvie. 'This morning we're

celebrating all being alive, with the bad guys behind bars. Mimosas?'

I accepted one gladly. 'They say I don't have a concussion, so I can drink this with impunity. Thank you!'

'Anyway, it's pretty light on alcohol.'

'True. My first husband used to call it a waste of perfectly good champagne. But I love them.' I lifted my glass. 'Here's to us!'

'I've invited Judith, too, and Andrew,' said Rob. He hadn't risen for the toast, and I saw that one foot was wrapped in bandages. So he, too, was among the walking wounded. 'Sammy isn't quite ready to leave the hospital,' he went on, 'but we'll have a little party for him later. Large groups tend to confuse him.'

The bell rang, Judith and Andrew came in and were provided with Mimosas, and Sylvie served us with a variety of pastries and a tray of cold meats and cheeses. 'I hope you don't mind,' she said. 'I just wasn't up to cooking this morning. We all got to bed rather late last night.'

'No kidding.' I looked around the room. 'And rather worse for wear. Sylvie, you're a saint to entertain at all. Did the madwoman get you, too?'

'Just a few tufts of hair. It hurt quite a lot, but it isn't serious. I'm happy she's restrained now.'

'All right,' said Rob, calling us to order. 'There's a lot you don't know about last night.'

'All we know is what we read in the paper,' said Judith, deadpan.

'First Mark Twain, now Will Rogers! You Brits are well up on American authors this morning.'

'Right,' said Alan. 'Now you can quote us some Shakespeare to get even.'

'Let me think about it. Proceed, Rob.'

He did a quick recap of the night's events that we already knew about, the set-up, the brouhaha, the woman's capture. 'At that point she was still Jane Doe. But we reckoned the news story would bring responses, and it did. The most interesting, and the most reliable, came from a pair of infuriated Druids.'

'Ah,' said Alan. 'Upset about the bad publicity.'

'Upset about the whole situation. It seems that our Priestess is a woman named Charity Walcot.'

'Charity!' I burst out. 'What a desperately inappropriate name! Sorry. I interrupted.'

'You're right, though. The Druids told us that she's been relatively harmless until recently. A pain in the neck, quarrelling with everyone else in her group, but not really crazy until lately.

'Modern Druids, you see, are pretty tolerant of differences of opinion. The basic tenets, respect for the earth and so on, are fundamental, but beyond that, there's no required set of beliefs or essential rituals, nothing of that kind. Miss Walcot didn't approve of that. She wanted to set up a temple whose members would swear to her ideas of what Druids are and were and should be, based on her misreading and outright invention of ancient texts.'

'But I thought there wasn't much written about them, at least not until the Romans came,' said Judith.

'You're quite right. So Miss Walcot was free, actually, to make up history as she went along. And that was fine until she started pressuring everyone to agree with her. The Druids did build Stonehenge, according to her version. The modern enclosure of it, the encouragement of tourism, all that is anathema. Profaning a holy place. And all of Bath is a sacrilege. The Romans built those baths over a holy place. Destroy them! The abbey, a monument to a false god – destroy it! Even the Jane Austen Centre is a place of homage to a blasphemous woman. Destroy it!'

'Oh!' said several of us together. 'Then the fire and the oak leaf—'

'Got it in one. It's fortunate that she wasn't a competent arsonist.' Rob helped himself to a chocolate croissant and a Bath bun. 'Have I left any loose ends?'

'What's going to happen to them?' asked Andrew, setting down his mimosa so he could take a bite of pastry. Eating with one hand is a challenge.

'That's up to a jury, of course, later on. Miss Walcot will certainly be declared unfit to stand trial. Broadmoor for the rest of her life, I'd imagine. Robinson is another question. He actually did very little. Trafficking in stolen goods is about it. We can't even charge him with corrupting a minor; Sammy is nearly thirty in actual calendar years. Robinson and his lawyer will claim he was unduly influenced by Miss Walcot, and he can be such a charming and plausible fellow, he'll probably get off with a light sentence.'

'And what about Sammy?' asked Judith. Her voice was quiet, but we could all feel the tension.

Rob smiled. 'Sammy who? I know of no one named Sammy who's been involved in anything criminal. And I don't intend to know. Cheers!'

'So "All's well that ends well."'

That got me a resounding chorus of boos.

After the others had left we gave Andrew his chess set. He was speechless. 'Let this be a memento of a case you'll never forget,' said Alan, 'the amazing case that happened even before you joined the force.'

We went to Evensong that afternoon and listened to the choir sing the Psalms and canticles in timeless Anglican chant. We prayed and gave thanks. And that evening we told Amy we'd be leaving in the morning. We called Jane to say we were coming home. And just before we went to bed Alan handed me a box. 'Happy birthday, love.'

In the box was the round brooch I had so admired at the Baths. 'But how . . . where—?'

'Rob retrieved it from Caine's loot. Drat, I can't stop calling him that. Rob took it back to the shop with my credit card, but they refused to let me pay. So it's your souvenir of probably the most memorable birthday trip of your life. Good night, darling.'

And all night I dreamed, not of the brooch, not of the tumultuous two weeks, but sweetly, of home.